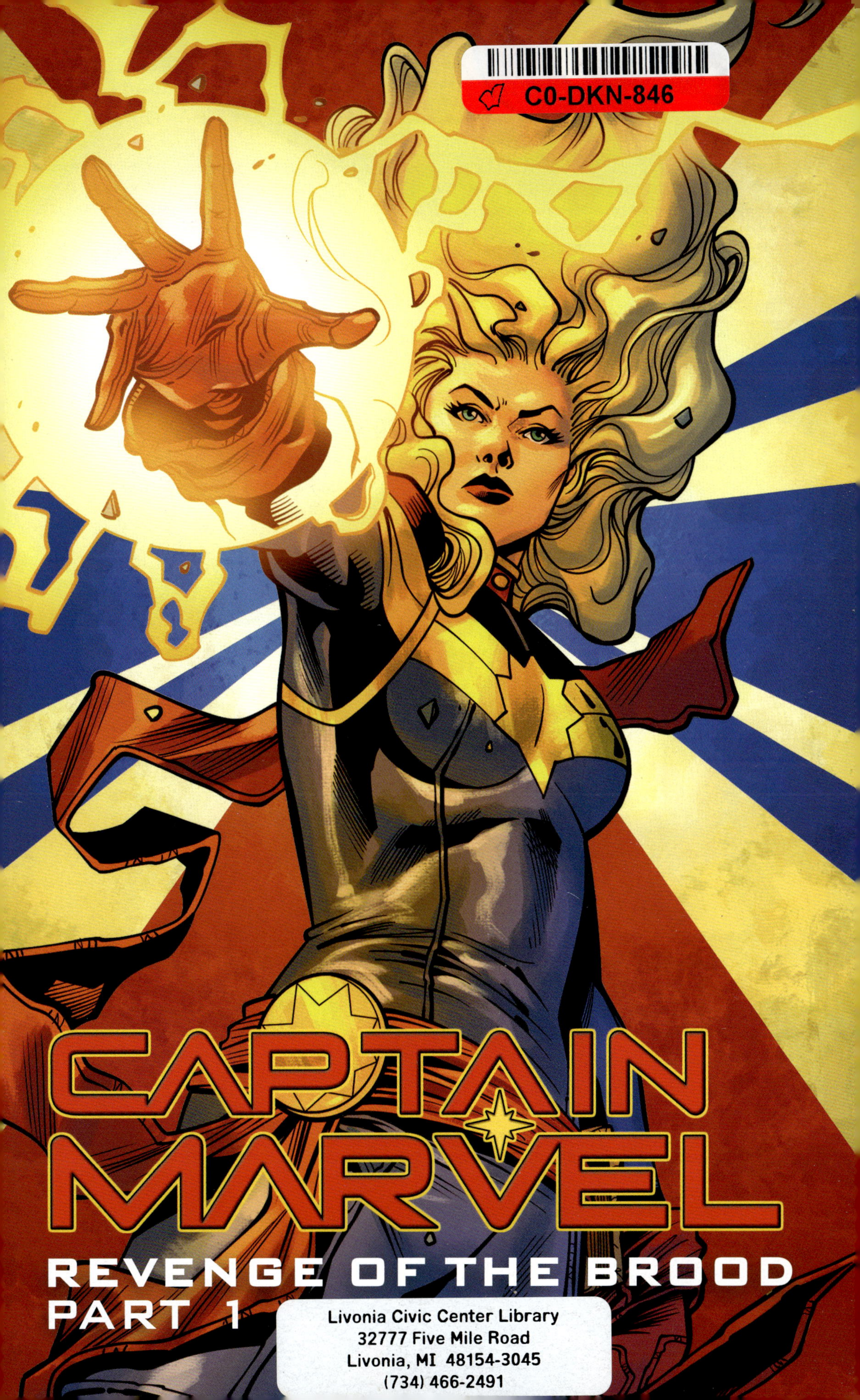
CAPTAIN MARVEL
REVENGE OF THE BROOD
PART 1

The Eternals went to war with the mutant nation of **Krakoa** over mutants' ability to resurrect themselves. A group of the Eternals opposed to the conflict allied themselves with the **Avengers**. Together, they used the Avengers headquarters, the deceased body of a Celestial, to create a new, living god: the **Progenitor**. Once awakened, the Progenitor announced to everyone on Earth that within 24 hours, they will all be judged. And if found lacking...all will die!

Now the heroes of Earth have their own personalized Progenitors following them around, testing and judging them. But Captain Marvel isn't the only sentient, super-powered being in her apartment building. What will a Flerken do under the eyes of god?!

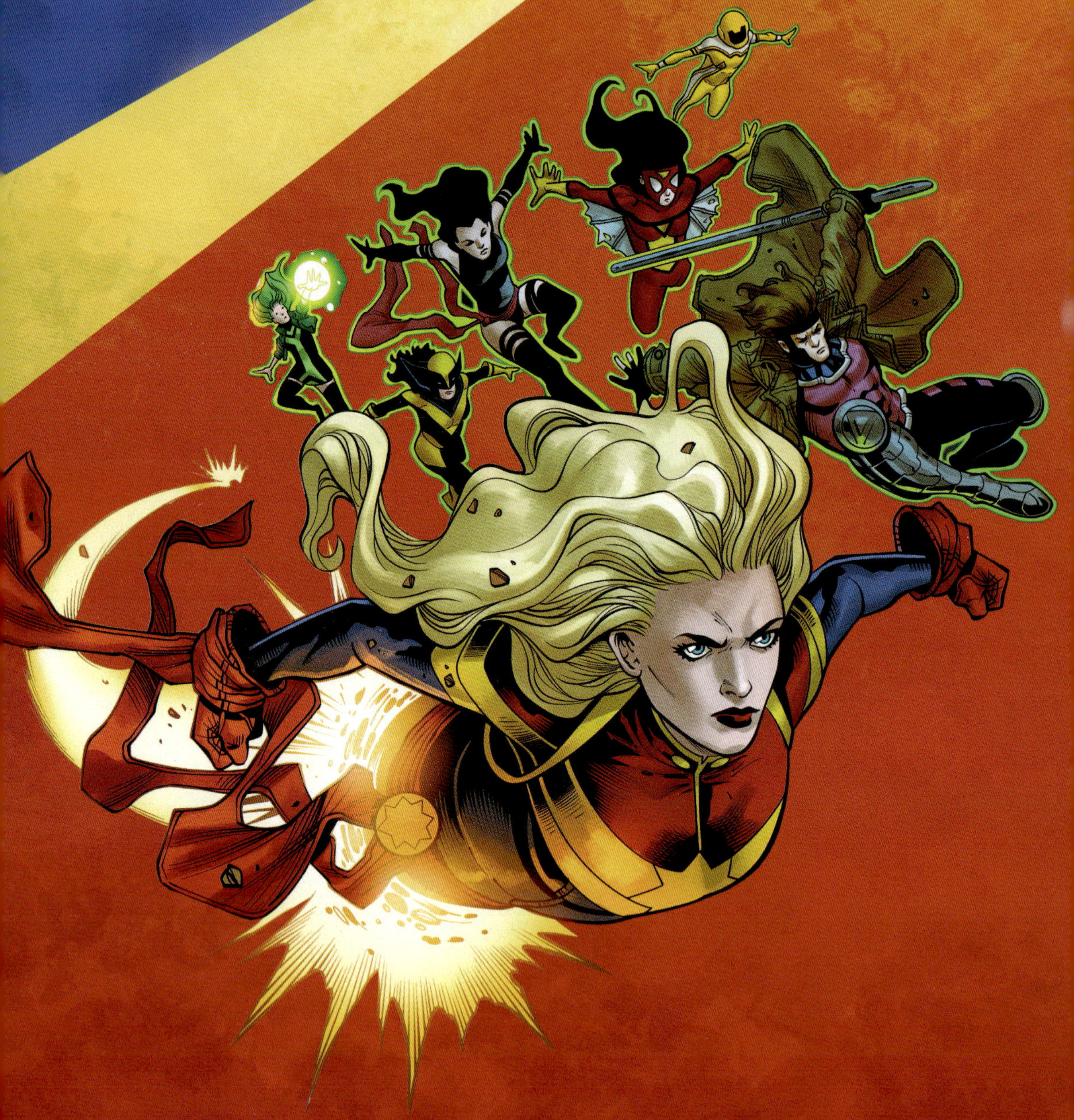

CAPTAIN MARVEL VOL. 9: REVENGE OF THE BROOD PART 1. Contains material originally published in magazine form as CAPTAIN MARVEL (2019) #42-46. First printing 2023. ISBN 978-1-302-94762-0. Published by MARVEL WORLDWIDE, INC., a subsidiary of MARVEL ENTERTAINMENT, LLC. OFFICE OF PUBLICATION: 1290 Avenue of the Americas, New York, NY 10104. **Printed in the U.S.A.** KEVIN FEIGE, Chief Creative Officer; DAN BUCKLEY, President, Marvel Entertainment; DAVID BOGART, Associate Publisher & SVP of Talent Affairs; TOM BREVOORT, VP, Executive Editor; NICK LOWE, Executive Editor, VP of Content, Digital Publishing; DAVID GABRIEL, VP of Print & Digital Publishing; SVEN LARSEN, VP of Licensed Publishing; MARK ANNUNZIATO, VP of Planning & Forecasting; JEFF YOUNGQUIST, VP of Production & Special Projects; ALEX MORALES, Director of Publishing Operations; DAN EDINGTON, Director of Editorial Operations; RICKEY PURDIN, Director of Talent Relations; JENNIFER GRÜNWALD, Director of Production & Special Projects; SUSAN CRESPI, Production Manager; STAN LEE, Chairman Emeritus. For information regarding advertising in Marvel Comics or on Marvel.com, please contact Vit DeBellis, Custom Solutions & Integrated Advertising Manager, at vdebellis@marvel.com. For Marvel subscription inquiries, please call 888-511-5480. **Manufactured between 3/3/2023 and 4/4/2023 by SEAWAY PRINTING, GREEN BAY, WI, USA.**

10 9 8 7 6 5 4 3 2 1

Born to a Kree mother and human father, former U.S. Air Force pilot **CAROL DANVERS** became a super hero when a Kree device activated her latent powers. Now she's an Avenger and Earth's Mightiest Hero.

CAPTAIN MARVEL

REVENGE OF THE BROOD
PART 1

KELLY THOMPSON
Writer

#42

ANDREA DI VITO
Artist

NOLAN WOODARD
Color Artist

JUAN FRIGERI & JESUS ABURTOV
Cover Art

#43-45

SERGIO DÁVILA
Penciler

SEAN PARSONS with **ELISABETTA D'AMICO** [#45]
Inkers

ARIF PRIANTO with **YEN NITRO** [#45]
Color Artists

JUAN FRIGERI & JESUS ABURTOV
Cover Art

#46

JAVIER PINA
Artist

YEN NITRO
Color Artist

JUAN FRIGERI & DAVID CURIEL
Cover Art

VC's CLAYTON COWLES
Letterer

ANITA OKOYE
Assistant Editor

SARAH BRUNSTAD
Editor

TOM BREVOORT
Executive Editor

Collection Editor: JENNIFER GRÜNWALD
Assistant Editor: DANIEL KIRCHHOFFER
Assistant Managing Editor: MAIA LOY
Associate Manager, Talent Relations: LISA MONTALBANO

VP Production & Special Projects: JEFF YOUNGQUIST
Book Designers: STACIE ZUCKER with ADAM DEL RE
SVP Print, Sales & Marketing: DAVID GABRIEL
Editor in Chief: C.B. CEBULSKI

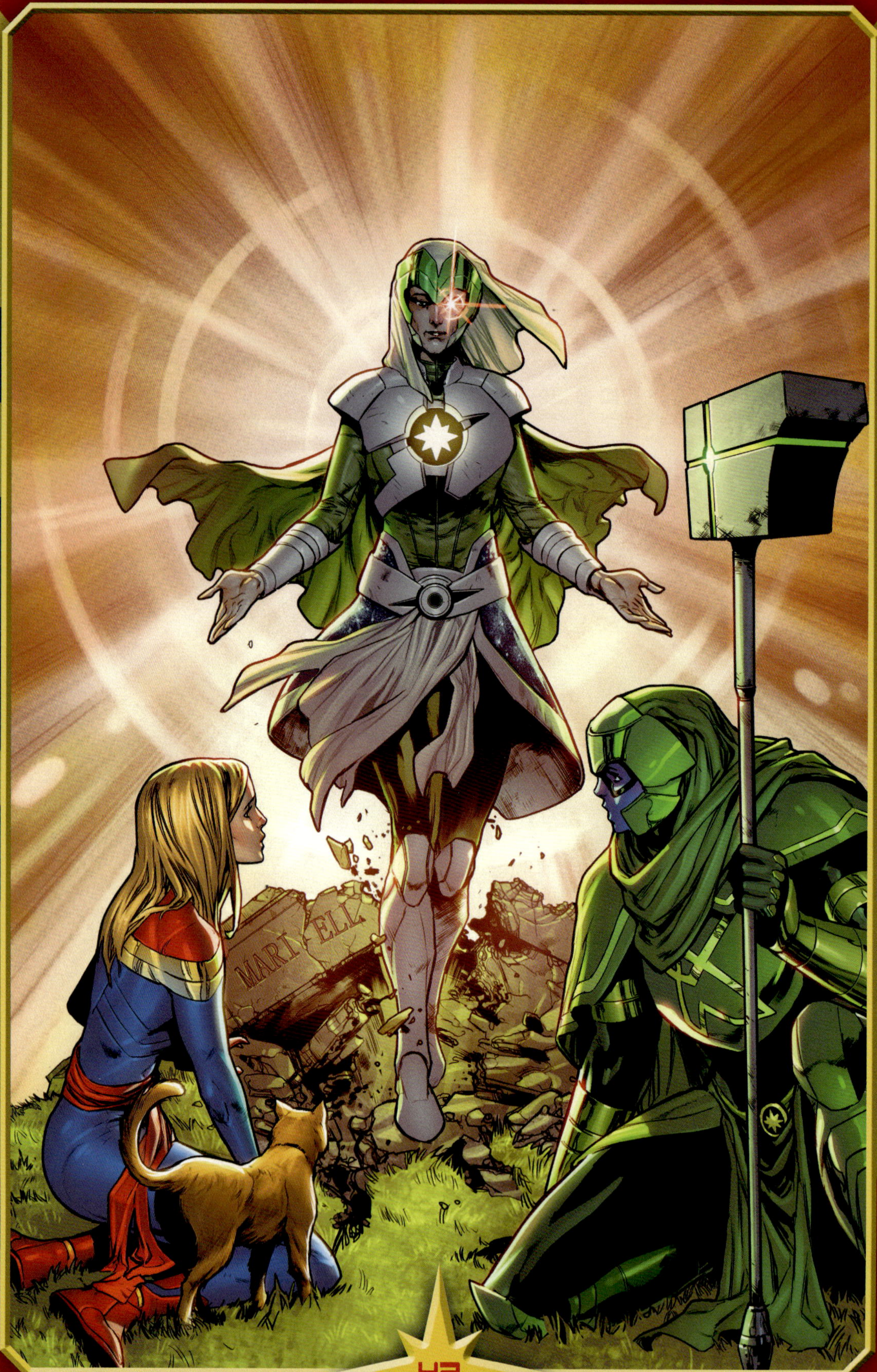
MARI-ELL

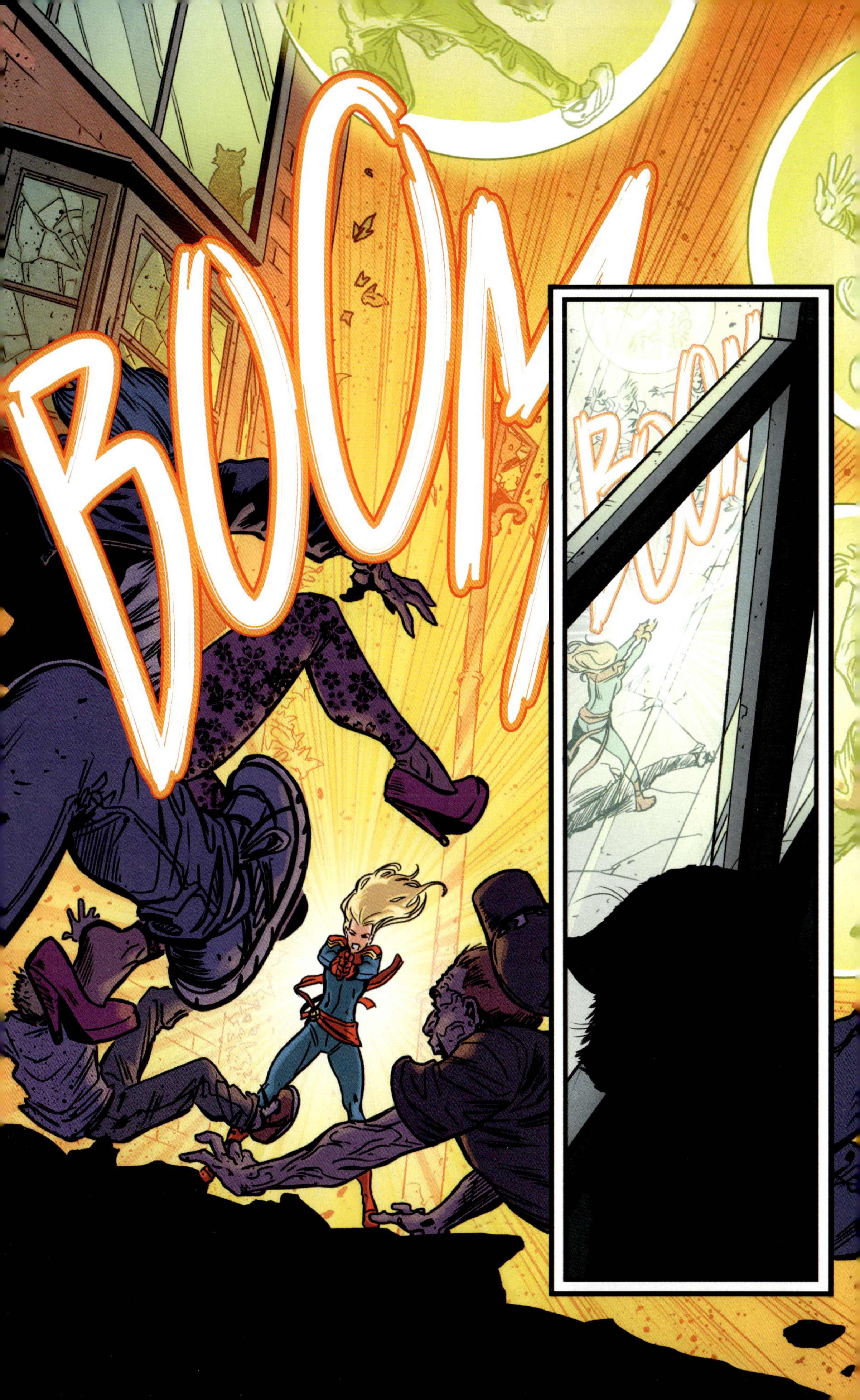
BOOM

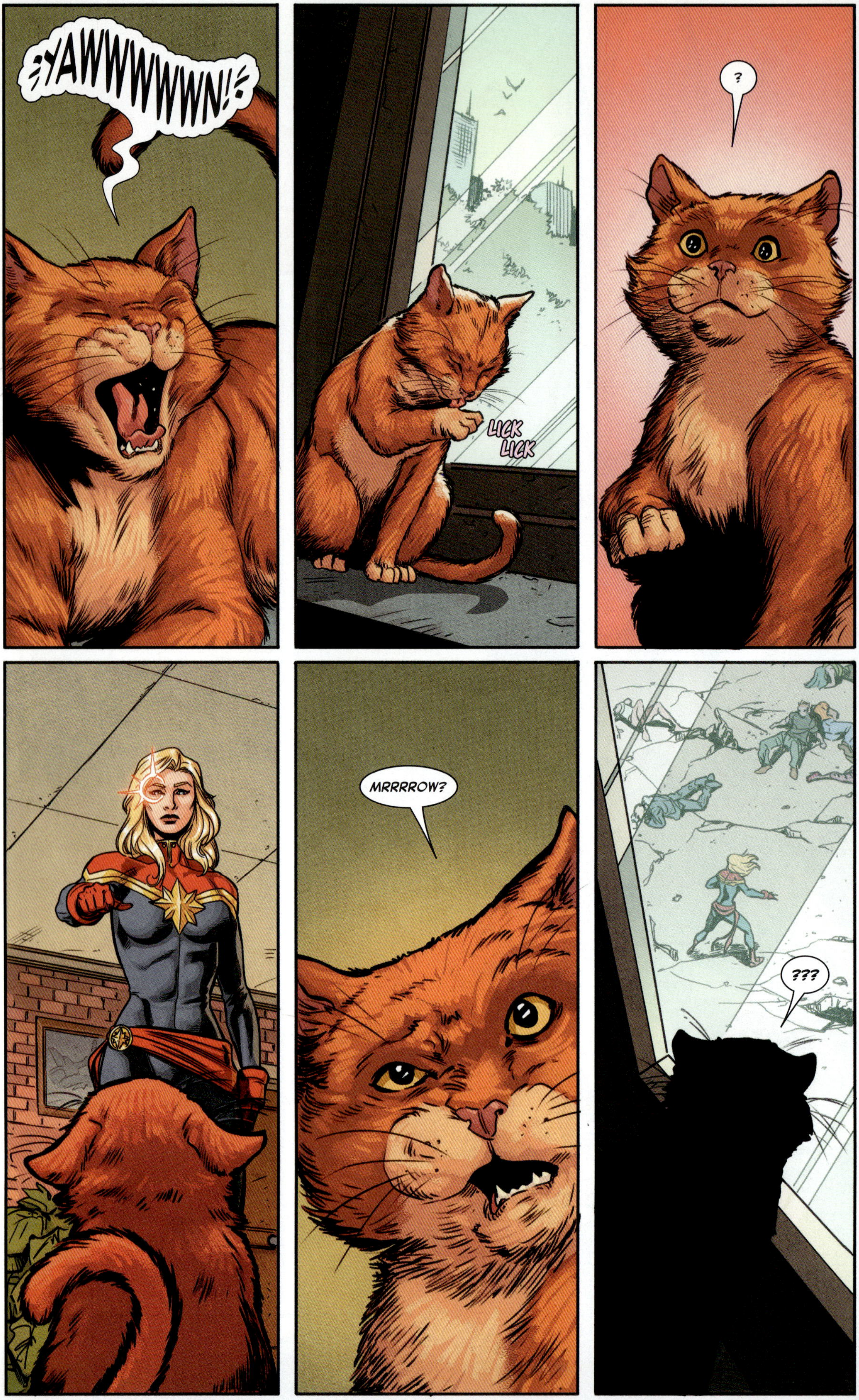

YAWWWWWN!
LICK
LICK
?
MRRRROW?
???

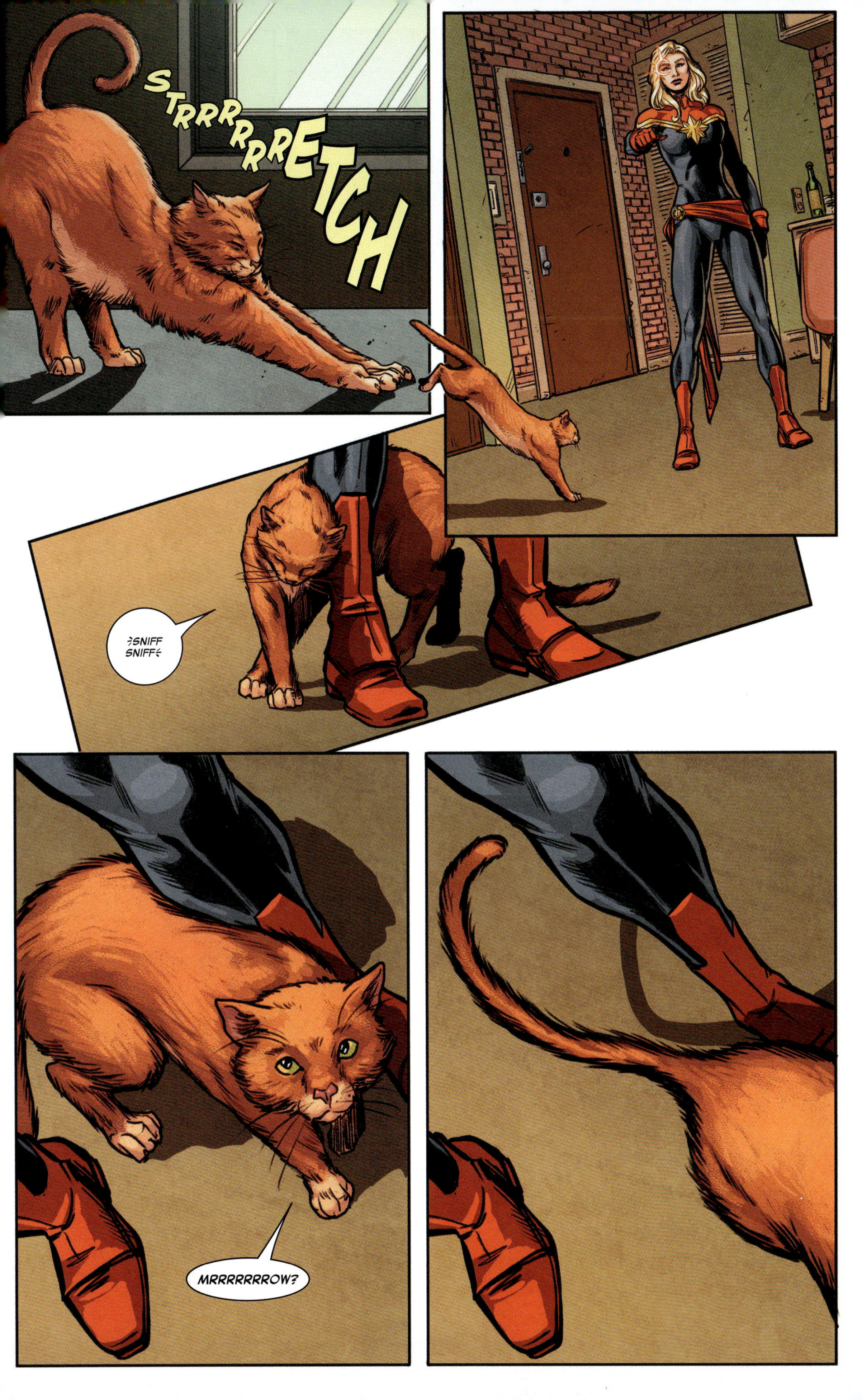
STRRRRRRRETCH
SNIFF SNIFF
MRRRRRRROW?

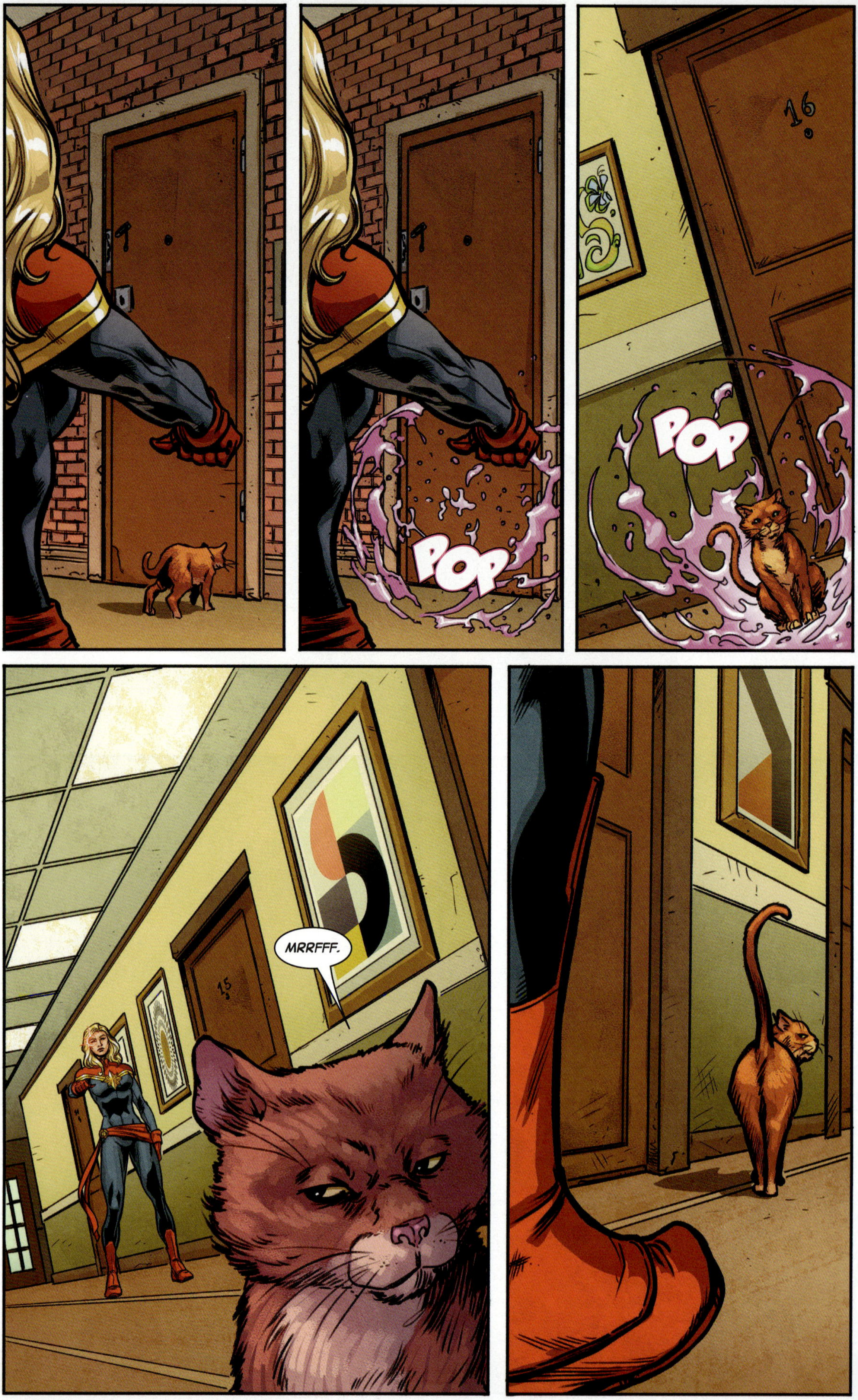
POP
POP
MRRFFF.

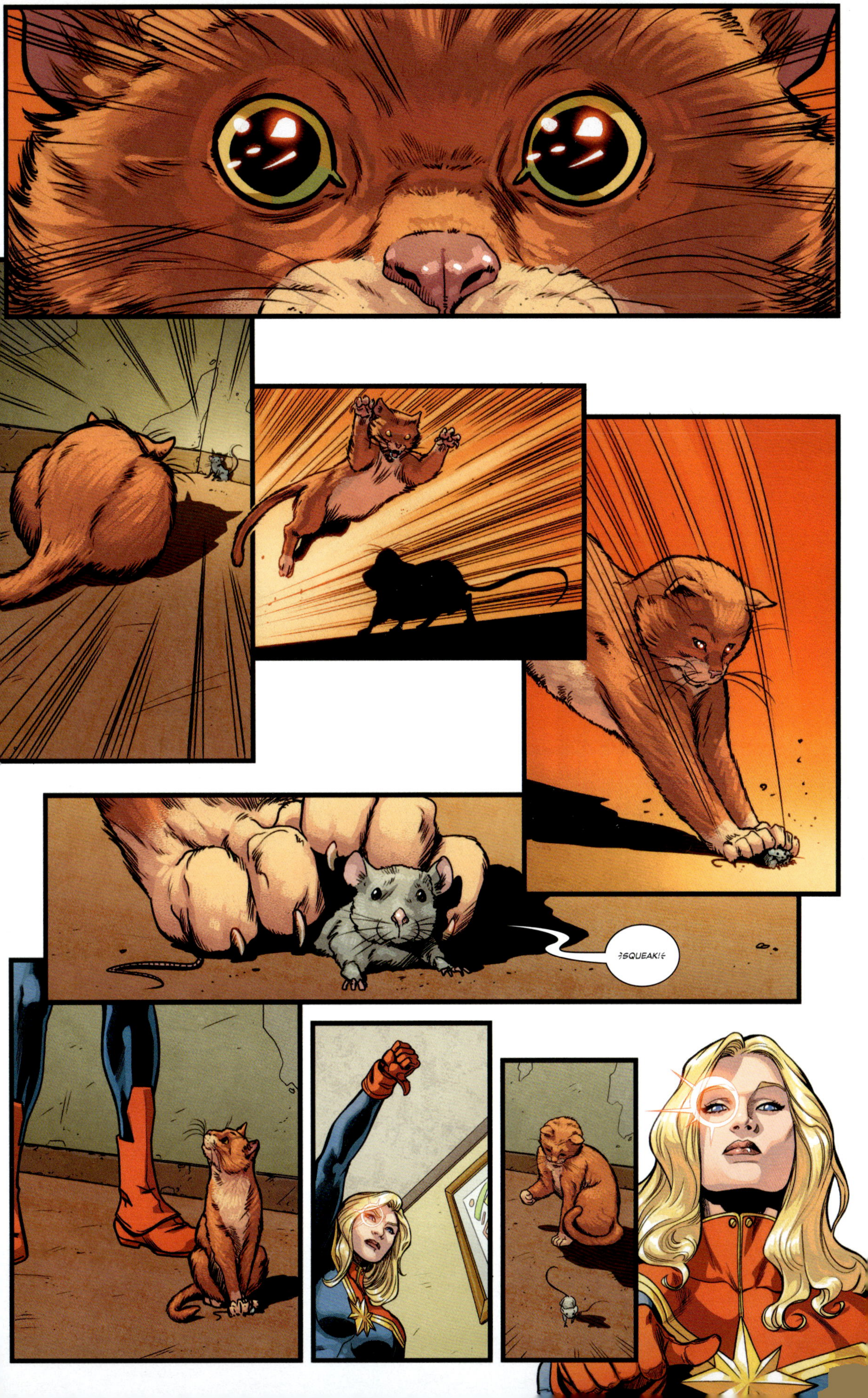
SQUEAK!

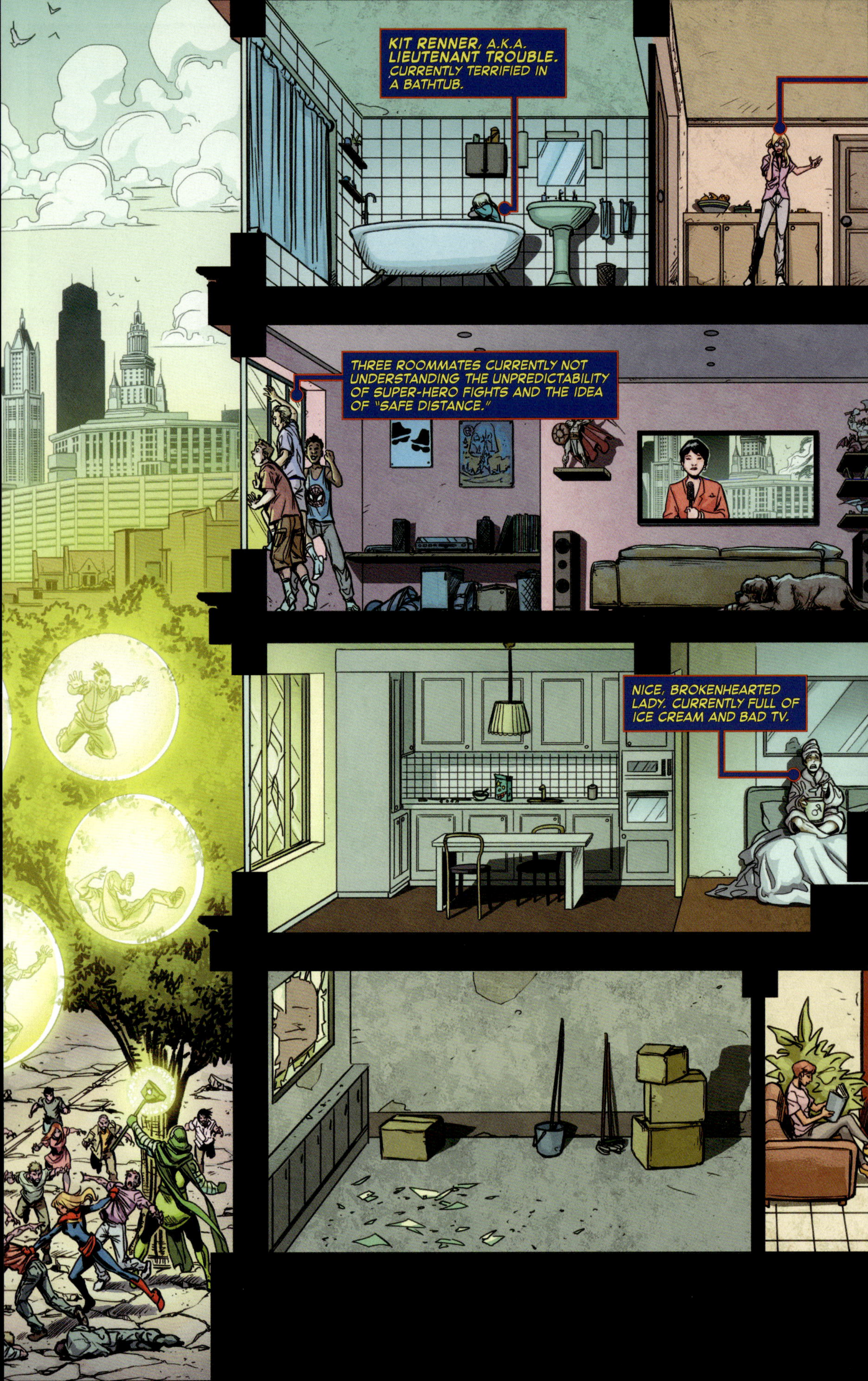

KIT RENNER, A.K.A. LIEUTENANT TROUBLE. CURRENTLY TERRIFIED IN A BATHTUB.
THREE ROOMMATES CURRENTLY NOT UNDERSTANDING THE UNPREDICTABILITY OF SUPER-HERO FIGHTS AND THE IDEA OF "SAFE DISTANCE."
NICE, BROKENHEARTED LADY. CURRENTLY FULL OF ICE CREAM AND BAD TV.

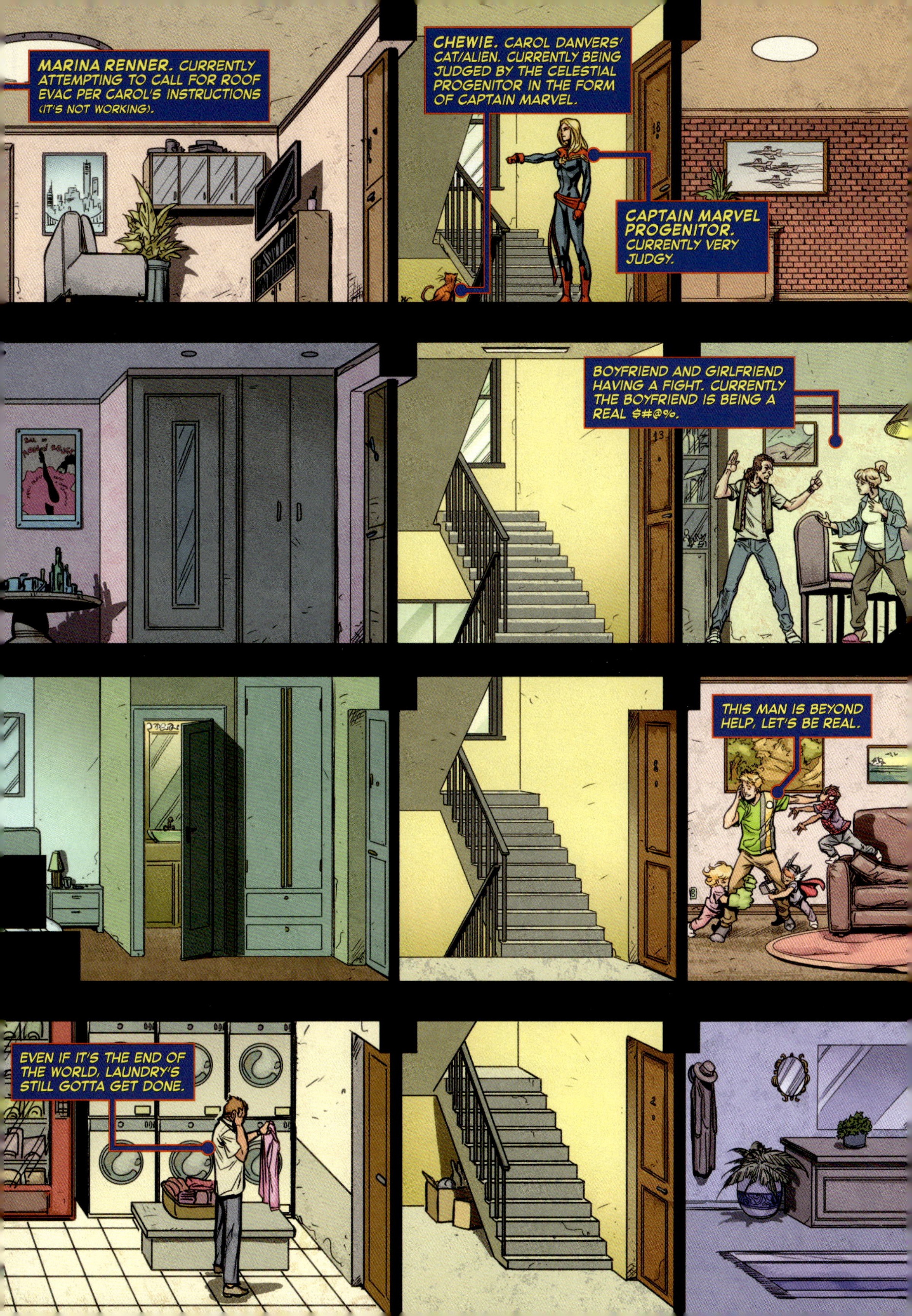
MARINA RENNER. CURRENTLY ATTEMPTING TO CALL FOR ROOF EVAC PER CAROL'S INSTRUCTIONS (IT'S NOT WORKING).
CHEWIE. CAROL DANVERS' CAT/ALIEN. CURRENTLY BEING JUDGED BY THE CELESTIAL PROGENITOR IN THE FORM OF CAPTAIN MARVEL.
CAPTAIN MARVEL PROGENITOR. CURRENTLY VERY JUDGY.
BOYFRIEND AND GIRLFRIEND HAVING A FIGHT. CURRENTLY THE BOYFRIEND IS BEING A REAL $#@%.
THIS MAN IS BEYOND HELP, LET'S BE REAL.
EVEN IF IT'S THE END OF THE WORLD, LAUNDRY'S STILL GOTTA GET DONE.

BOYFRIEND AND GIRLFRIEND.
ARRGGHHH! WHAT IS THAT?!
POP
UH, I--I THINK IT'S C-CAPTAIN MARVEL'S CAT.
HOW THE HELL DID IT GET IN HERE?!
I THINK IT CAN TELEPORT?
GET OUT OF HERE, CAT!
MRRRFF.
RAAAAAAAAAA!
POP
AHHHHHHHH! I HATE CATS!

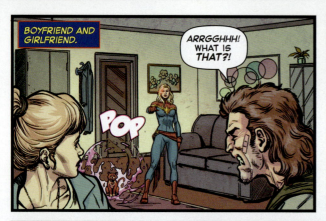

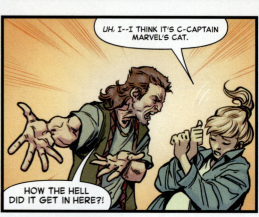

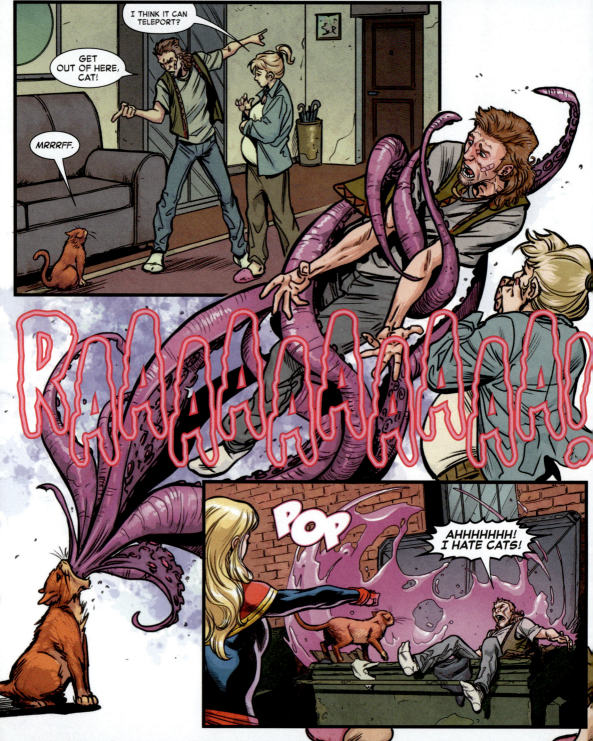

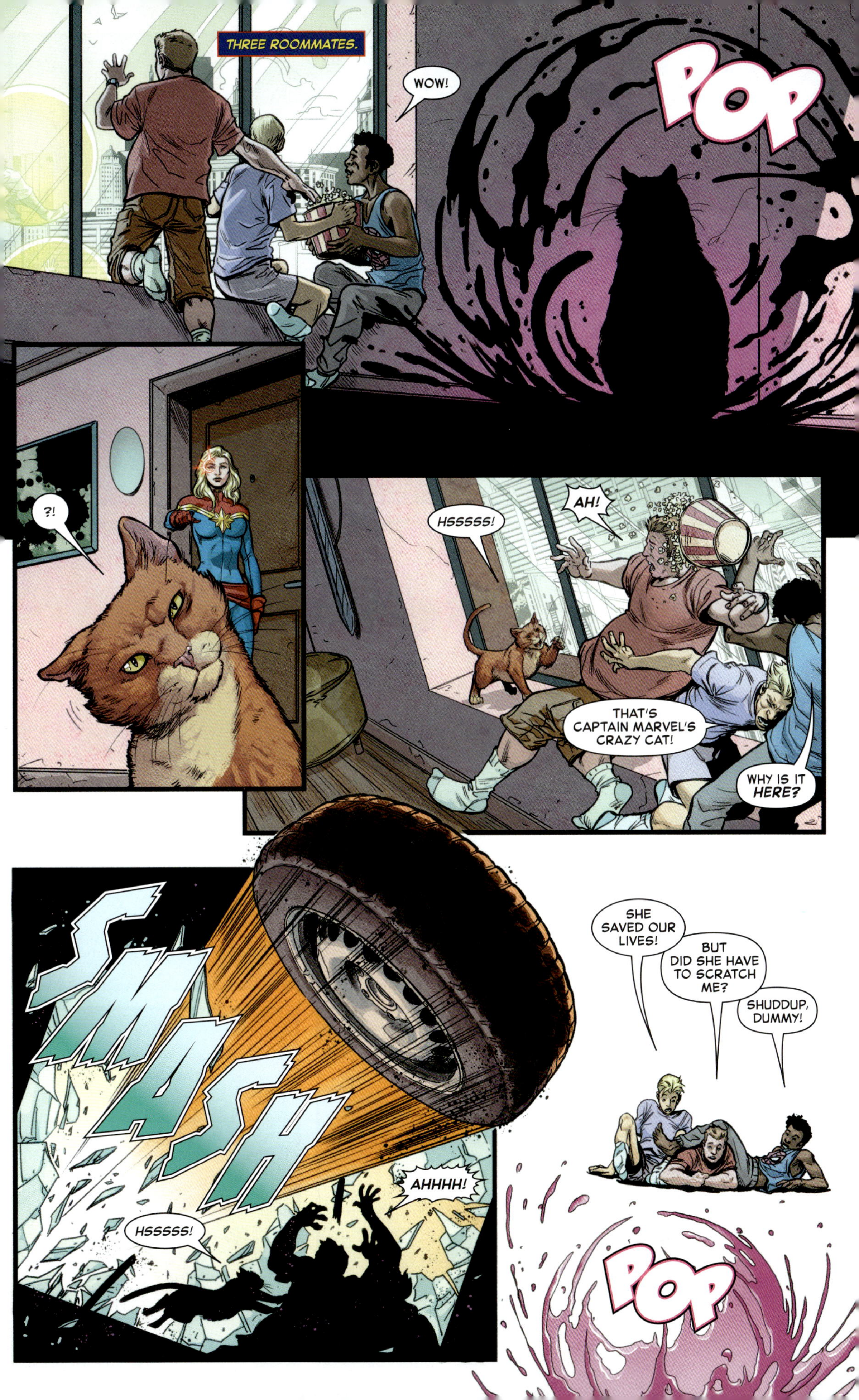
THREE ROOMMATES.
WOW!
POP
?!
HSSSSS!
AH!
THAT'S CAPTAIN MARVEL'S CRAZY CAT!
WHY IS IT HERE?
SMASH
AHHHH!
HSSSSS!
SHE SAVED OUR LIVES!
BUT DID SHE HAVE TO SCRATCH ME?
SHUDDUP, DUMMY!
POP

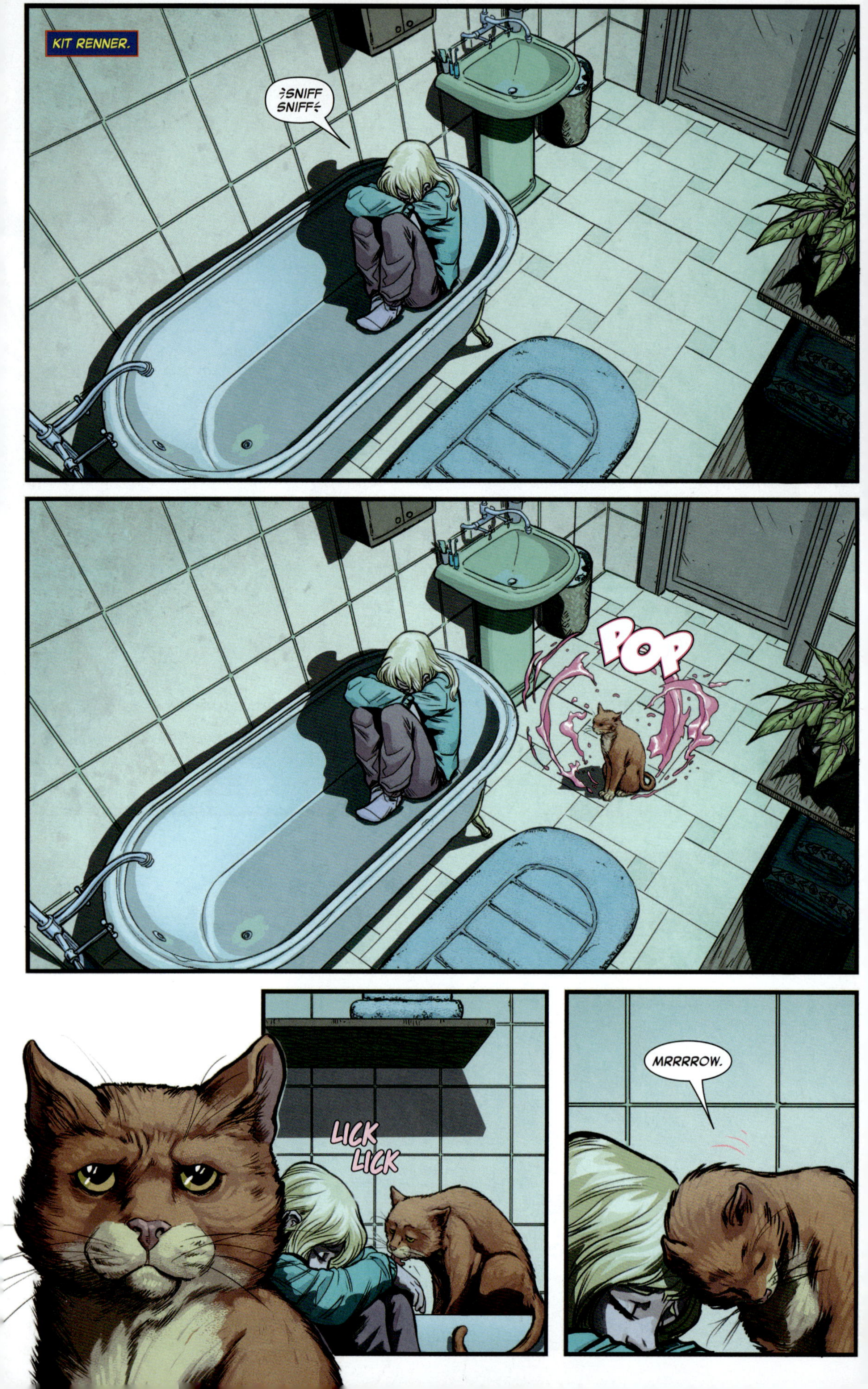
KIT RENNER.
SNIFF SNIFF
POP
LICK LICK
MRRRROW.

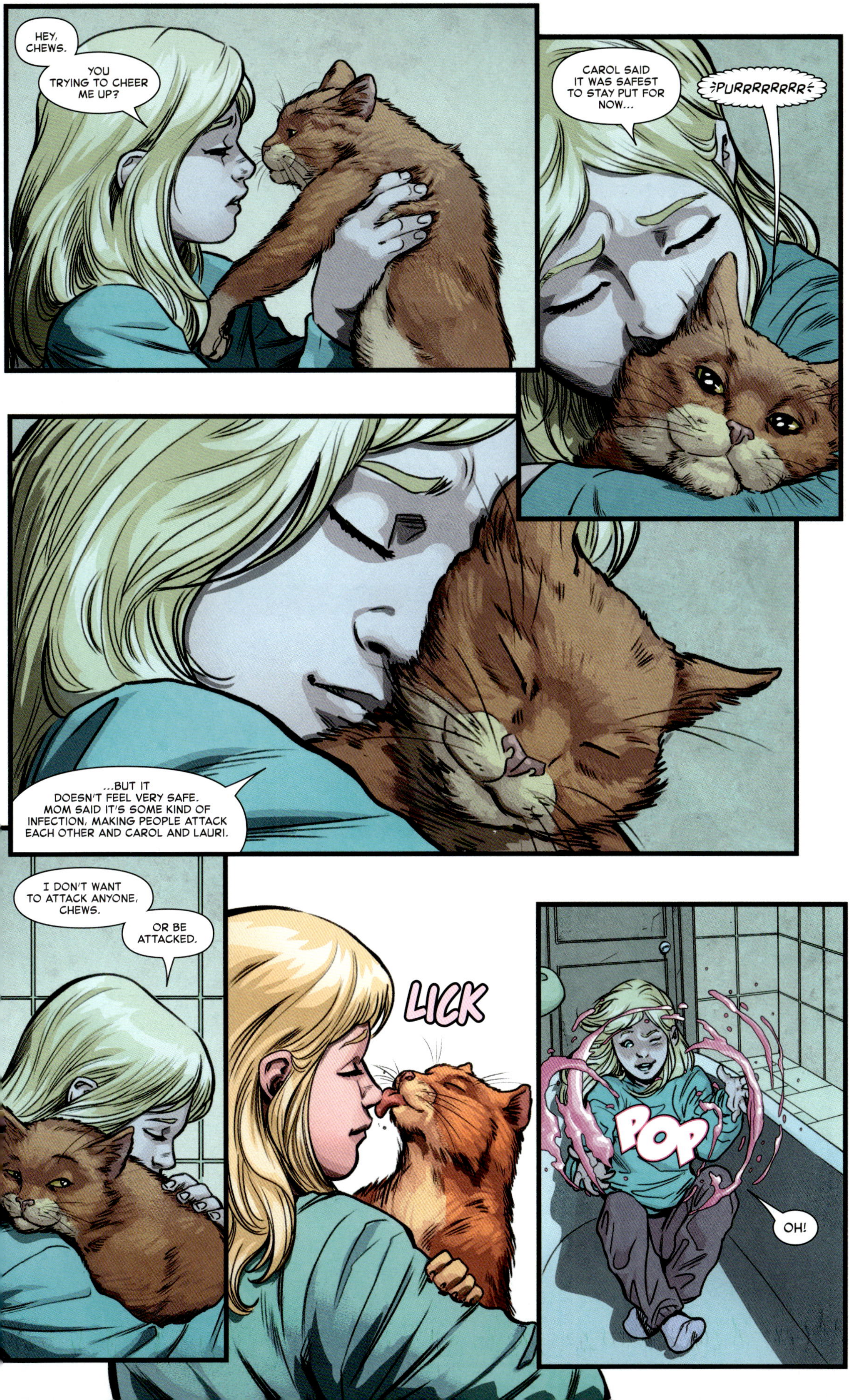
HEY, CHEWS.
YOU TRYING TO CHEER ME UP?
CAROL SAID IT WAS SAFEST TO STAY PUT FOR NOW...
PURRRRRRRR
...BUT IT DOESN'T FEEL VERY SAFE. MOM SAID IT'S SOME KIND OF INFECTION, MAKING PEOPLE ATTACK EACH OTHER AND CAROL AND LAURI.
I DON'T WANT TO ATTACK ANYONE, CHEWS.
OR BE ATTACKED.
LICK
POP
OH!

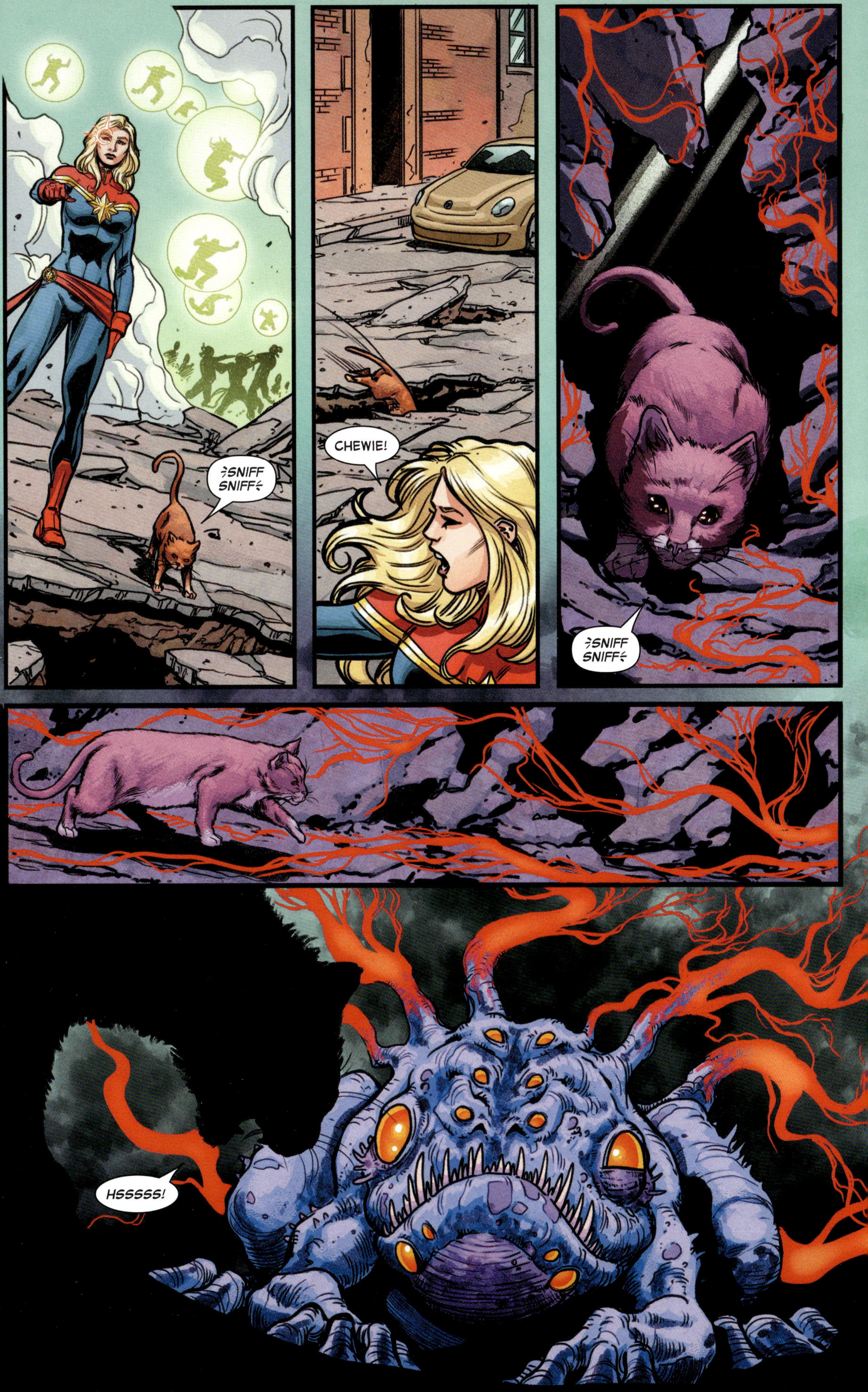
SNIFF SNIFF
CHEWIE!
SNIFF SNIFF
HSSSSS!

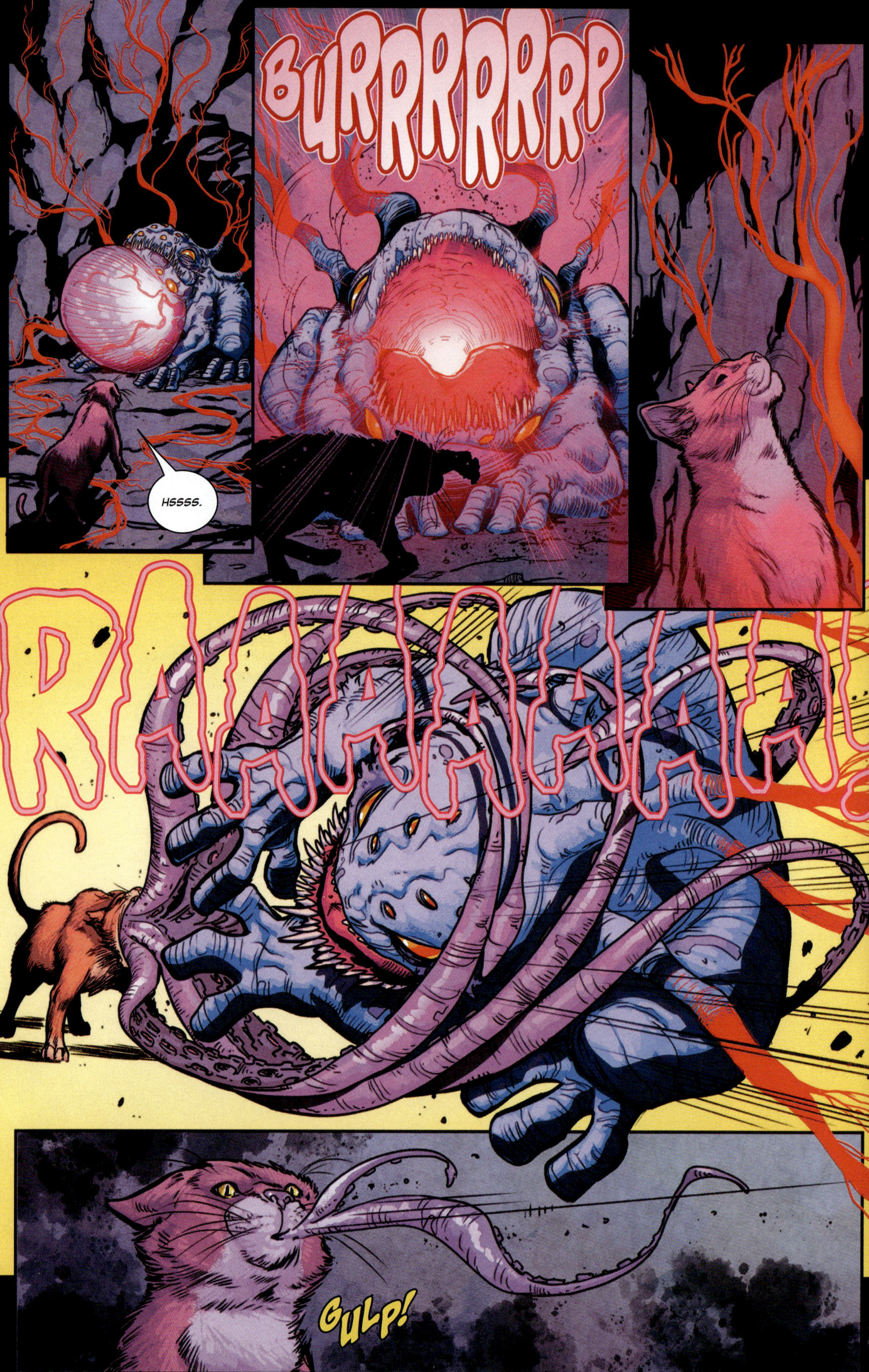
HSSSS.
BURRRRRRP
RAAAAAAA!
GULP!

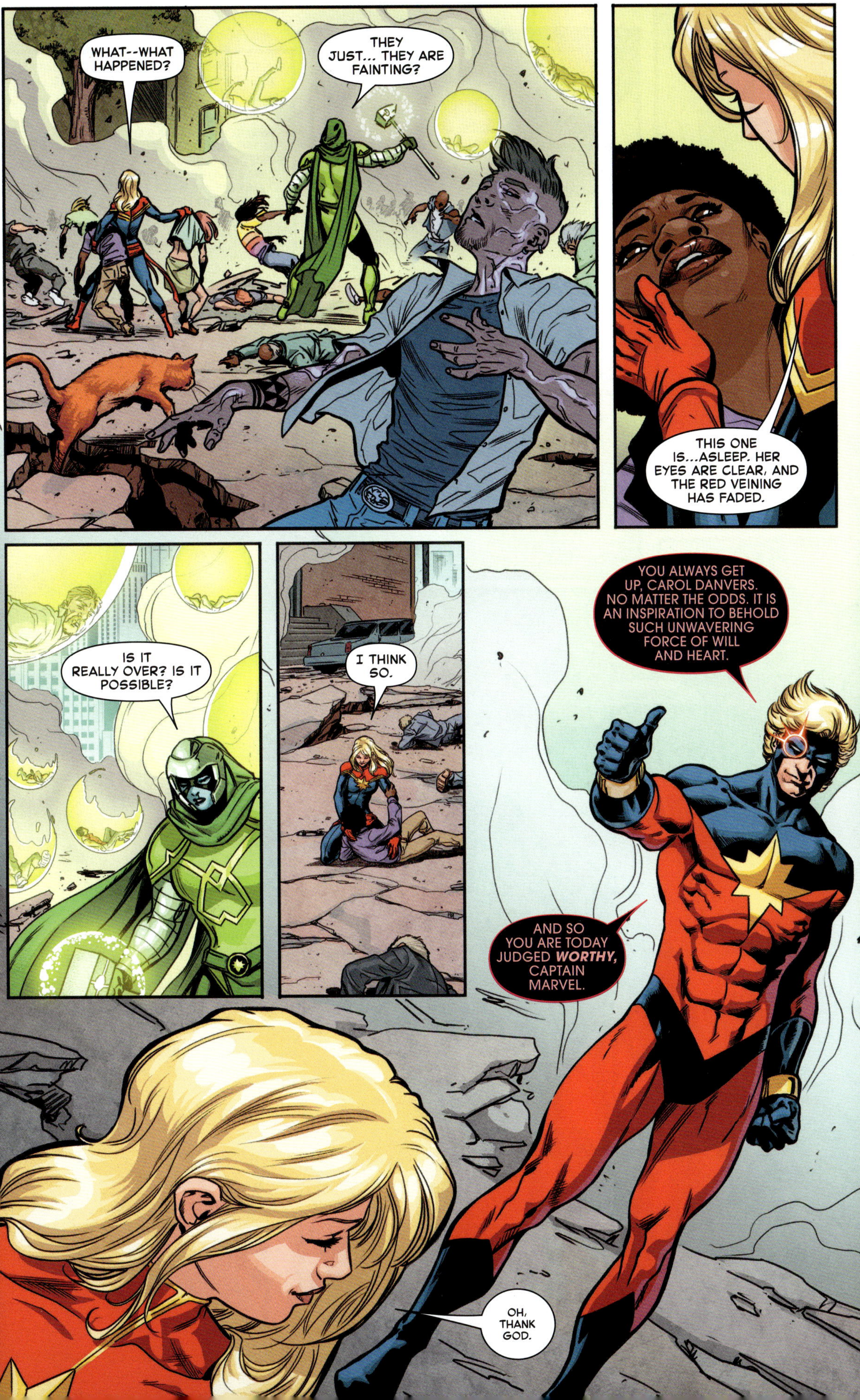
WHAT--WHAT HAPPENED?
THEY JUST... THEY ARE FAINTING?
THIS ONE IS...ASLEEP. HER EYES ARE CLEAR, AND THE RED VEINING HAS FADED.
IS IT REALLY OVER? IS IT POSSIBLE?
I THINK SO.
YOU ALWAYS GET UP, CAROL DANVERS. NO MATTER THE ODDS. IT IS AN INSPIRATION TO BEHOLD SUCH UNWAVERING FORCE OF WILL AND HEART.
AND SO YOU ARE TODAY JUDGED WORTHY, CAPTAIN MARVEL.
OH, THANK GOD.

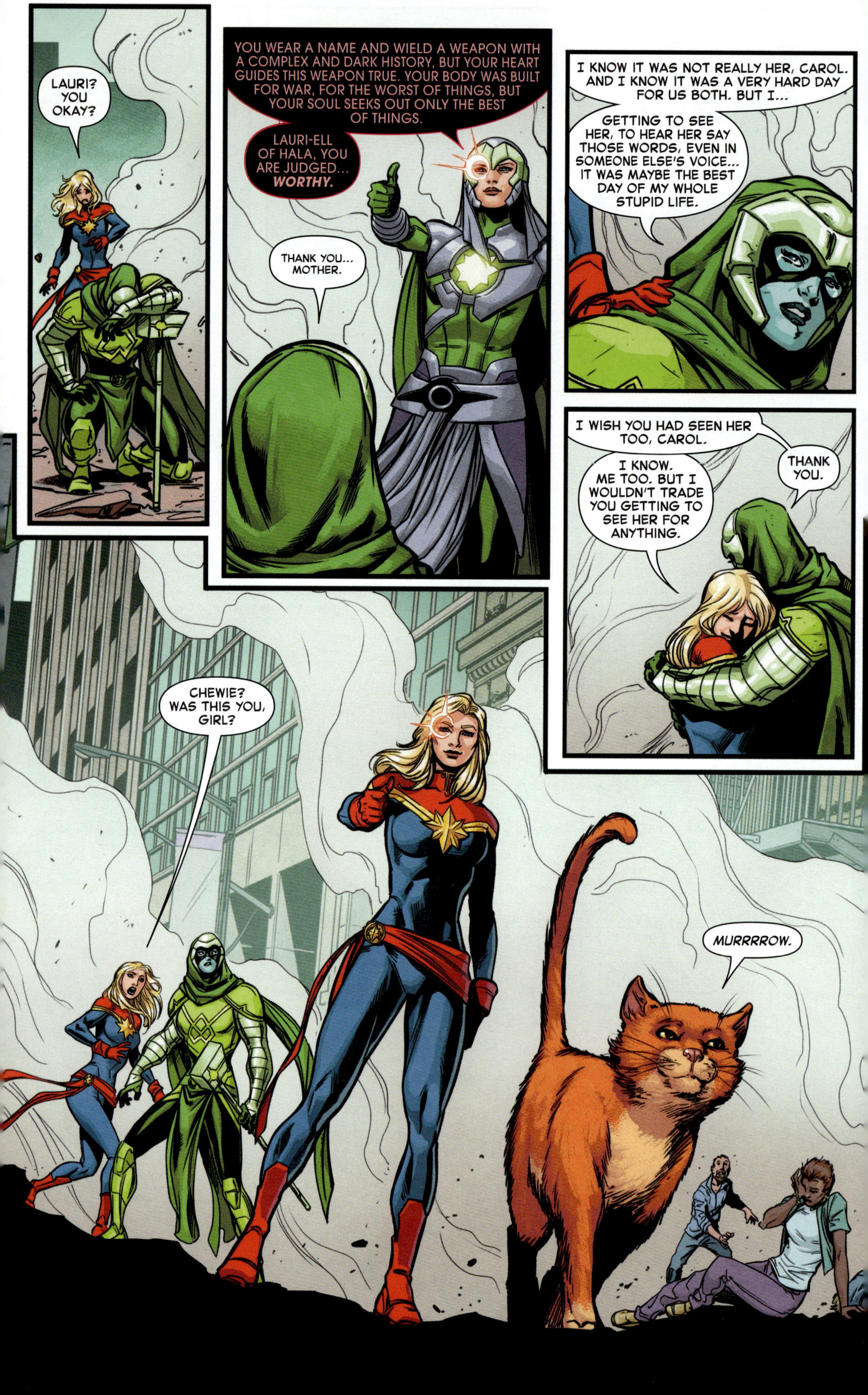
LAURI? YOU OKAY?
YOU WEAR A NAME AND WIELD A WEAPON WITH A COMPLEX AND DARK HISTORY, BUT YOUR HEART GUIDES THIS WEAPON TRUE. YOUR BODY WAS BUILT FOR WAR, FOR THE WORST OF THINGS, BUT YOUR SOUL SEEKS OUT ONLY THE BEST OF THINGS.
LAURI-ELL OF HALA, YOU ARE JUDGED... WORTHY.
THANK YOU... MOTHER.
I KNOW IT WAS NOT REALLY HER, CAROL. AND I KNOW IT WAS A VERY HARD DAY FOR US BOTH. BUT I...
GETTING TO SEE HER, TO HEAR HER SAY THOSE WORDS, EVEN IN SOMEONE ELSE'S VOICE... IT WAS MAYBE THE BEST DAY OF MY WHOLE STUPID LIFE.
I WISH YOU HAD SEEN HER TOO, CAROL.
I KNOW. ME TOO. BUT I WOULDN'T TRADE YOU GETTING TO SEE HER FOR ANYTHING.
THANK YOU.
CHEWIE? WAS THIS YOU, GIRL?
MURRRROW.

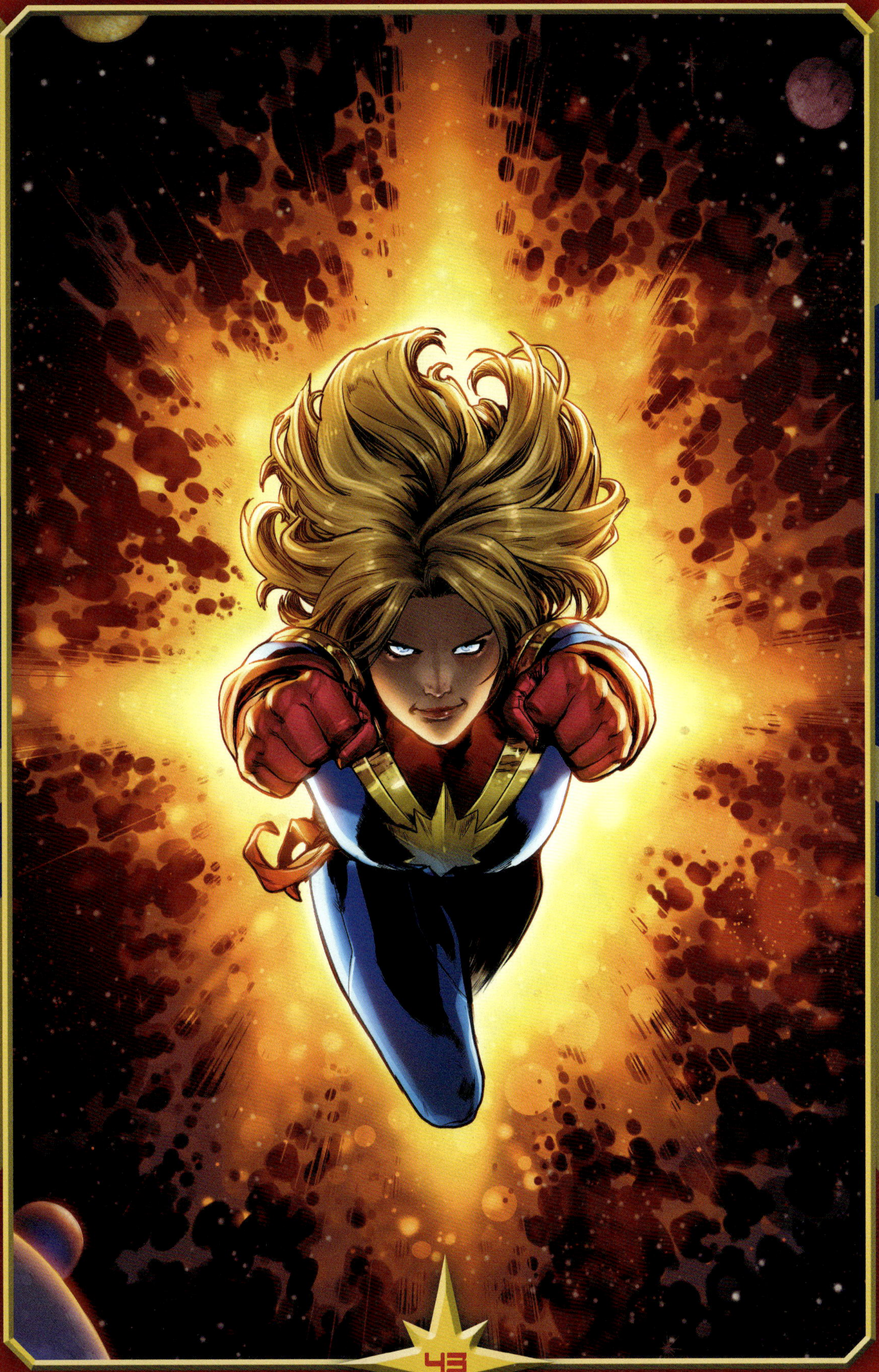

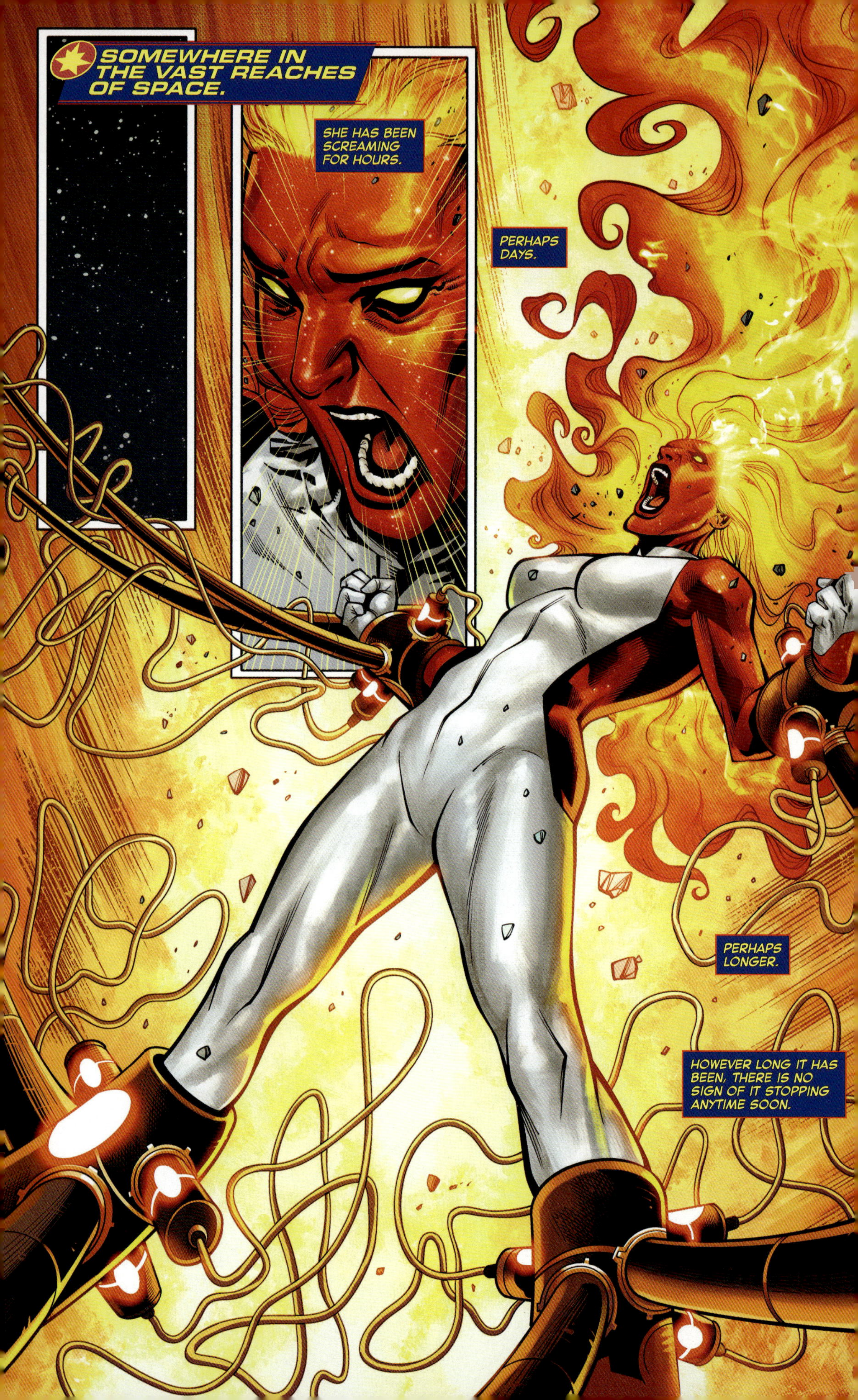
SOMEWHERE IN THE VAST REACHES OF SPACE.
SHE HAS BEEN SCREAMING FOR HOURS.
PERHAPS DAYS.
PERHAPS LONGER.
HOWEVER LONG IT HAS BEEN, THERE IS NO SIGN OF IT STOPPING ANYTIME SOON.

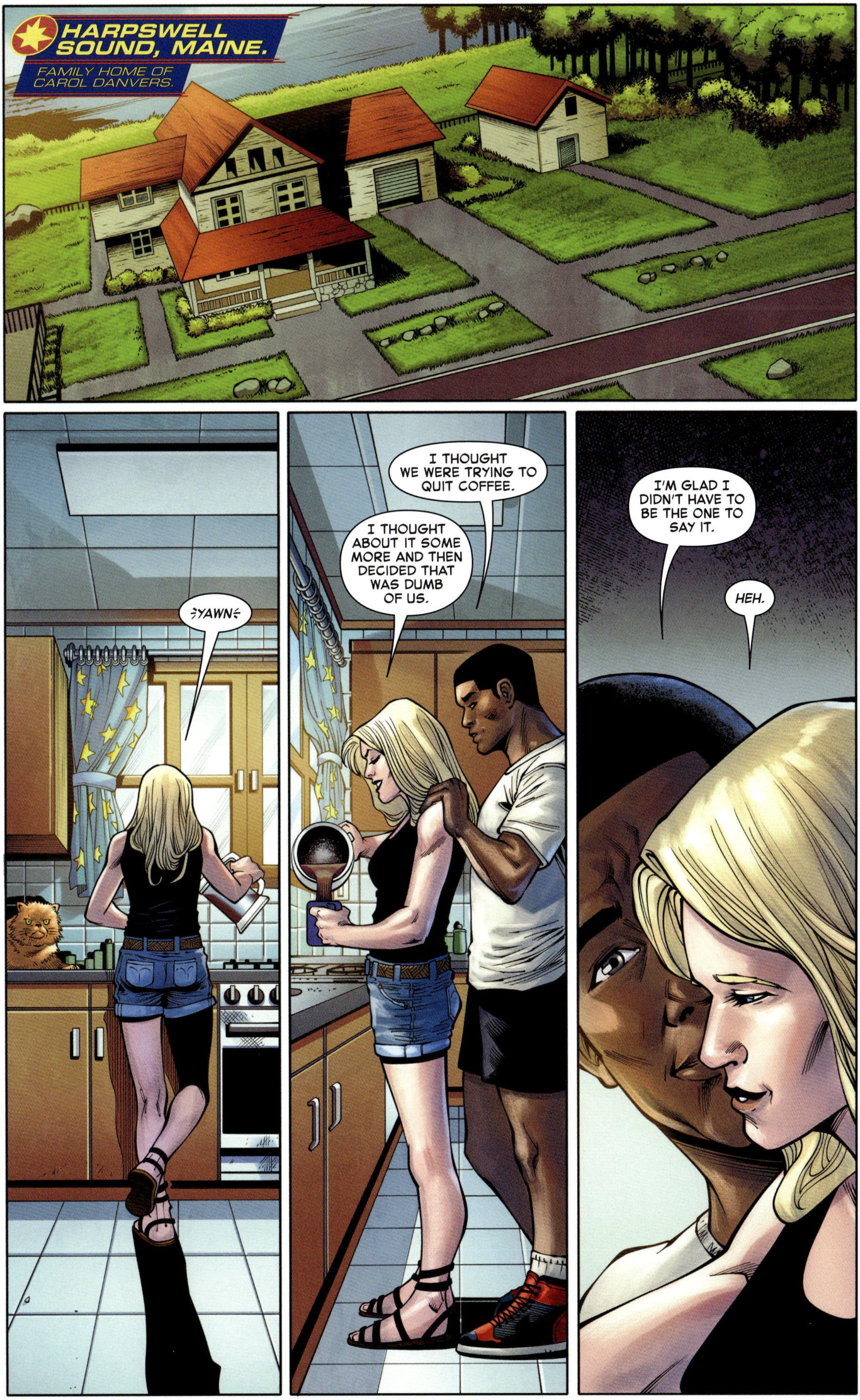
HARPSWELL SOUND, MAINE.
FAMILY HOME OF CAROL DANVERS.
YAWN
I THOUGHT WE WERE TRYING TO QUIT COFFEE.
I THOUGHT ABOUT IT SOME MORE AND THEN DECIDED THAT WAS DUMB OF US.
I'M GLAD I DIDN'T HAVE TO BE THE ONE TO SAY IT.
HEH.

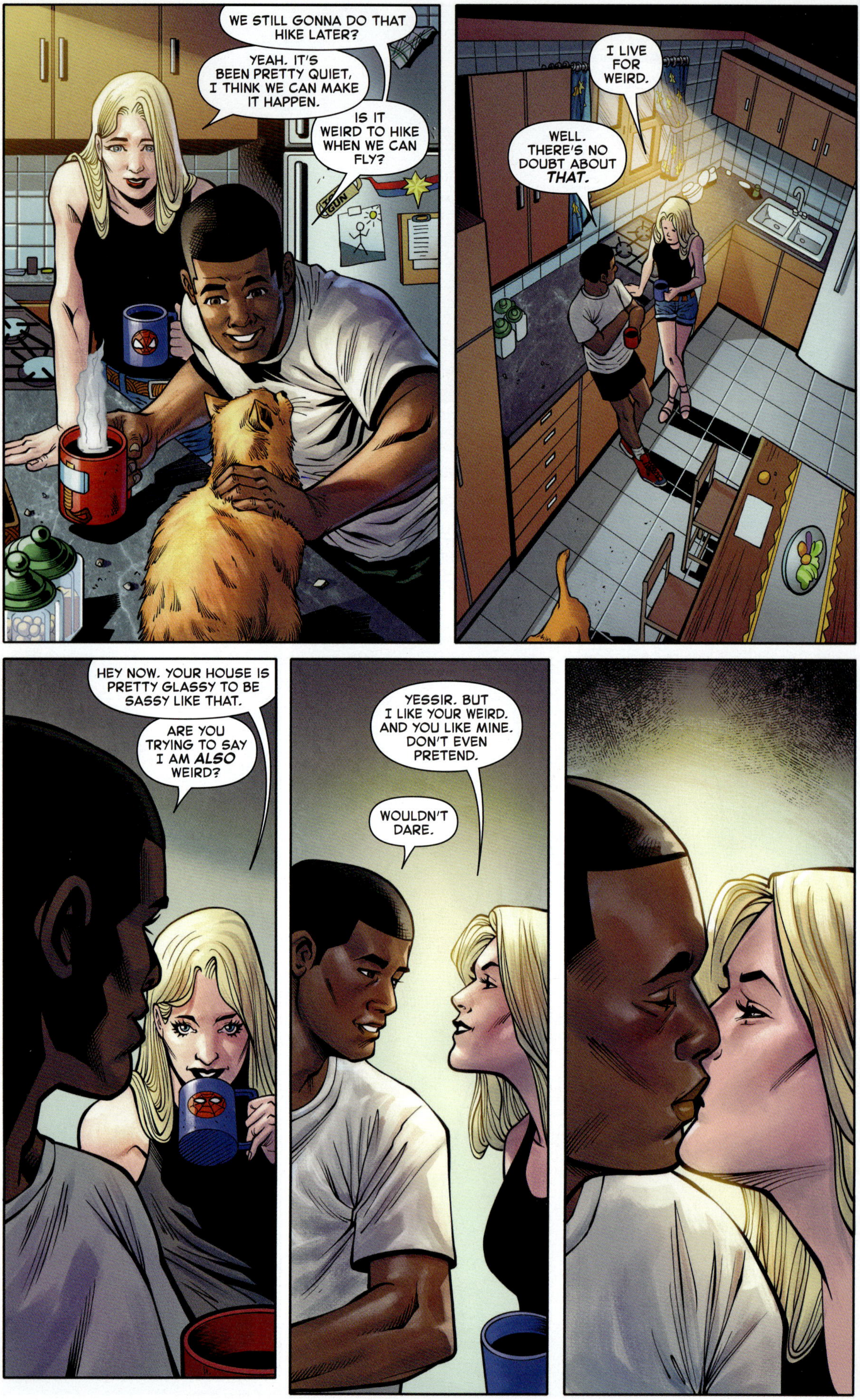
WE STILL GONNA DO THAT HIKE LATER?
YEAH. IT'S BEEN PRETTY QUIET, I THINK WE CAN MAKE IT HAPPEN.
IS IT WEIRD TO HIKE WHEN WE CAN FLY?
I LIVE FOR WEIRD.
WELL. THERE'S NO DOUBT ABOUT *THAT.*
HEY NOW. YOUR HOUSE IS PRETTY GLASSY TO BE SASSY LIKE THAT.
ARE YOU TRYING TO SAY I AM *ALSO* WEIRD?
YESSIR. BUT I LIKE YOUR WEIRD. AND YOU LIKE MINE. DON'T EVEN PRETEND.
WOULDN'T DARE.

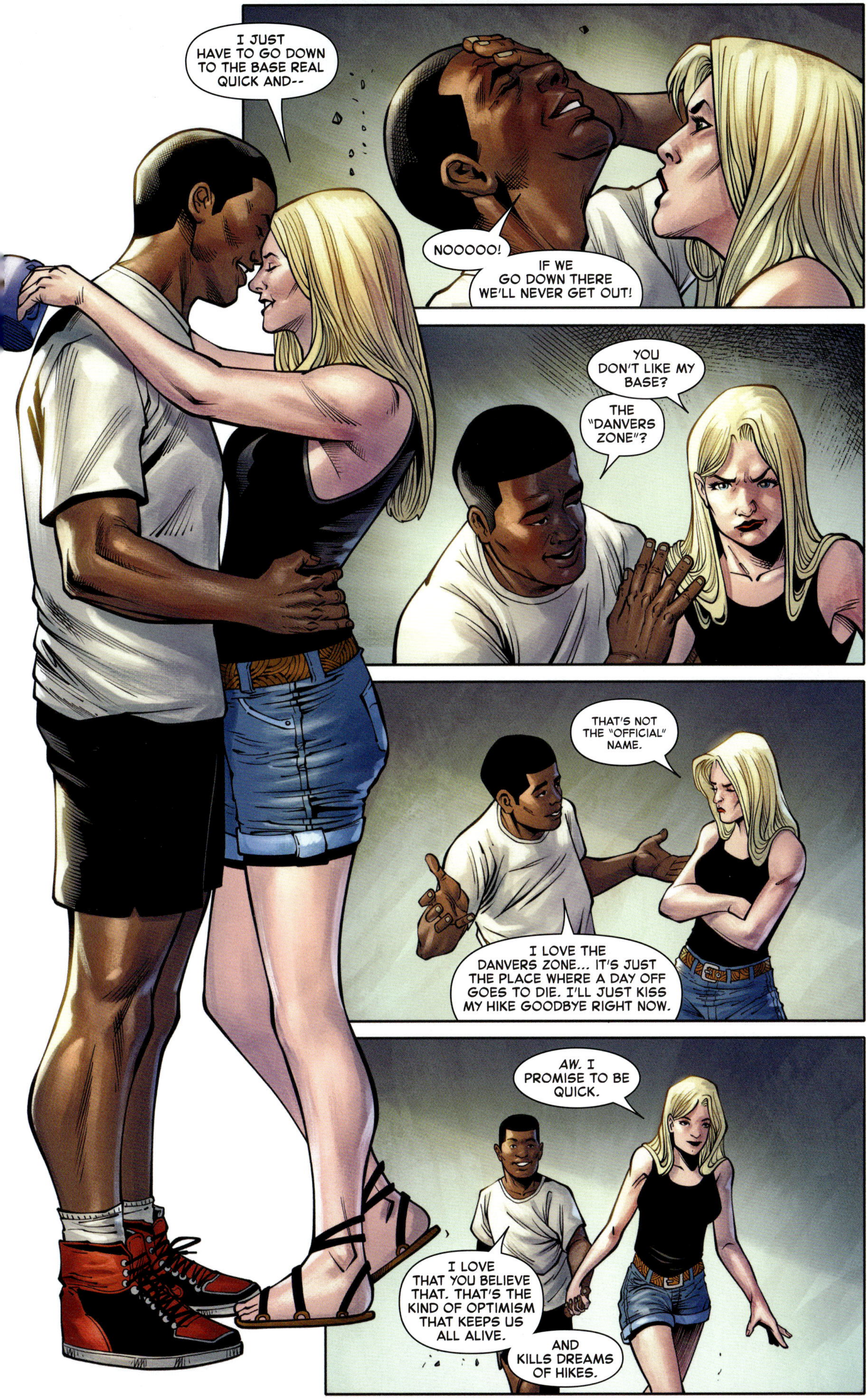
I JUST HAVE TO GO DOWN TO THE BASE REAL QUICK AND--
NOOOOO!
IF WE GO DOWN THERE WE'LL NEVER GET OUT!
YOU DON'T LIKE MY BASE?
THE "DANVERS ZONE"?
THAT'S NOT THE "OFFICIAL" NAME.
I LOVE THE DANVERS ZONE... IT'S JUST THE PLACE WHERE A DAY OFF GOES TO DIE. I'LL JUST KISS MY HIKE GOODBYE RIGHT NOW.
AW. I PROMISE TO BE QUICK.
I LOVE THAT YOU BELIEVE THAT. THAT'S THE KIND OF OPTIMISM THAT KEEPS US ALL ALIVE.
AND KILLS DREAMS OF HIKES.

SEE, WE DIDN'T EVEN DRESS FOR THE CAVE...WE'RE HAVING A DAY OFF, I PROMISE!
CAPTAIN MARVEL'S SECRET BASE.
PING PING PING PING
THAT PINGING CAN'T BE GOOD.
YEAH... I CAN'T EVEN PRETEND THAT'S NOT A PROBLEM.
IT SEEMS LIKE IT'S COMING THROUGH AN OLD BACK CHANNEL.
PING
PLEASE BE SOMETHING EASY, PLEASE BE SOMETHING EASY.

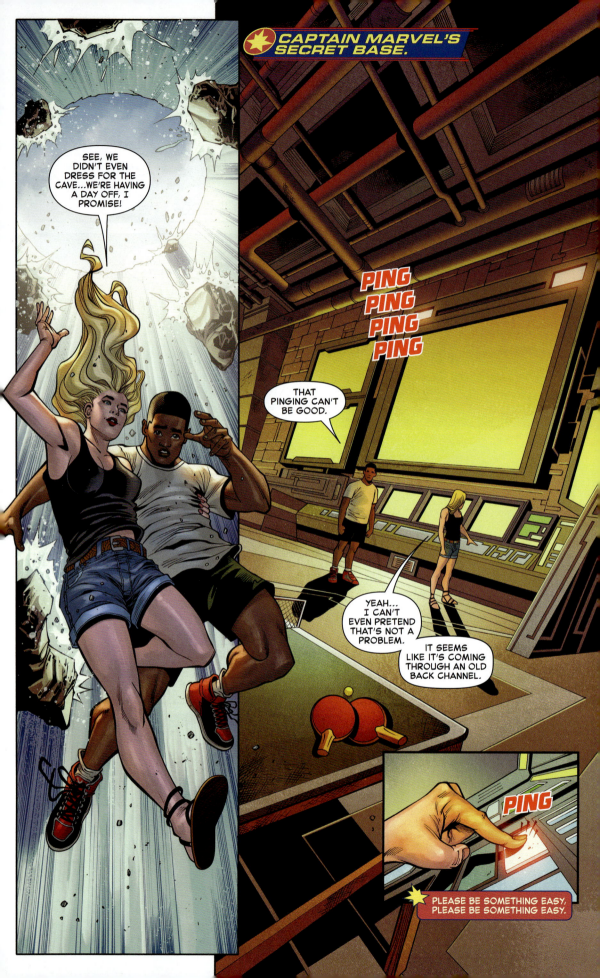

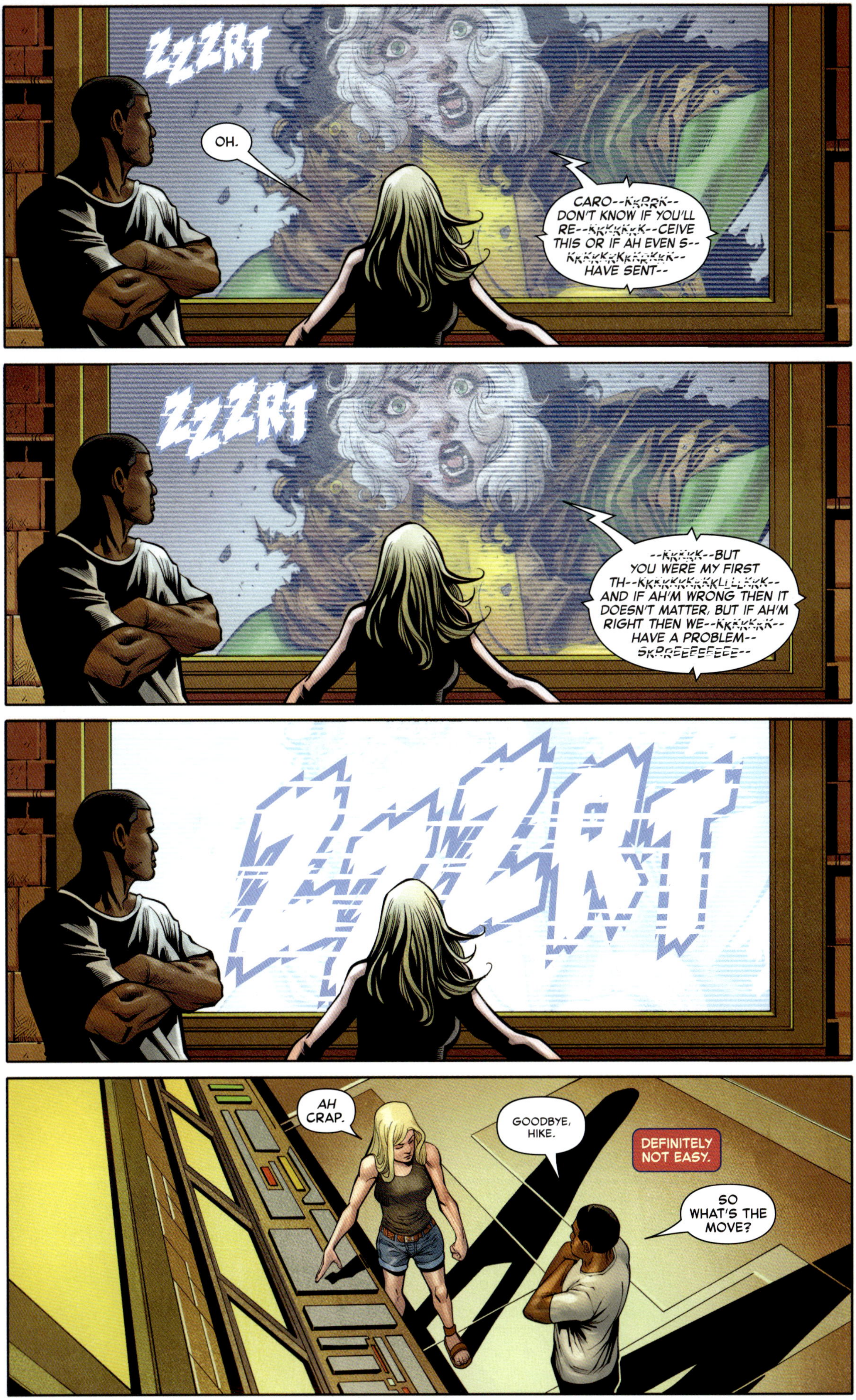
ZZZZRT
OH.
CARO--KKRRK--DON'T KNOW IF YOU'LL RE--KKKKKKK--CEIVE THIS OR IF AH EVEN S--KKKKKKKRKKK--HAVE SENT--
ZZZZRT
--KKKKK--BUT YOU WERE MY FIRST TH--KKKKKKKKKKLLLKKK--AND IF AH'M WRONG THEN IT DOESN'T MATTER, BUT IF AH'M RIGHT THEN WE--KKKKKKK--HAVE A PROBLEM--SKREEEEEEEEE--
ZZZRT
AH CRAP.
GOODBYE, HIKE.
DEFINITELY NOT EASY.
SO WHAT'S THE MOVE?

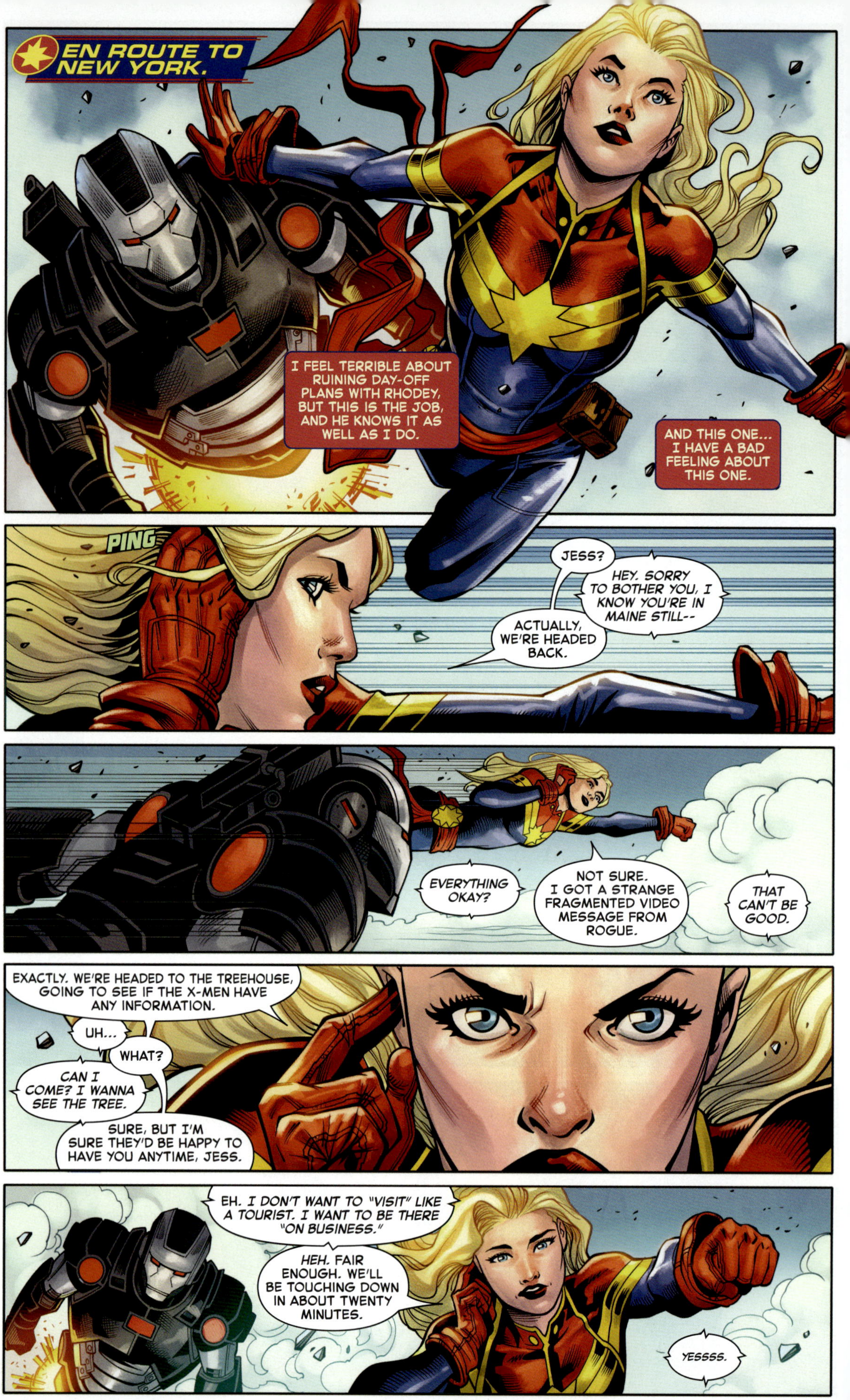
EN ROUTE TO NEW YORK.
I FEEL TERRIBLE ABOUT RUINING DAY-OFF PLANS WITH RHODEY, BUT THIS IS THE JOB, AND HE KNOWS IT AS WELL AS I DO.
AND THIS ONE... I HAVE A BAD FEELING ABOUT THIS ONE.
PING
JESS?
HEY. SORRY TO BOTHER YOU, I KNOW YOU'RE IN MAINE STILL--
ACTUALLY, WE'RE HEADED BACK.
EVERYTHING OKAY?
NOT SURE. I GOT A STRANGE FRAGMENTED VIDEO MESSAGE FROM ROGUE.
THAT CAN'T BE GOOD.
EXACTLY. WE'RE HEADED TO THE TREEHOUSE, GOING TO SEE IF THE X-MEN HAVE ANY INFORMATION.
UH...
WHAT?
CAN I COME? I WANNA SEE THE TREE.
SURE, BUT I'M SURE THEY'D BE HAPPY TO HAVE YOU ANYTIME, JESS.
EH. I DON'T WANT TO "VISIT" LIKE A TOURIST. I WANT TO BE THERE "ON BUSINESS."
HEH. FAIR ENOUGH. WE'LL BE TOUCHING DOWN IN ABOUT TWENTY MINUTES.
YESSSS.

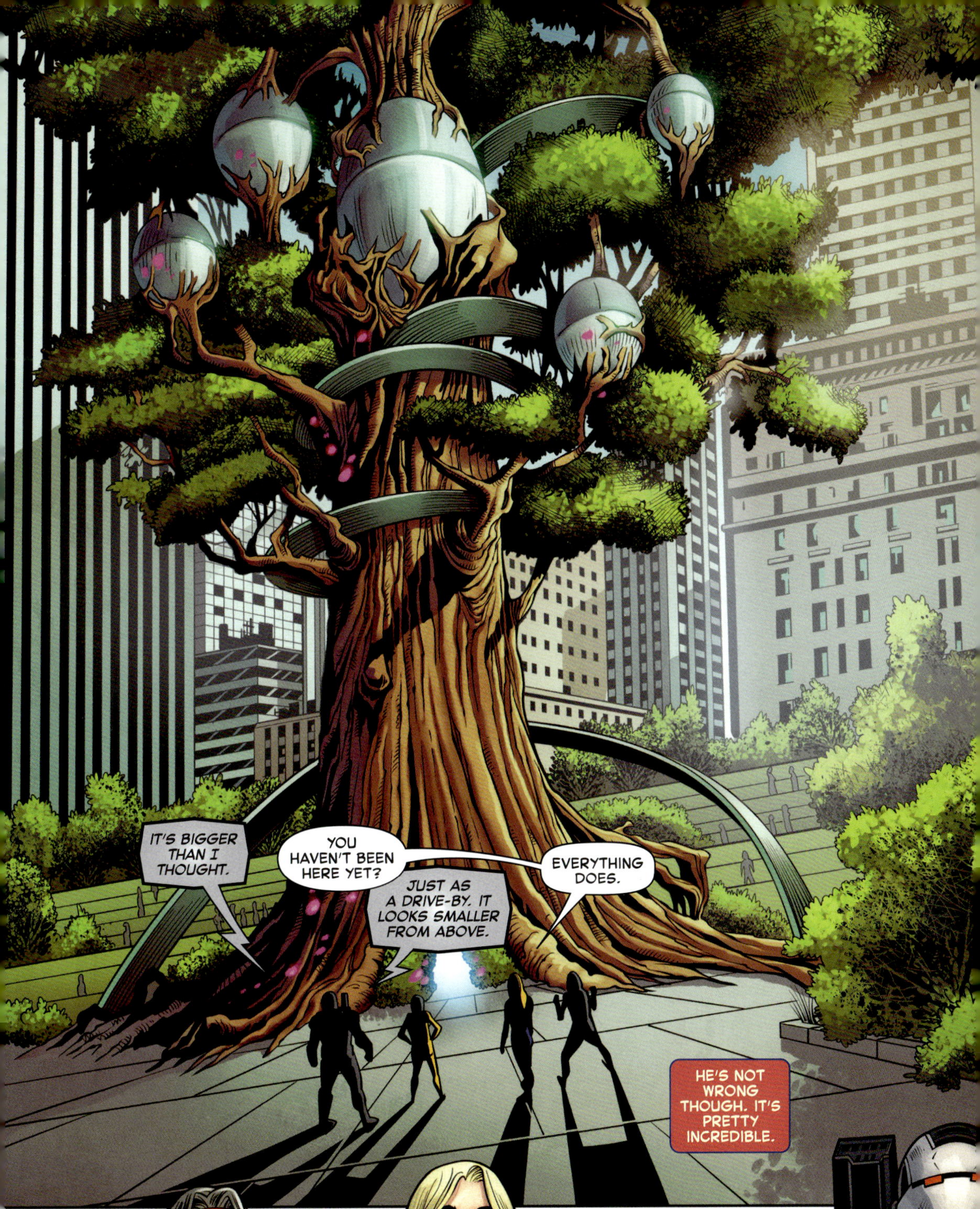
IT'S BIGGER THAN I THOUGHT.
YOU HAVEN'T BEEN HERE YET?
JUST AS A DRIVE-BY. IT LOOKS SMALLER FROM ABOVE.
EVERYTHING DOES.
HE'S NOT WRONG THOUGH. IT'S PRETTY INCREDIBLE.

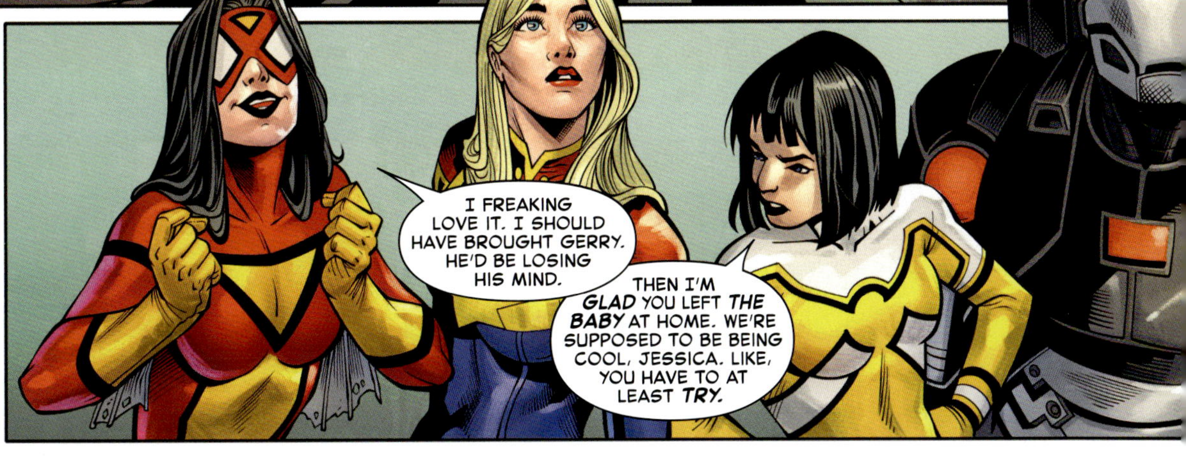
I FREAKING LOVE IT. I SHOULD HAVE BROUGHT GERRY. HE'D BE LOSING HIS MIND.
THEN I'M GLAD YOU LEFT THE BABY AT HOME. WE'RE SUPPOSED TO BE BEING COOL, JESSICA. LIKE, YOU HAVE TO AT LEAST TRY.

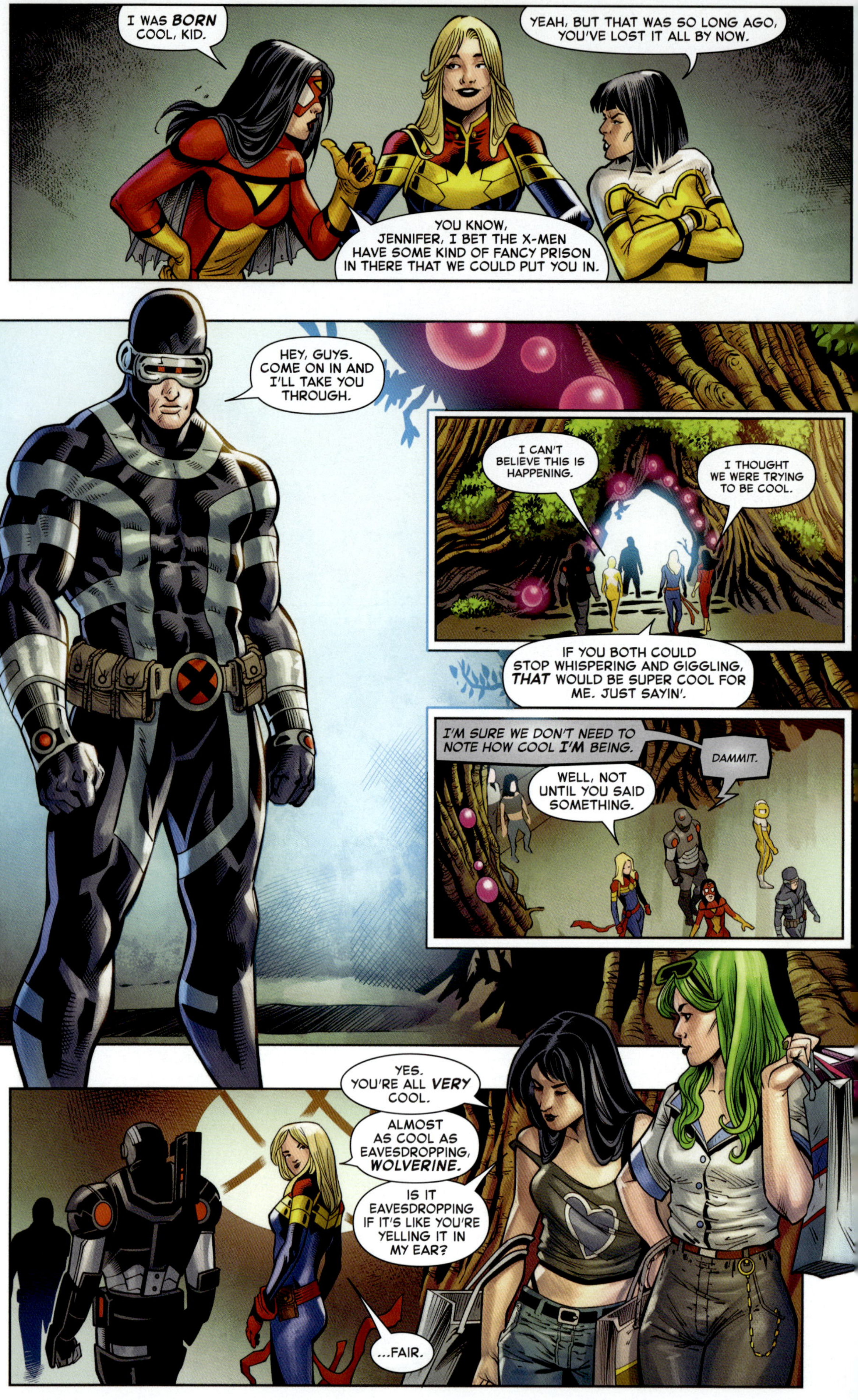

I WAS **BORN** COOL, KID.
YEAH, BUT THAT WAS SO LONG AGO, YOU'VE LOST IT ALL BY NOW.
YOU KNOW, JENNIFER, I BET THE X-MEN HAVE SOME KIND OF FANCY PRISON IN THERE THAT WE COULD PUT YOU IN.
HEY, GUYS. COME ON IN AND I'LL TAKE YOU THROUGH.
I CAN'T BELIEVE THIS IS HAPPENING.
I THOUGHT WE WERE TRYING TO BE COOL.
IF YOU BOTH COULD STOP WHISPERING AND GIGGLING, **THAT** WOULD BE SUPER COOL FOR ME. JUST SAYIN'.
*I'M SURE WE DON'T NEED TO NOTE HOW COOL **I'M** BEING.*
DAMMIT.
WELL, NOT UNTIL YOU SAID SOMETHING.
YES. YOU'RE ALL **VERY** COOL.
ALMOST AS COOL AS EAVESDROPPING, **WOLVERINE.**
IS IT EAVESDROPPING IF IT'S LIKE YOU'RE YELLING IT IN MY EAR?
...FAIR.

SHE DID NOT. WE'RE NOT EXACTLY DE CODEPENDENT TYPES.

DID YOU HAVE ANY THOUGHTS, CAROL, ON WHAT DIS MIGHT BE? DE REASON SHE MIGHT CONTACT YOU 'STEAD OF... WELL, *US?*

GO ON.

I ONLY HAD ONE IDEA, BUT I SHOULD TELL YOU I HAVE ZERO FACTS TO BACK IT UP.

LAST TIME I SAW ROGUE FOR ANY LENGTH OF TIME, IT WAS WHEN NUCLEAR MAN LURED US ONTO ROOSEVELT ISLAND.*

HE PITTED ROGUE AND I AGAINST ONE ANOTHER AND ORIGINALLY LURED HER THERE BY SENDING A FAKE MESSAGE FROM *ME.* IT DOESN'T SEEM WILDLY OUT OF POCKET THAT HE'D TRY THE SAME TRICK AGAIN, BUT REVERSED.

BUT THAT'S IT--IT'S A WILD GUESS AT BEST. EITHER WAY, IT HAS TO BE LOOKED INTO IF SHE'S UNACCOUNTED FOR.

*IT HAPPENED WAY BACK IN *MR. & MRS. X #10* AND *CAPTAIN MARVEL #3!* --SB

I KNOW SHE'S FAMILY, BUT I'D LIKE TO TAKE THE LEAD HERE, IF YOU DON'T MIND. SINCE THE MESSAGE CAME TO ME.

AGREED. BUT WE'D LIKE TO SEND SOME X-MEN WITH YOU TO ASSIST.

IT'S ALMOST LIKE OLD TIMES.

I ASSUME I DON' HAVE TA LET YOU KNOW I'M IN.

I KIND OF FIGURED.

I'M IN.

SECONDING POLARIS.

THANKS GUYS, APPRECIATE IT. IF WE'RE JUST GIVING AWAY X-MEN, CAN I REQUEST A *TELEPATH?* JEAN, YOU WANNA GO FOR A RIDE?

UNFORTUNATELY I'M BOOKED, BUT I THINK WE CAN HELP YOU OUT WITH--

CAROL? CAROL, ARE YOU THERE? KKKKKKRRRRK KKRKKK--

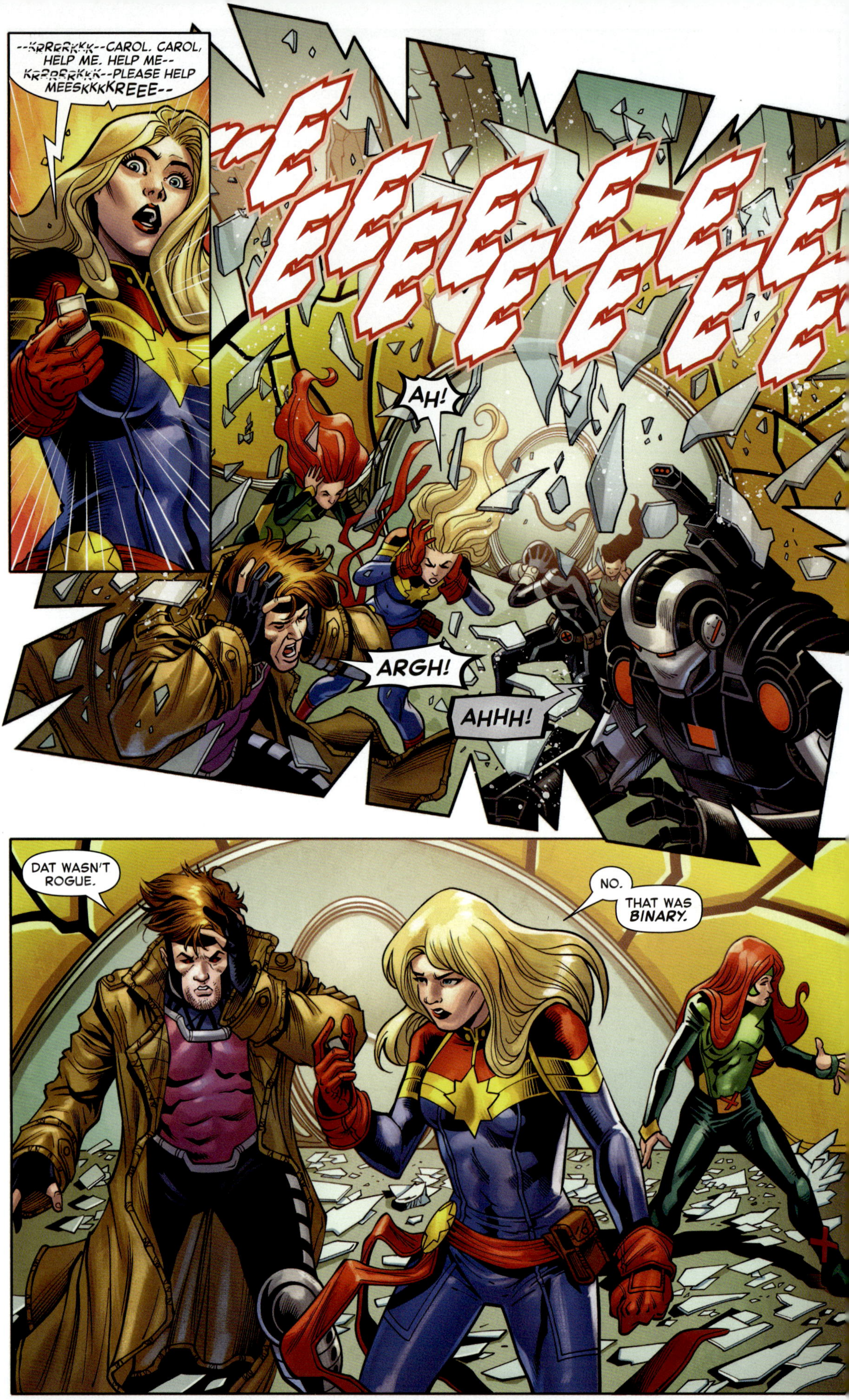
--KRRRRKKK--CAROL. CAROL, HELP ME. HELP ME--KRRRRRKKK--PLEASE HELP MEESKKKKREEE--
--EEEEEEEEEEEEEEE
AH!
ARGH!
AHHH!
DAT WASN'T ROGUE.
NO.
THAT WAS *BINARY.*

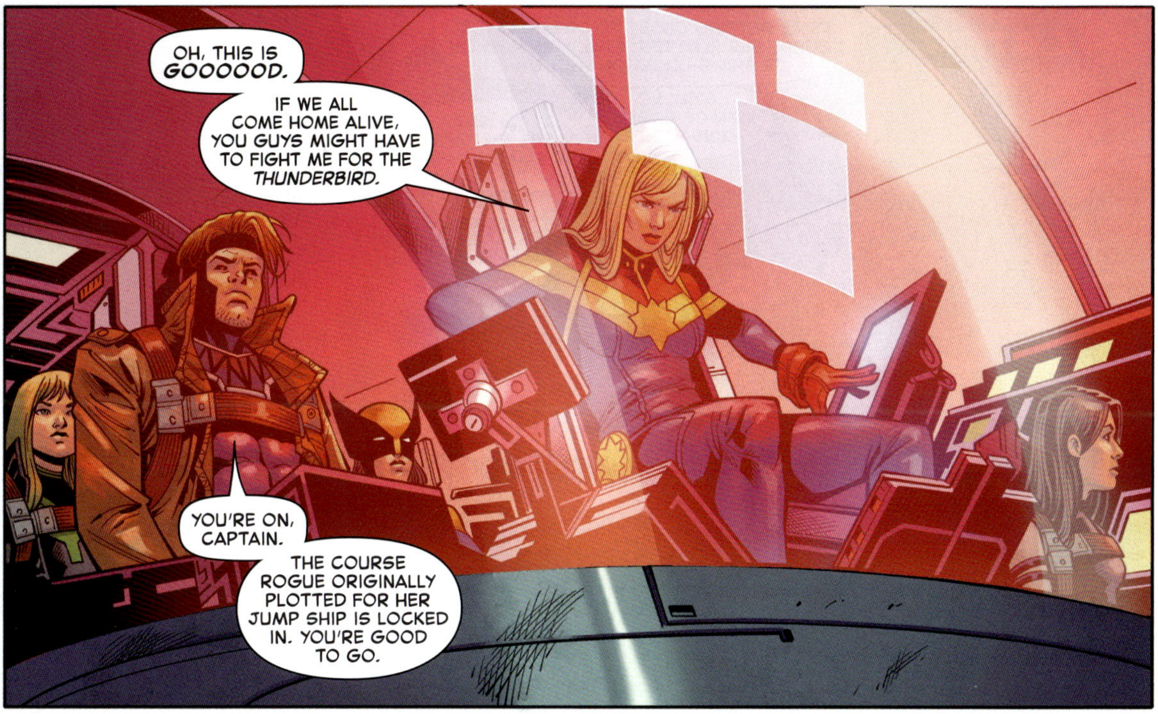
OH, THIS IS *GOOOOOD.*
IF WE ALL COME HOME ALIVE, YOU GUYS MIGHT HAVE TO FIGHT ME FOR THE *THUNDERBIRD.*
YOU'RE ON, CAPTAIN.
THE COURSE ROGUE ORIGINALLY PLOTTED FOR HER JUMP SHIP IS LOCKED IN. YOU'RE GOOD TO GO.

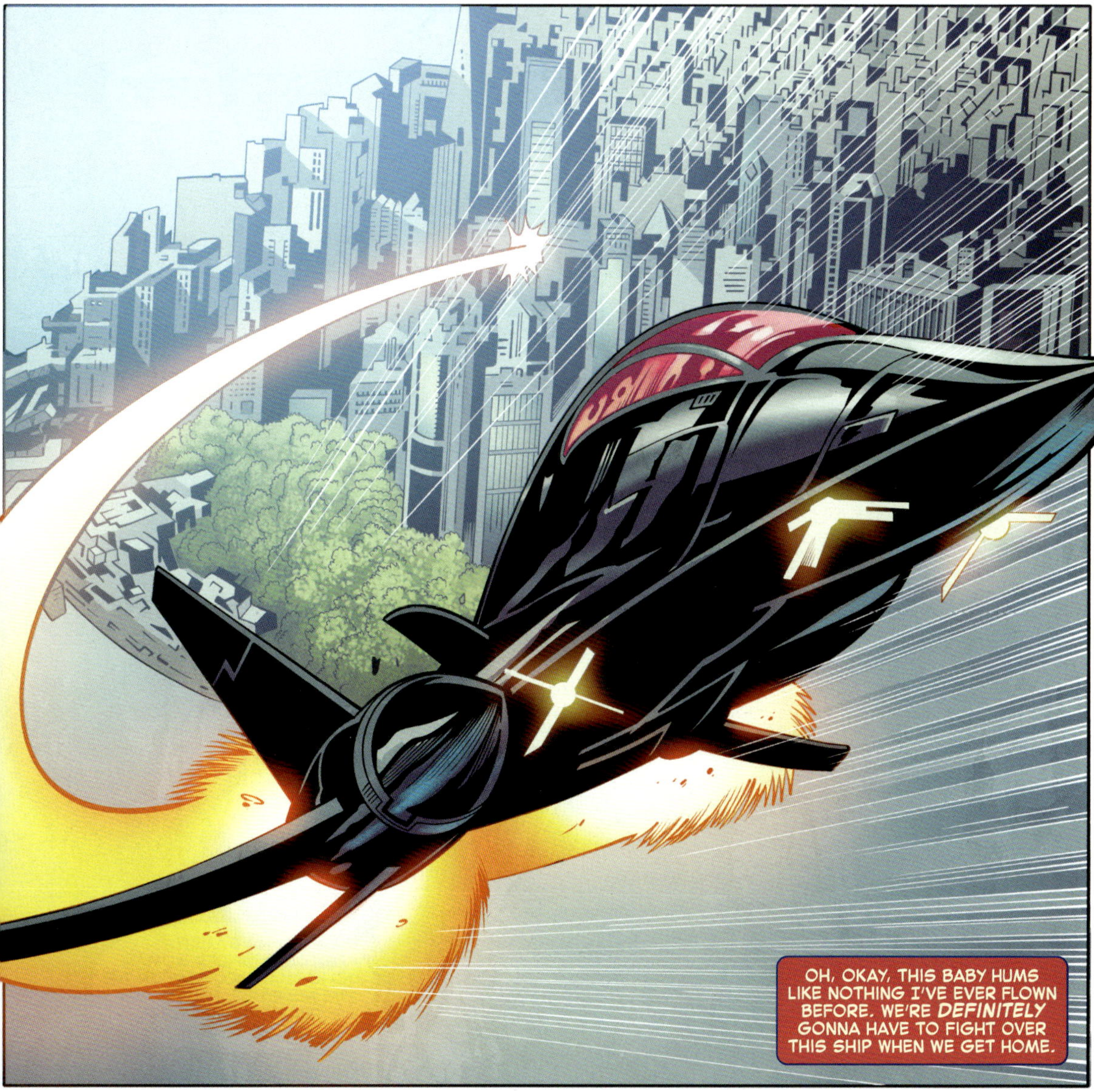
OH, OKAY, THIS BABY HUMS LIKE NOTHING I'VE EVER FLOWN BEFORE. WE'RE *DEFINITELY* GONNA HAVE TO FIGHT OVER THIS SHIP WHEN WE GET HOME.

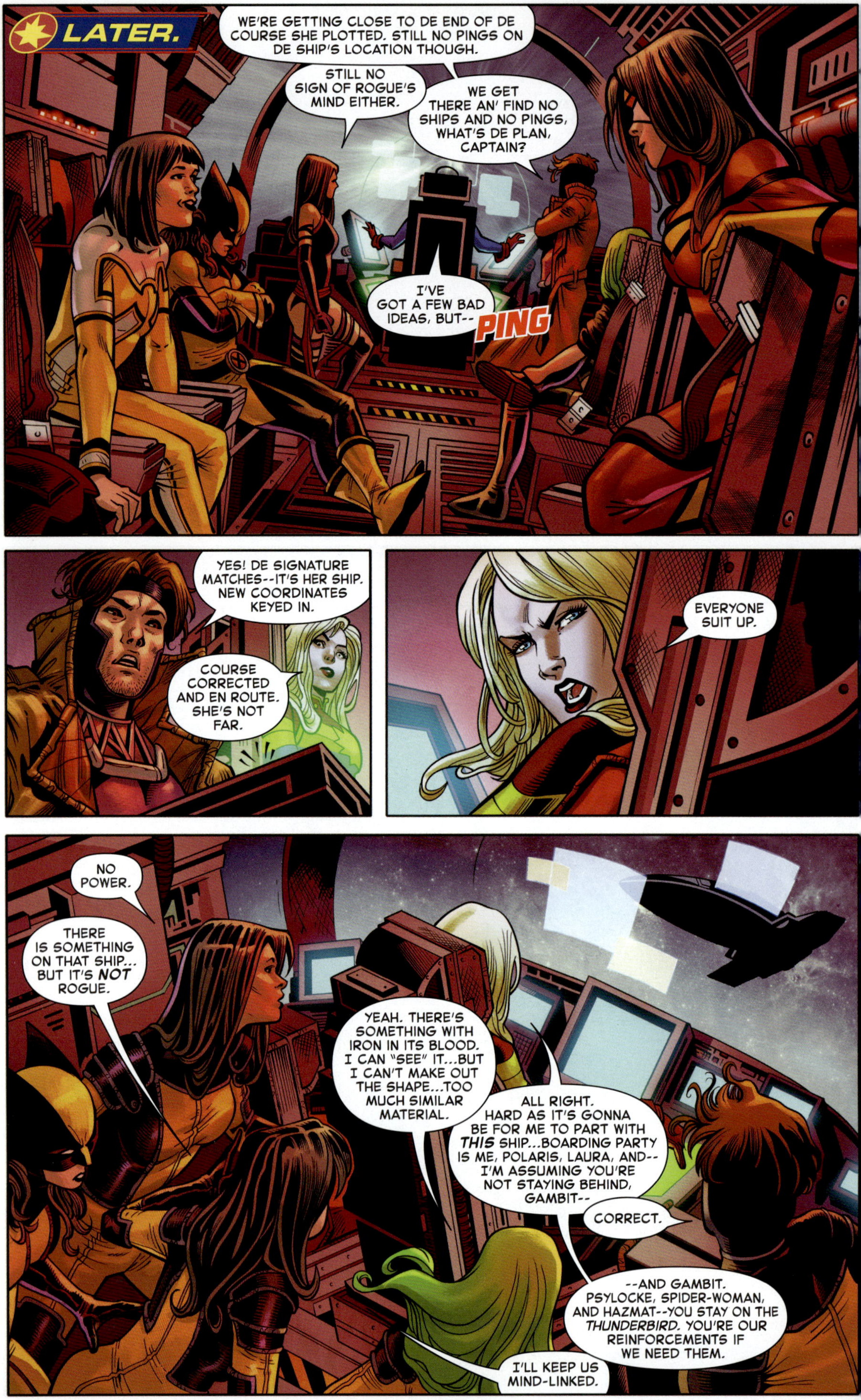
LATER.
WE'RE GETTING CLOSE TO DE END OF DE COURSE SHE PLOTTED. STILL NO PINGS ON DE SHIP'S LOCATION THOUGH.
STILL NO SIGN OF ROGUE'S MIND EITHER.
WE GET THERE AN' FIND NO SHIPS AND NO PINGS, WHAT'S DE PLAN, CAPTAIN?
I'VE GOT A FEW BAD IDEAS, BUT--
PING
YES! DE SIGNATURE MATCHES--IT'S HER SHIP. NEW COORDINATES KEYED IN.
COURSE CORRECTED AND EN ROUTE. SHE'S NOT FAR.
EVERYONE SUIT UP.
NO POWER.
THERE IS SOMETHING ON THAT SHIP... BUT IT'S NOT ROGUE.
YEAH. THERE'S SOMETHING WITH IRON IN ITS BLOOD. I CAN "SEE" IT...BUT I CAN'T MAKE OUT THE SHAPE...TOO MUCH SIMILAR MATERIAL.
ALL RIGHT. HARD AS IT'S GONNA BE FOR ME TO PART WITH THIS SHIP...BOARDING PARTY IS ME, POLARIS, LAURA, AND-- I'M ASSUMING YOU'RE NOT STAYING BEHIND, GAMBIT--
CORRECT.
--AND GAMBIT. PSYLOCKE, SPIDER-WOMAN, AND HAZMAT--YOU STAY ON THE THUNDERBIRD. YOU'RE OUR REINFORCEMENTS IF WE NEED THEM.
I'LL KEEP US MIND-LINKED.

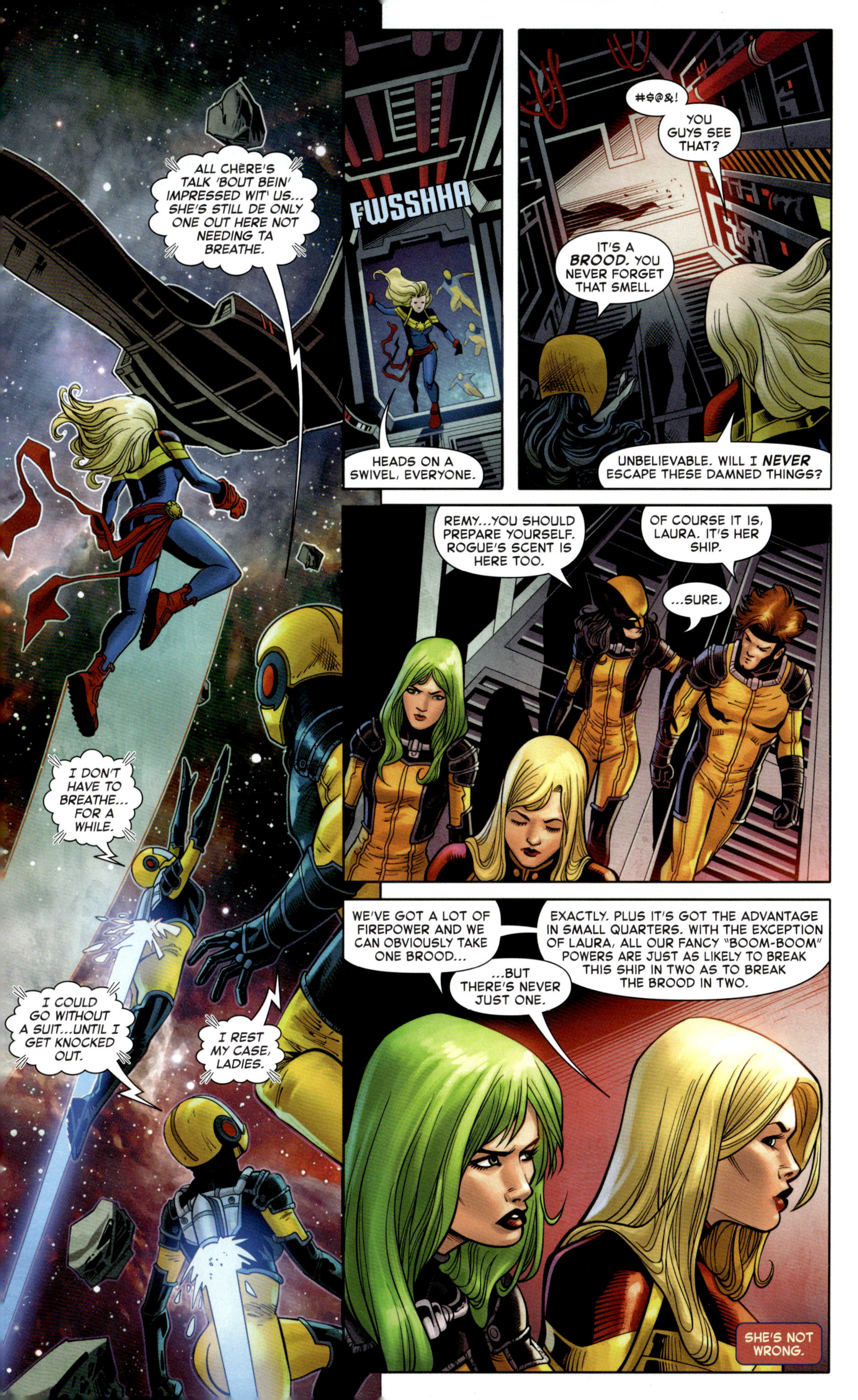

ALL CHÈRE'S TALK 'BOUT BEIN' IMPRESSED WIT' US... SHE'S STILL DE ONLY ONE OUT HERE NOT NEEDING TA BREATHE.
I DON'T HAVE TO BREATHE... FOR A WHILE.
I COULD GO WITHOUT A SUIT...UNTIL I GET KNOCKED OUT.
I REST MY CASE, LADIES.
FWSSHHA
HEADS ON A SWIVEL, EVERYONE.
#$@&!
YOU GUYS SEE THAT?
IT'S A BROOD. YOU NEVER FORGET THAT SMELL.
UNBELIEVABLE. WILL I NEVER ESCAPE THESE DAMNED THINGS?
REMY...YOU SHOULD PREPARE YOURSELF. ROGUE'S SCENT IS HERE TOO.
OF COURSE IT IS, LAURA. IT'S HER SHIP.
...SURE.
WE'VE GOT A LOT OF FIREPOWER AND WE CAN OBVIOUSLY TAKE ONE BROOD...
...BUT THERE'S NEVER JUST ONE.
EXACTLY. PLUS IT'S GOT THE ADVANTAGE IN SMALL QUARTERS. WITH THE EXCEPTION OF LAURA, ALL OUR FANCY "BOOM-BOOM" POWERS ARE JUST AS LIKELY TO BREAK THIS SHIP IN TWO AS TO BREAK THE BROOD IN TWO.
SHE'S NOT WRONG.

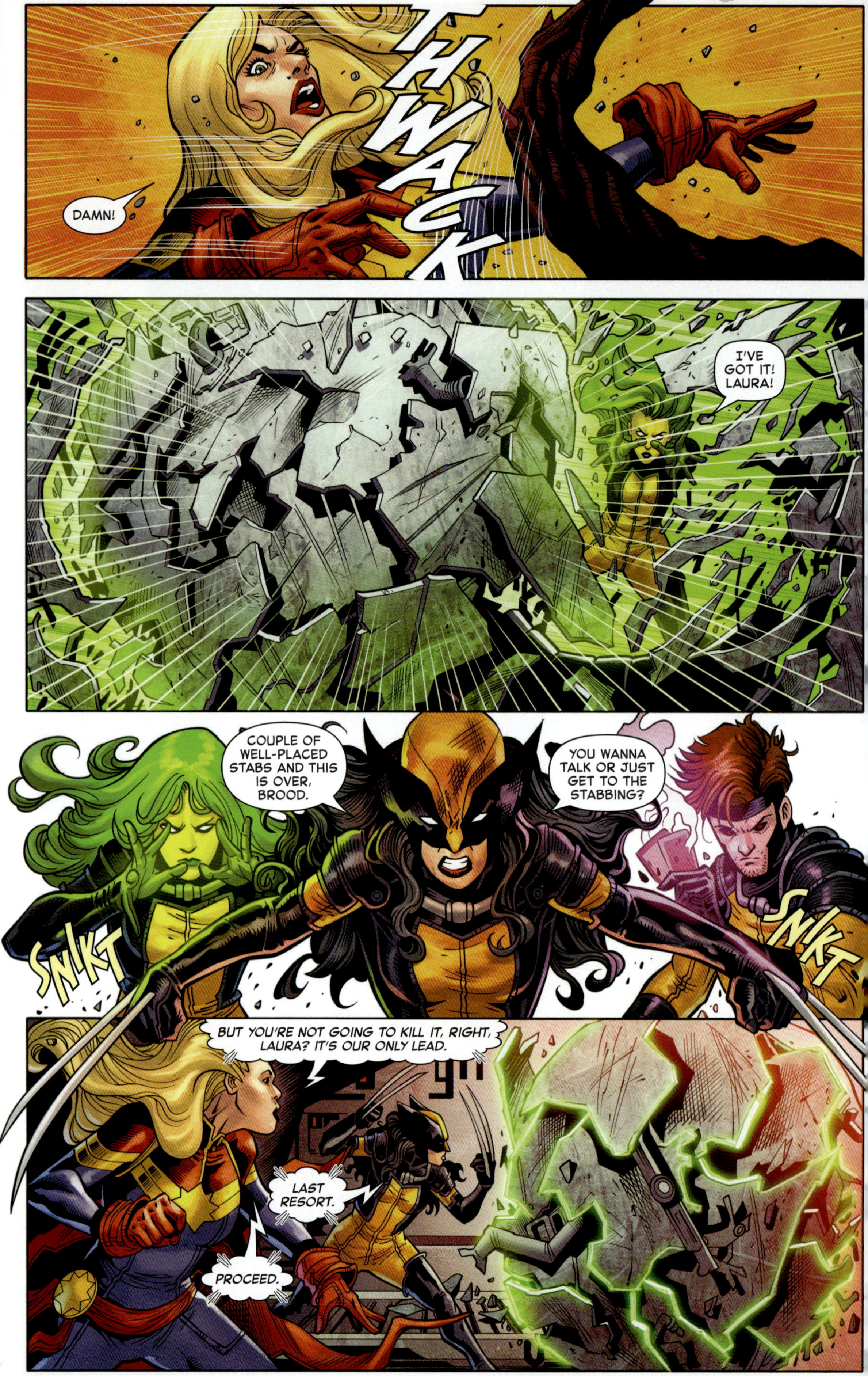
THWACK
DAMN!
I'VE GOT IT! LAURA!
COUPLE OF WELL-PLACED STABS AND THIS IS OVER, BROOD.
YOU WANNA TALK OR JUST GET TO THE STABBING?
SNIKT
SNIKT
BUT YOU'RE NOT GOING TO KILL IT, RIGHT, LAURA? IT'S OUR ONLY LEAD.
LAST RESORT.
PROCEED.

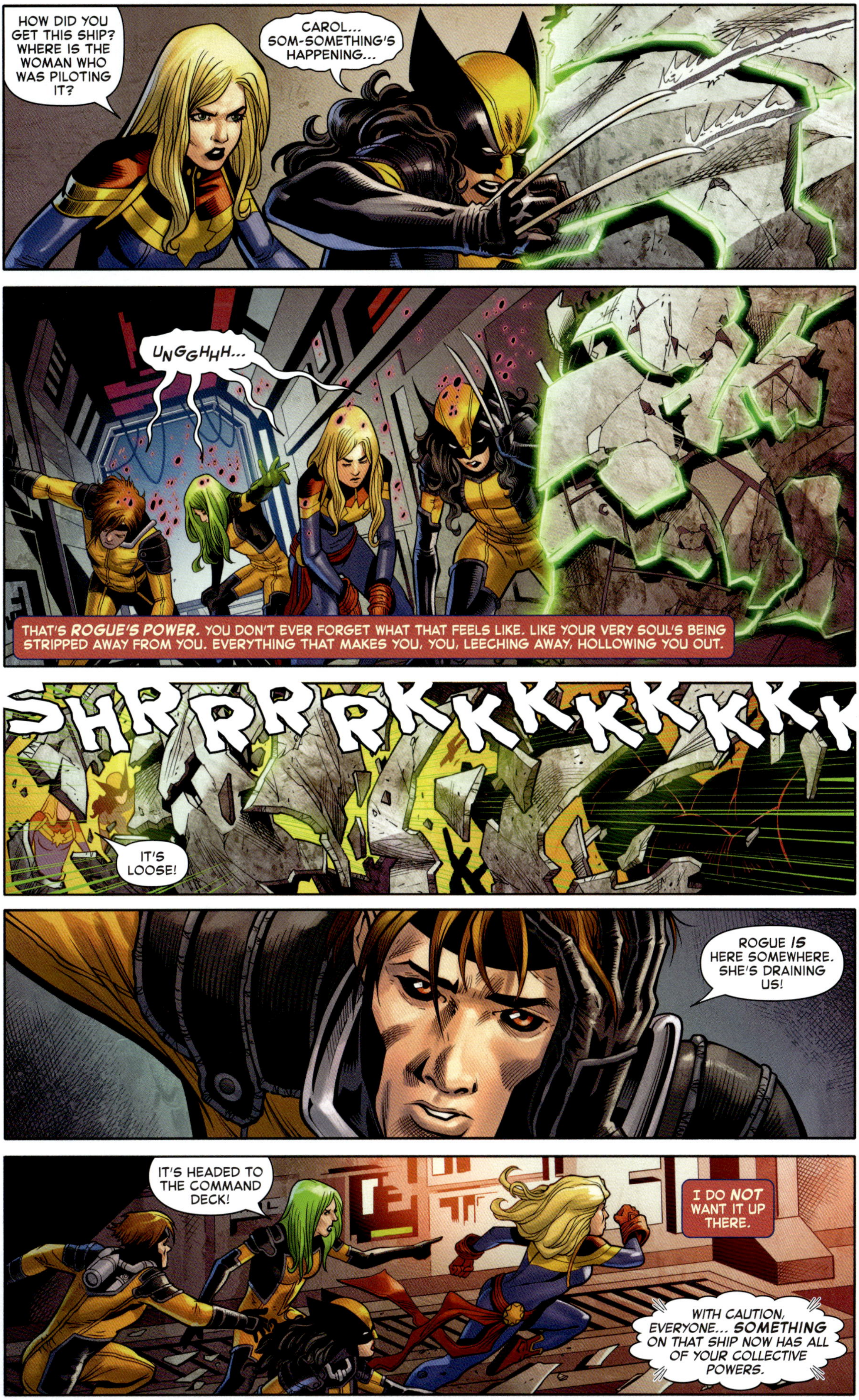
HOW DID YOU GET THIS SHIP? WHERE IS THE WOMAN WHO WAS PILOTING IT?
CAROL... SOM-SOMETHING'S HAPPENING...
UNGGHHH...
THAT'S ROGUE'S POWER. YOU DON'T EVER FORGET WHAT THAT FEELS LIKE. LIKE YOUR VERY SOUL'S BEING STRIPPED AWAY FROM YOU. EVERYTHING THAT MAKES YOU, YOU, LEECHING AWAY, HOLLOWING YOU OUT.
SHRRRKKKKKKK
IT'S LOOSE!
ROGUE IS HERE SOMEWHERE. SHE'S DRAINING US!
IT'S HEADED TO THE COMMAND DECK!
I DO NOT WANT IT UP THERE.
WITH CAUTION, EVERYONE... SOMETHING ON THAT SHIP NOW HAS ALL OF YOUR COLLECTIVE POWERS.

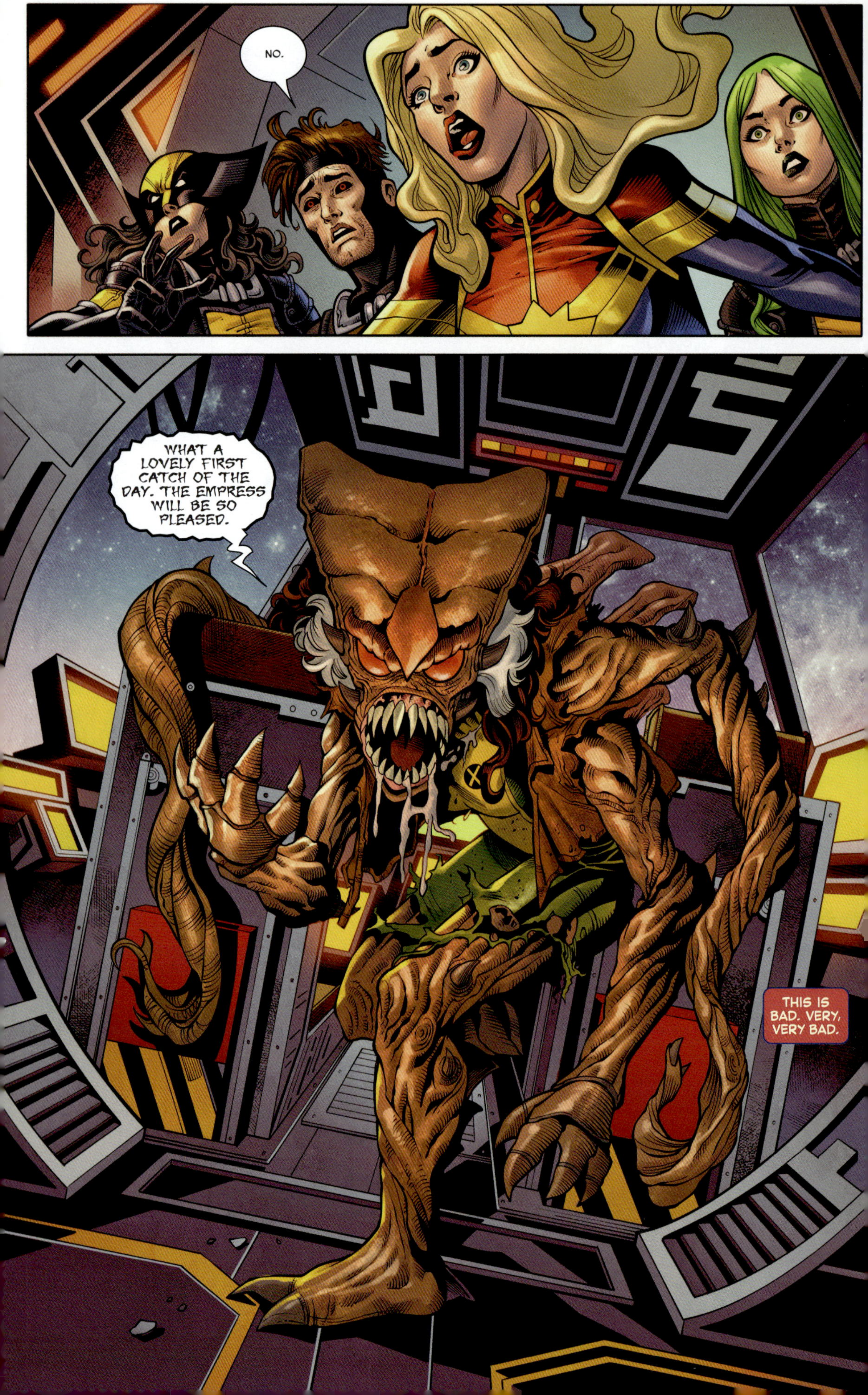
NO.
WHAT A LOVELY FIRST CATCH OF THE DAY. THE EMPRESS WILL BE SO PLEASED.
THIS IS BAD. VERY, VERY BAD.

SLAM

GAMBIT.

WE...WE DON' HAVE TA KILL HER.

NORMALLY, I KNOW...I KNOW, DAT FAR GONE TO BROOD INFECTION, SHE'D BE A LOST CAUSE. BUT DIS IS ROGUE. SHE'S SPECIAL. WE GOT LAURA RIGHT HERE--ROGUE ABSORBS THOSE HEALING POWERS AN' WE GET HER BACK.

REMY...

WE'LL TRY IT THAT WAY, BUT IF IT DOESN'T WORK OUT...IT WILL BE OKAY. WE CAN STILL RESURRECT HER. JUST HANG ONTO THAT.

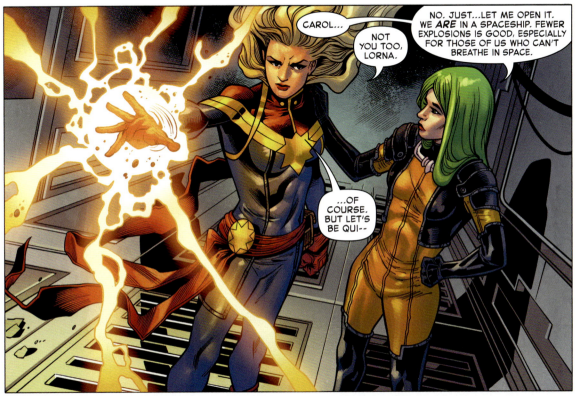

CAROL...

NOT YOU TOO, LORNA.

NO. JUST...LET ME OPEN IT. WE *ARE* IN A SPACESHIP. FEWER EXPLOSIONS IS GOOD, ESPECIALLY FOR THOSE OF US WHO CAN'T BREATHE IN SPACE.

...OF COURSE. BUT LET'S BE QUI--

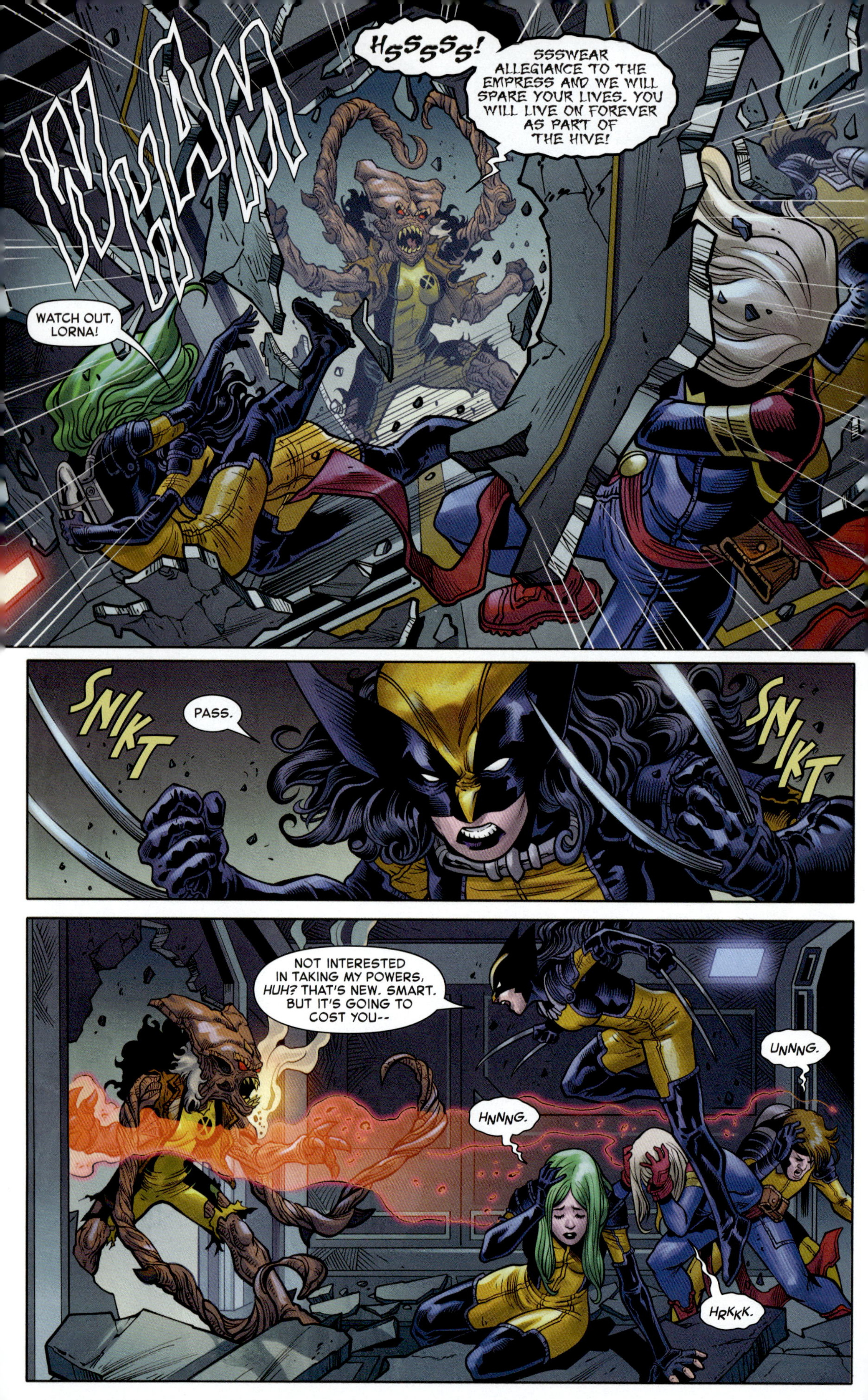
HSSSSS!
SSSWEAR ALLEGIANCE TO THE EMPRESS AND WE WILL SPARE YOUR LIVES. YOU WILL LIVE ON FOREVER AS PART OF THE HIVE!
WATCH OUT, LORNA!
SNIKT
PASS.
SNIKT
NOT INTERESTED IN TAKING MY POWERS, HUH? THAT'S NEW. SMART. BUT IT'S GOING TO COST YOU--
UNNNG.
HNNNG.
HRKKK.

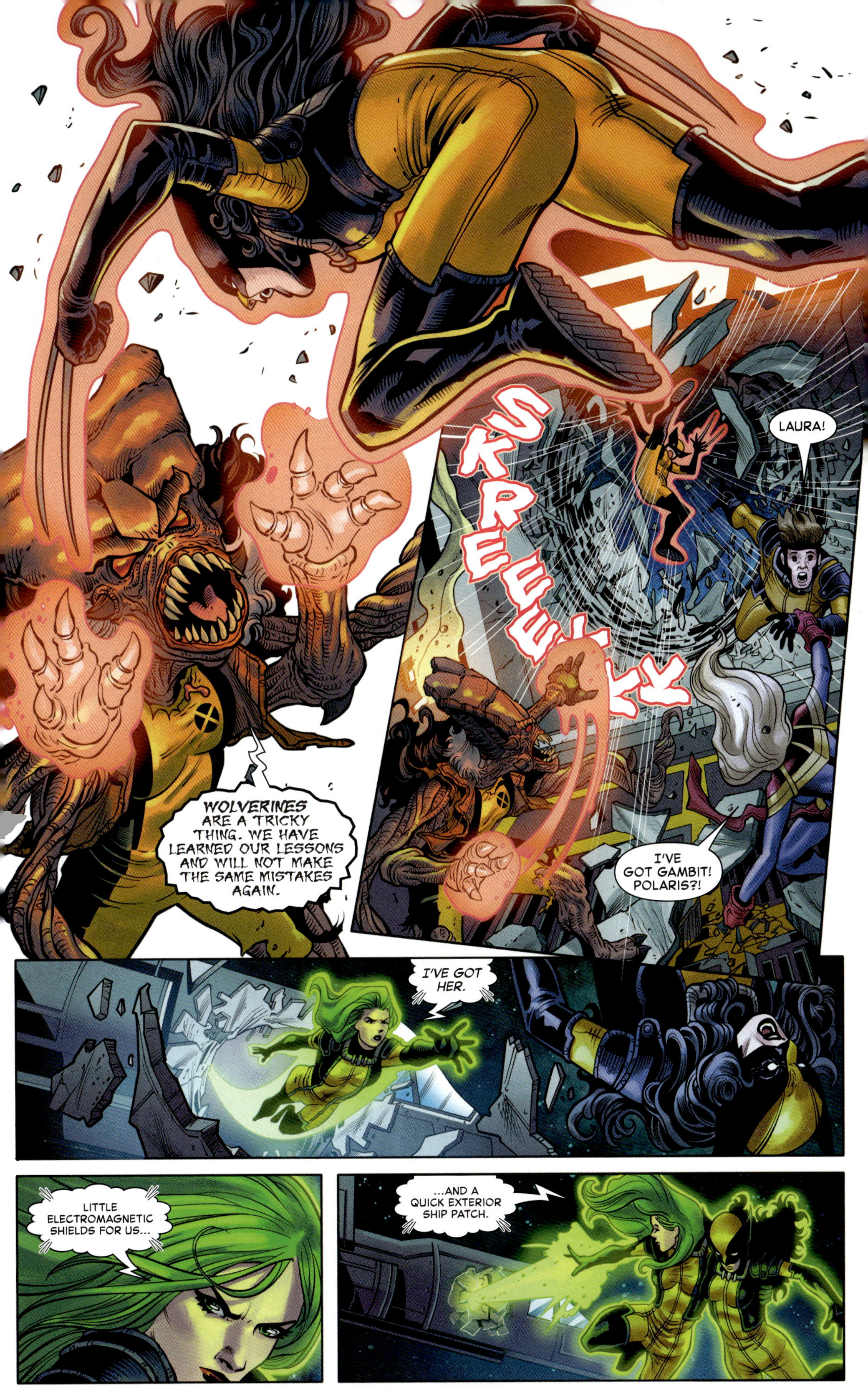

SKREEEKK
LAURA!
WOLVERINES ARE A TRICKY THING. WE HAVE LEARNED OUR LESSONS AND WILL NOT MAKE THE SAME MISTAKES AGAIN.
I'VE GOT GAMBIT! POLARIS?!
I'VE GOT HER.
LITTLE ELECTROMAGNETIC SHIELDS FOR US...
...AND A QUICK EXTERIOR SHIP PATCH.

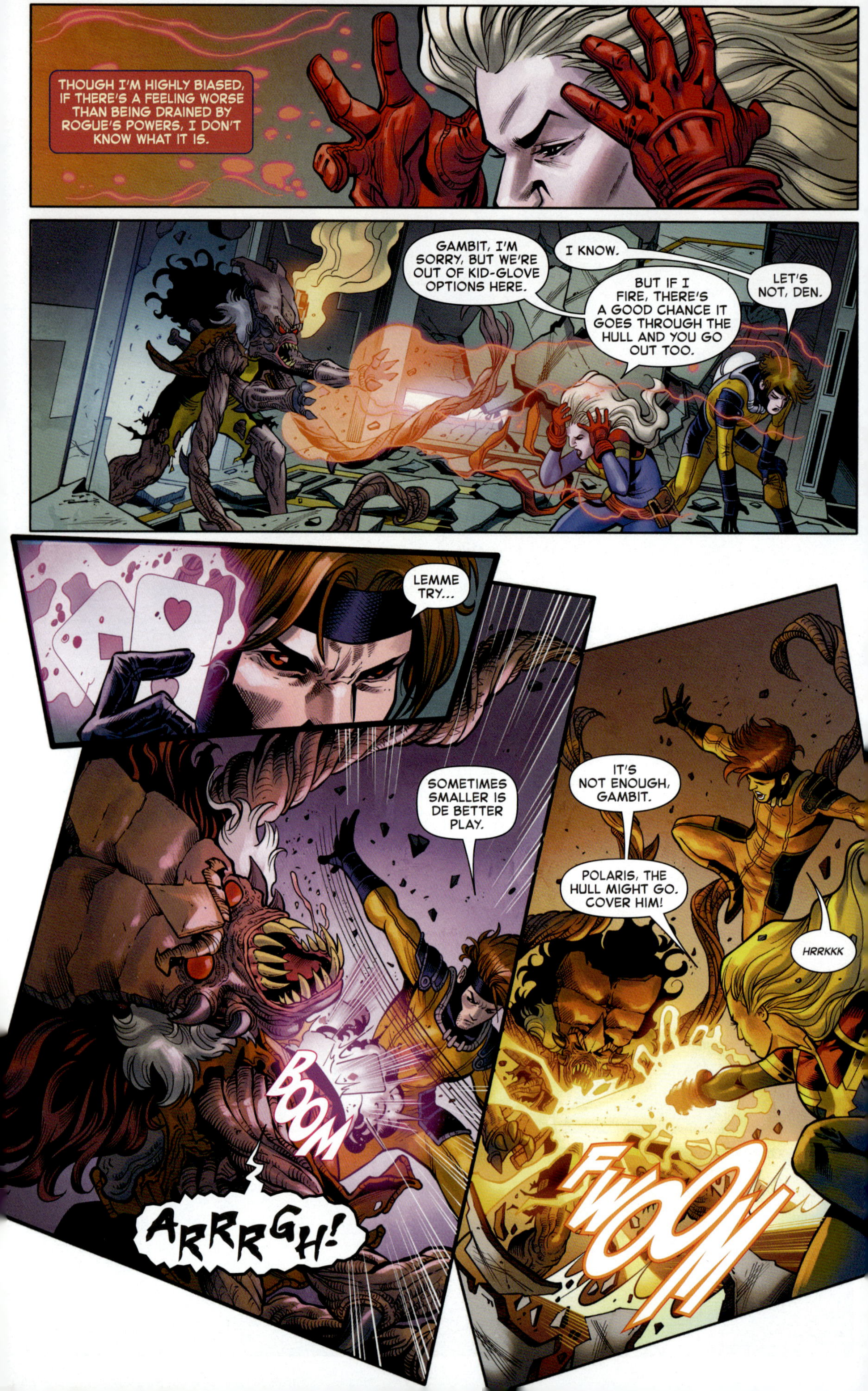
THOUGH I'M HIGHLY BIASED, IF THERE'S A FEELING WORSE THAN BEING DRAINED BY ROGUE'S POWERS, I DON'T KNOW WHAT IT IS.
GAMBIT, I'M SORRY, BUT WE'RE OUT OF KID-GLOVE OPTIONS HERE.
I KNOW.
BUT IF I FIRE, THERE'S A GOOD CHANCE IT GOES THROUGH THE HULL AND YOU GO OUT TOO.
LET'S NOT, DEN.
LEMME TRY...
SOMETIMES SMALLER IS DE BETTER PLAY.
BOOM
ARRRGH!
IT'S NOT ENOUGH, GAMBIT.
POLARIS, THE HULL MIGHT GO. COVER HIM!
HRRKKK
FWOOM

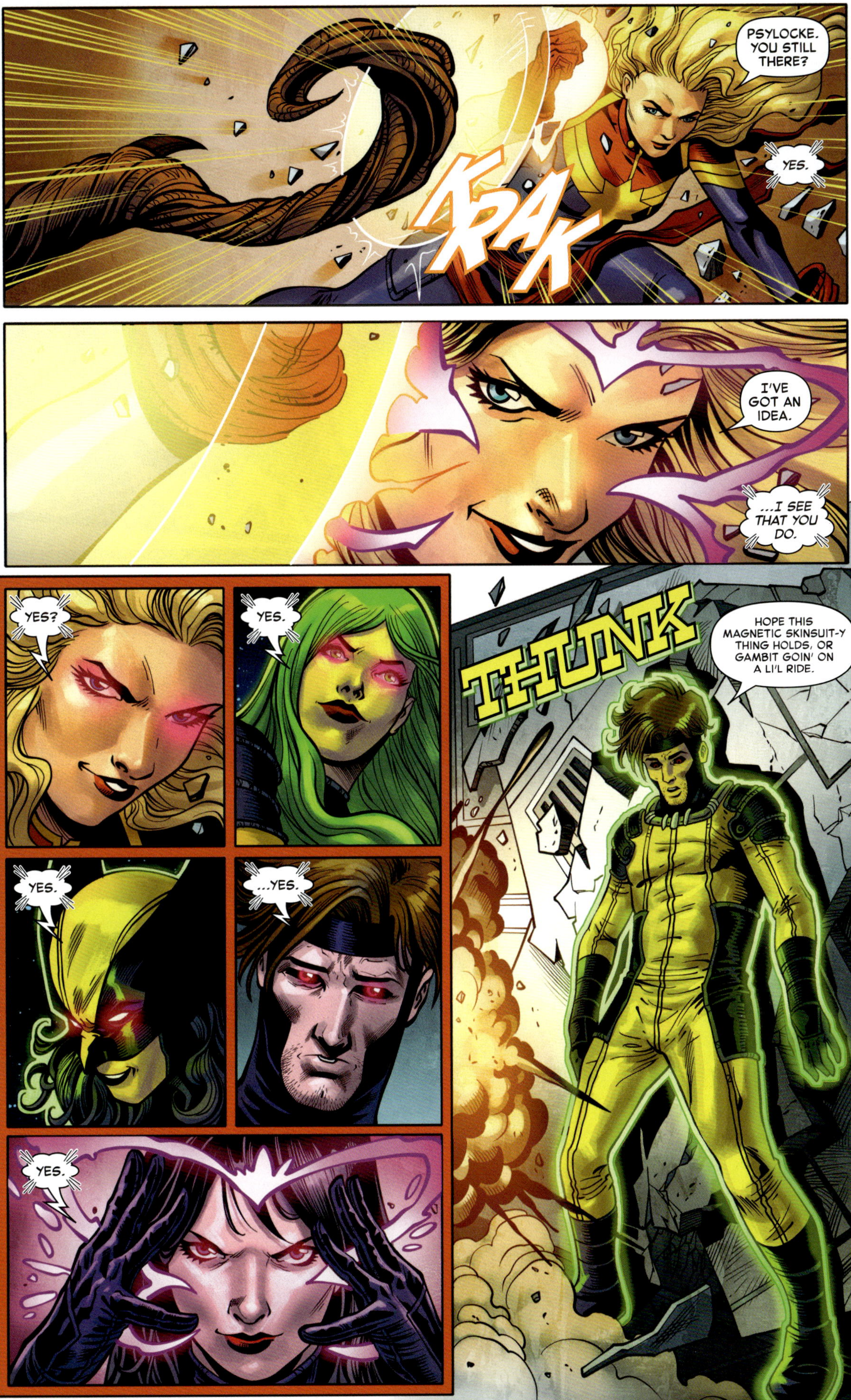
PSYLOCKE. YOU STILL THERE?
KRAK
YES.
I'VE GOT AN IDEA.
...I SEE THAT YOU DO.
YES?
YES.
YES.
...YES.
YES.
THUNK
HOPE THIS MAGNETIC SKINSUIT-Y THING HOLDS, OR GAMBIT GOIN' ON A LI'L RIDE.

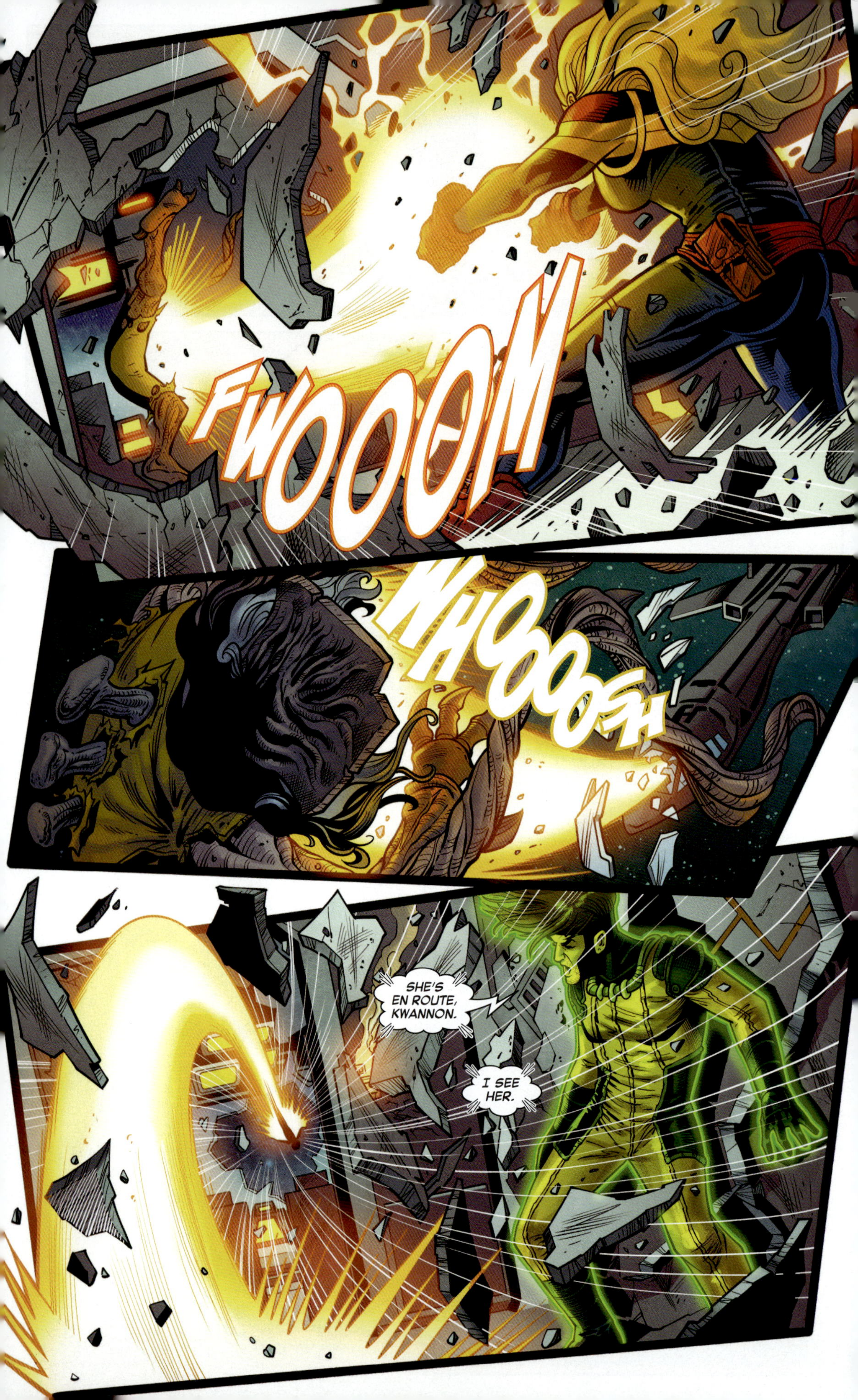
FWOOOM
WHOOOOSH
SHE'S EN ROUTE, KWANNON.
I SEE HER.

KWANNON, SHE'S IN POSITION. HIT IT.
I'M SORRY, ROGUE.
WHEN YOU WAKE ON KRAKOA, YOU WON'T REMEMBER THIS, AND I HOPE THAT'S FOR THE BEST.
FWOOM
GOOD NIGHT.

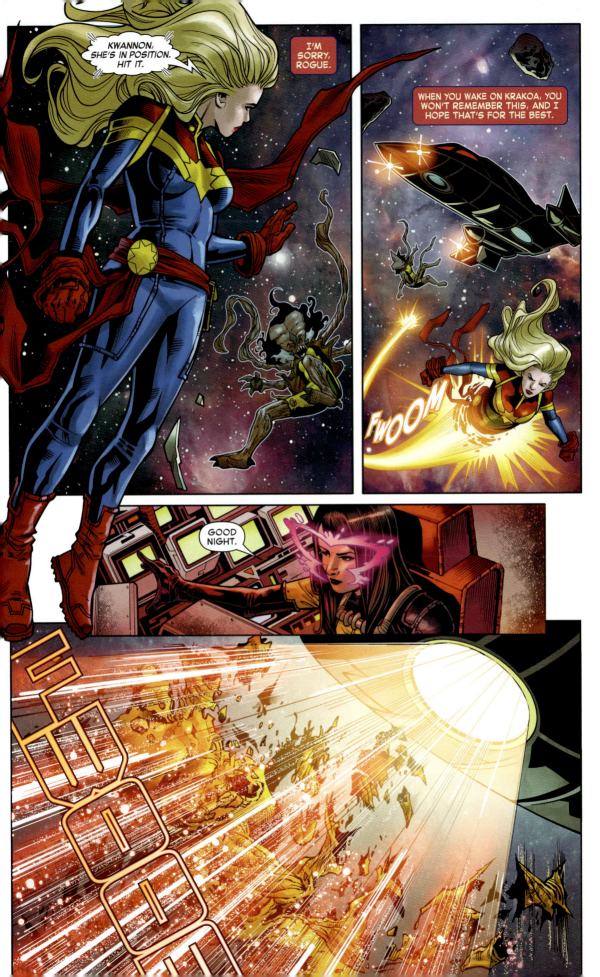

IT HAD ALL OUR POWERS... IT WAS IMPOSSIBLE TO GET CLOSE. WE DIDN'T...I DIDN'T SEE ANOTHER WAY.

WE KNOW.

DER WAS NONE.

I'M SORRY, REMY.

THA'S MY GIRL.

ALWAYS WAS TOO TOUGH FOR HER OWN GOOD.

I'VE SENT MESSAGES HOME... BOTH PSYCHIC AND VIA THE *THUNDERBIRD.* BUT WE'RE PRETTY FAR OUT OF POCKET. I DOUBT ANYONE HAS RECEIVED EITHER.

I JUST DON'T UNDERSTAND WHY THIS IS HAPPENING.

HOW DO YOU MEAN?

I DON'T KNOW HOW AWARE YOU ARE, CAROL, BUT THE SITUATION WITH THE BROOD HAS BEEN DRASTICALLY DIFFERENT EVER SINCE THE *KING EGG* ENTERED THE PICTURE.*

THE BROOD HAVE ESSENTIALLY BEEN *ALLIES* TO THE X-MEN--TO *EARTH*--EVER SINCE BROO CAME INTO POWER. WHAT WE'VE SEEN TODAY SUGGESTS A RATHER DRAMATIC SHIFT.

I'LL SAY.

*IN X-MEN (2019) #9! --S.B.

I UNDERSTAND IF YOU ALL FEEL YOU NEED TO GO BACK...TO WARN THE OTHERS THAT SOMETHING BAD IS GOING ON OUT HERE AND TO GET ROGUE BACK TO YOU ALL AS SOON AS POSSIBLE.

BUT I BELIEVE BINARY IS STILL OUT HERE, AND I CAN'T JUST LEAVE HER. SO I'M STAYING.

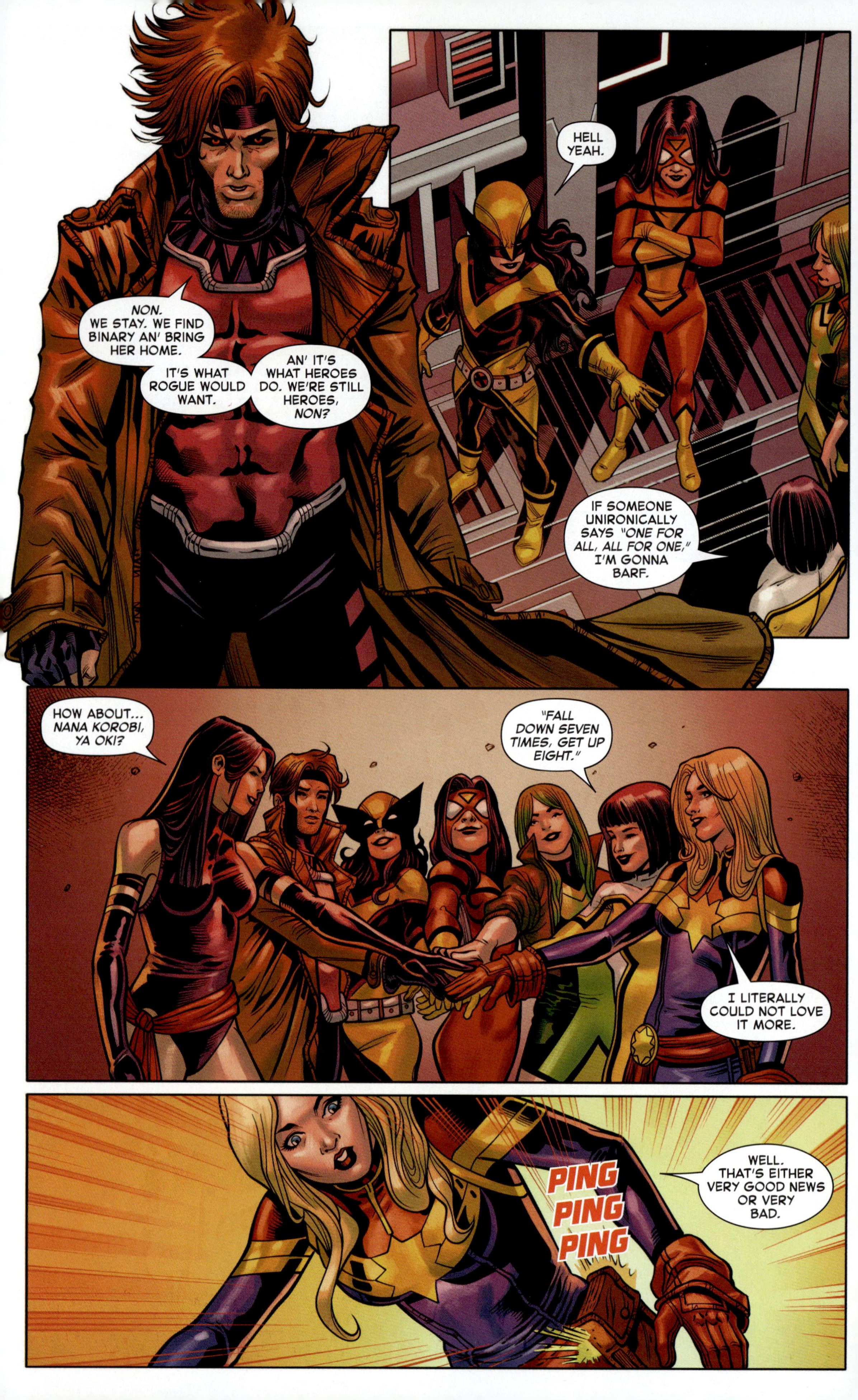
HELL YEAH.
NON. WE STAY. WE FIND BINARY AN' BRING HER HOME.
IT'S WHAT ROGUE WOULD WANT.
AN' IT'S WHAT HEROES DO. WE'RE STILL HEROES, NON?
IF SOMEONE UNIRONICALLY SAYS "ONE FOR ALL, ALL FOR ONE," I'M GONNA BARF.
HOW ABOUT... NANA KOROBI, YA OKI?
"FALL DOWN SEVEN TIMES, GET UP EIGHT."
I LITERALLY COULD NOT LOVE IT MORE.
PING PING PING
WELL. THAT'S EITHER VERY GOOD NEWS OR VERY BAD.

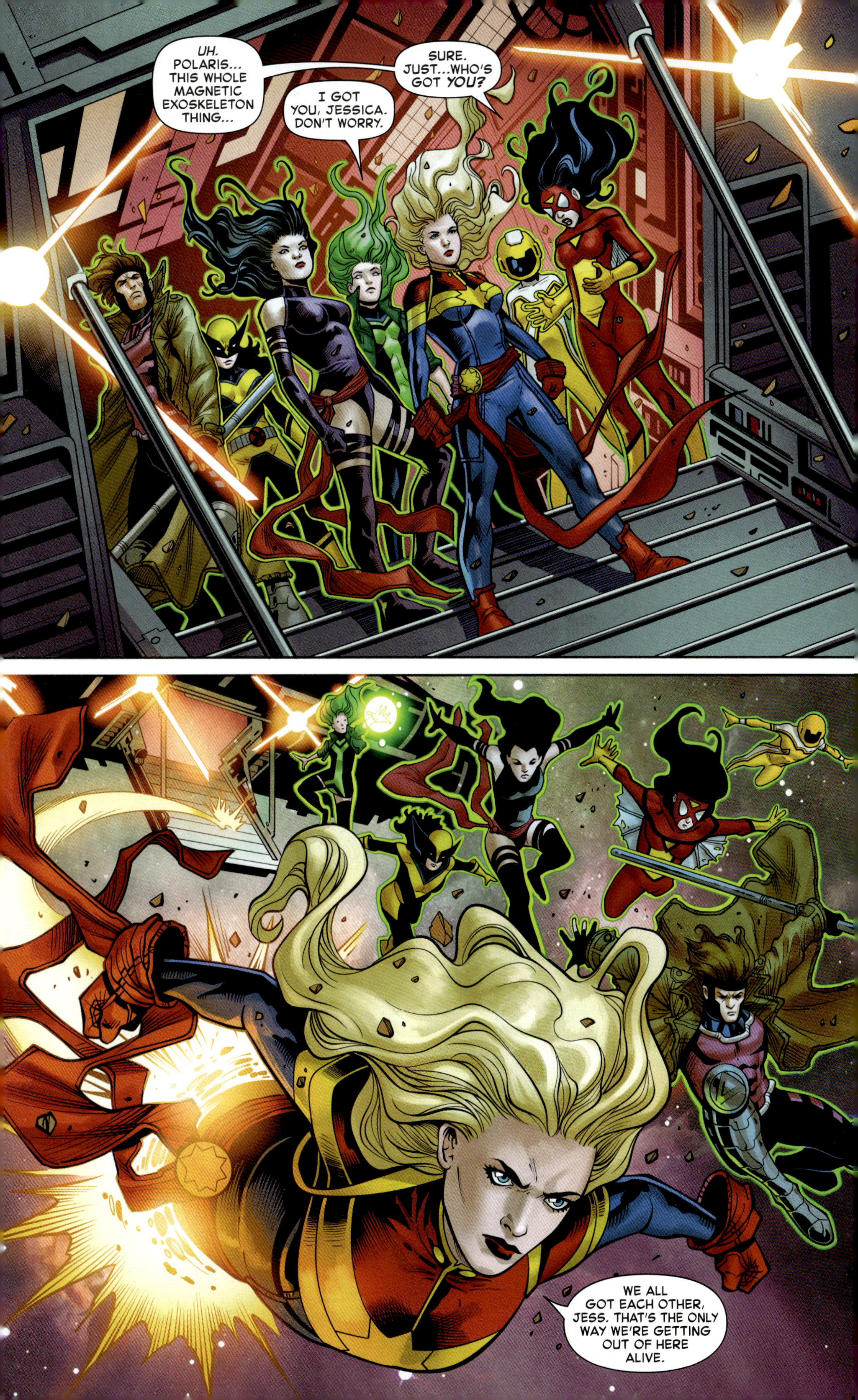
UH. POLARIS... THIS WHOLE MAGNETIC EXOSKELETON THING...
I GOT YOU, JESSICA. DON'T WORRY.
SURE. JUST...WHO'S GOT *YOU?*
WE ALL GOT EACH OTHER, JESS. THAT'S THE ONLY WAY WE'RE GETTING OUT OF HERE ALIVE.

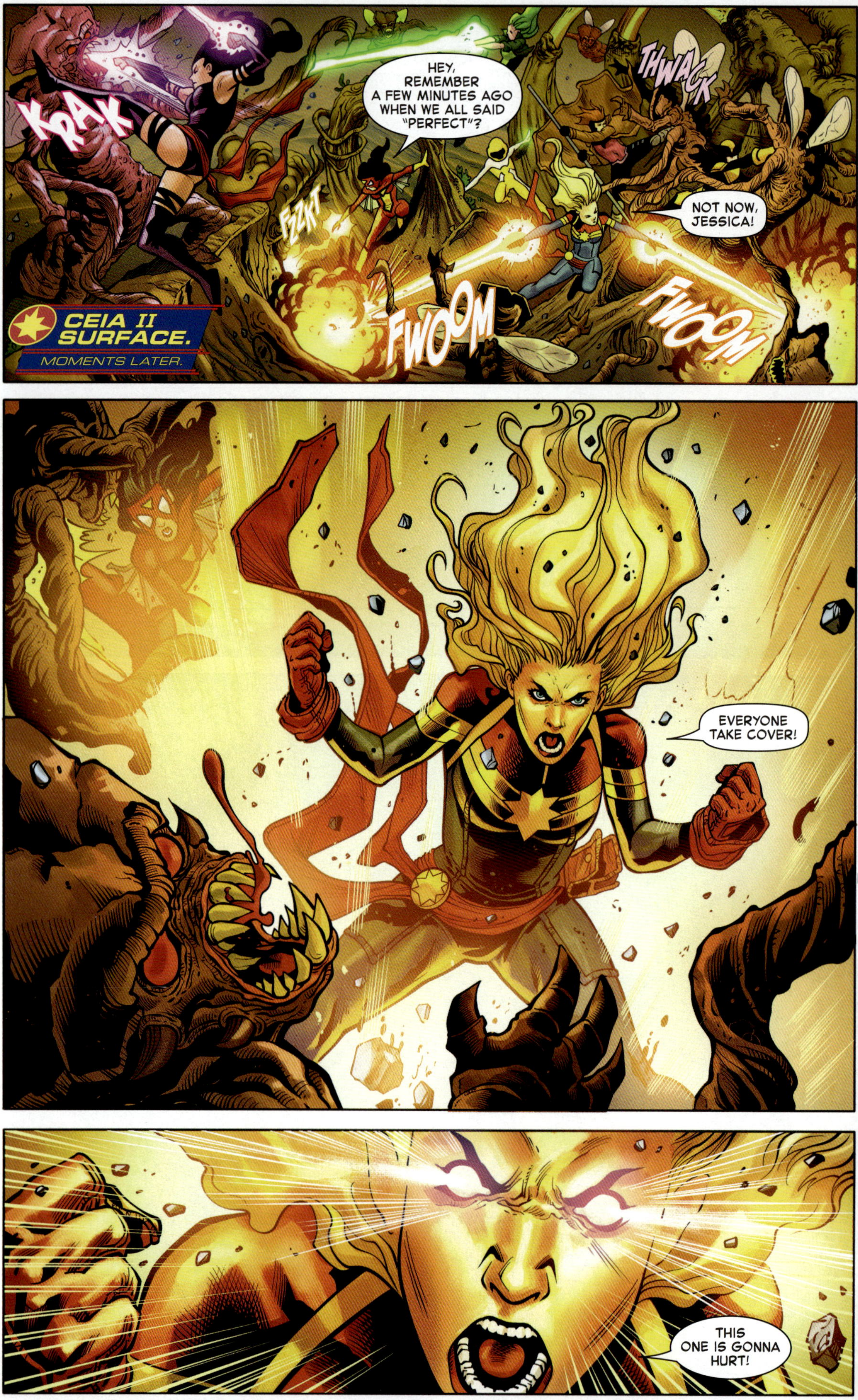
KRAK
HEY, REMEMBER A FEW MINUTES AGO WHEN WE ALL SAID "PERFECT"?
THWACK
NOT NOW, JESSICA!
FZZKT
CEIA II SURFACE.
MOMENTS LATER.
FWOOM
FWOOM
EVERYONE TAKE COVER!
THIS ONE IS GONNA HURT!

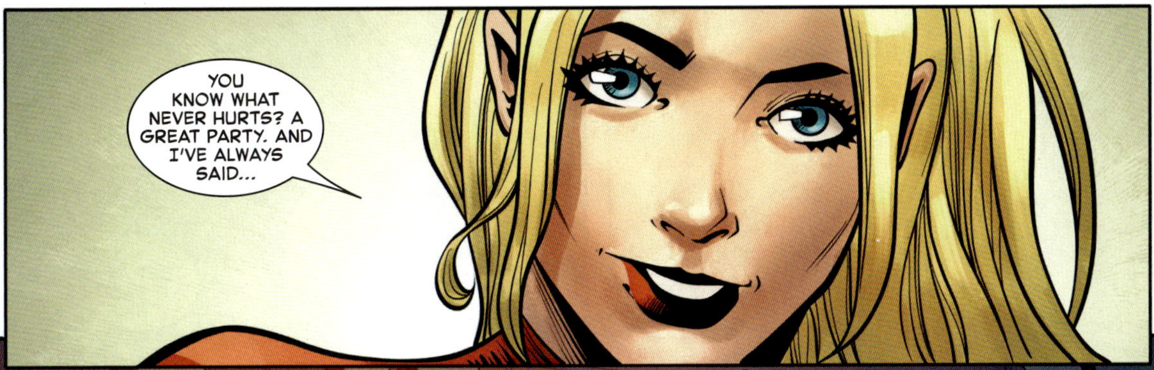
YOU KNOW WHAT NEVER HURTS? A GREAT PARTY. AND I'VE ALWAYS SAID...

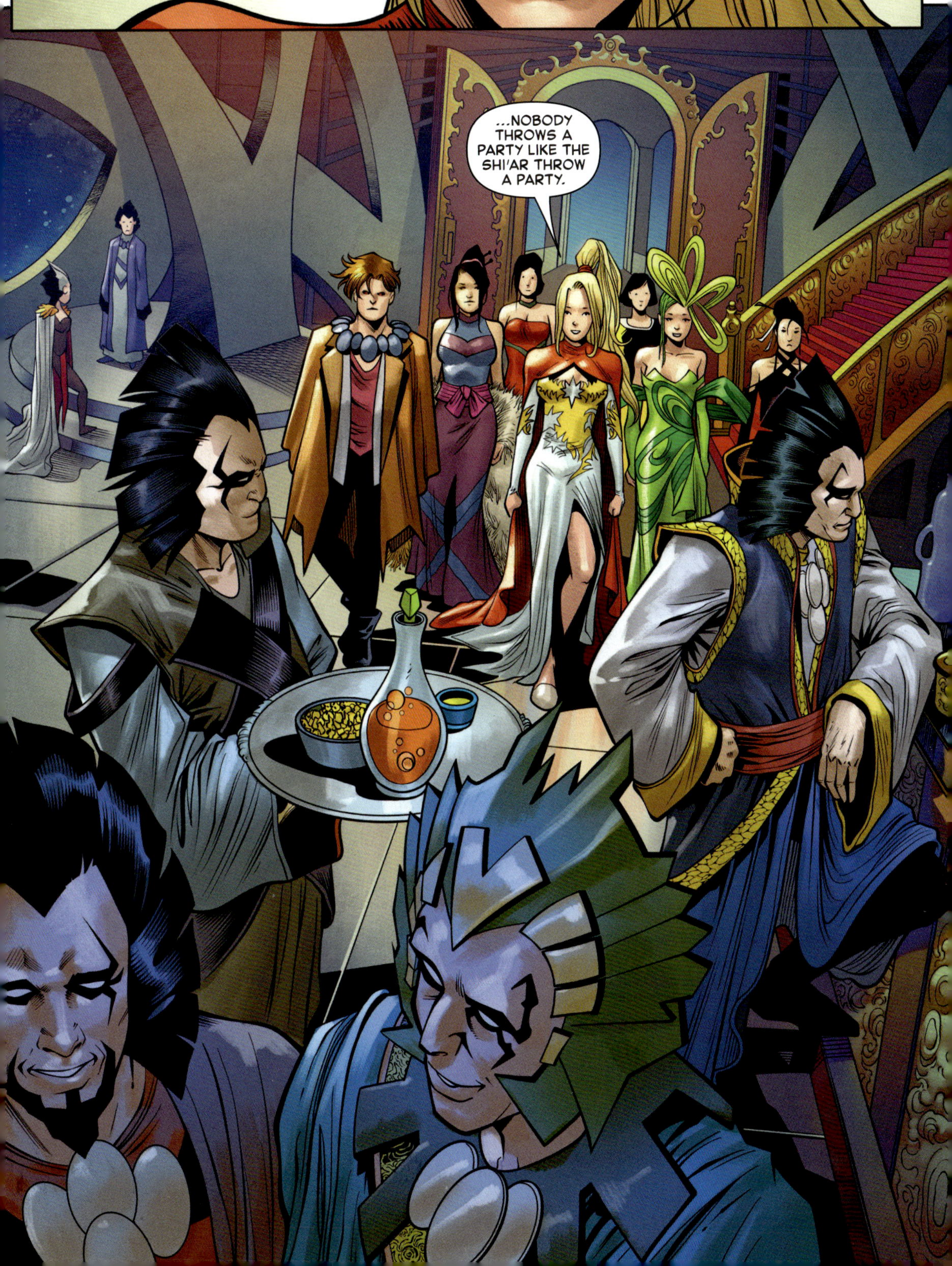
...NOBODY THROWS A PARTY LIKE THE SHI'AR THROW A PARTY.

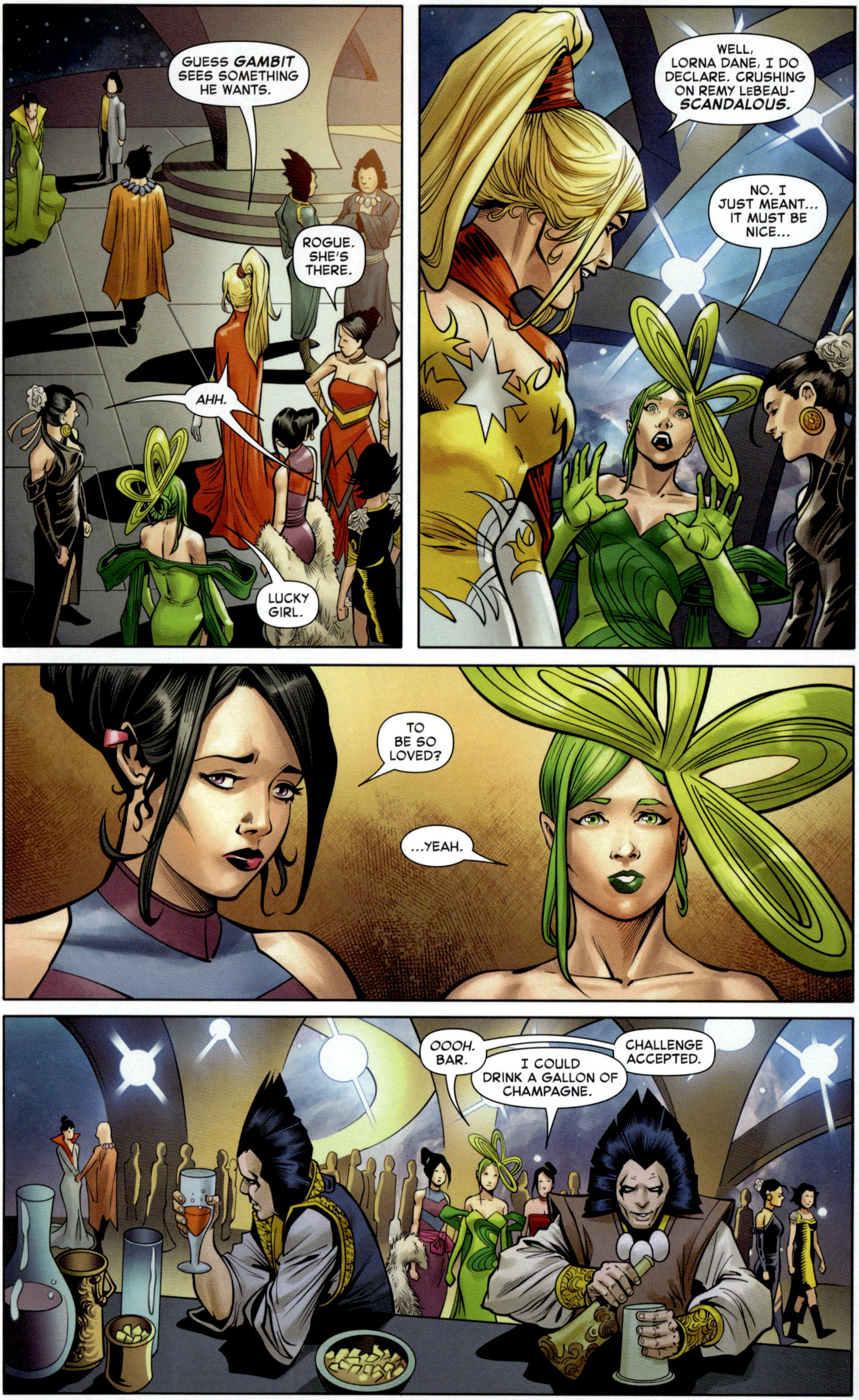
GUESS GAMBIT SEES SOMETHING HE WANTS.
ROGUE. SHE'S THERE.
AHH.
LUCKY GIRL.
WELL, LORNA DANE, I DO DECLARE. CRUSHING ON REMY LEBEAU-SCANDALOUS.
NO. I JUST MEANT... IT MUST BE NICE...
TO BE SO LOVED?
...YEAH.
OOOH. BAR.
I COULD DRINK A GALLON OF CHAMPAGNE.
CHALLENGE ACCEPTED.

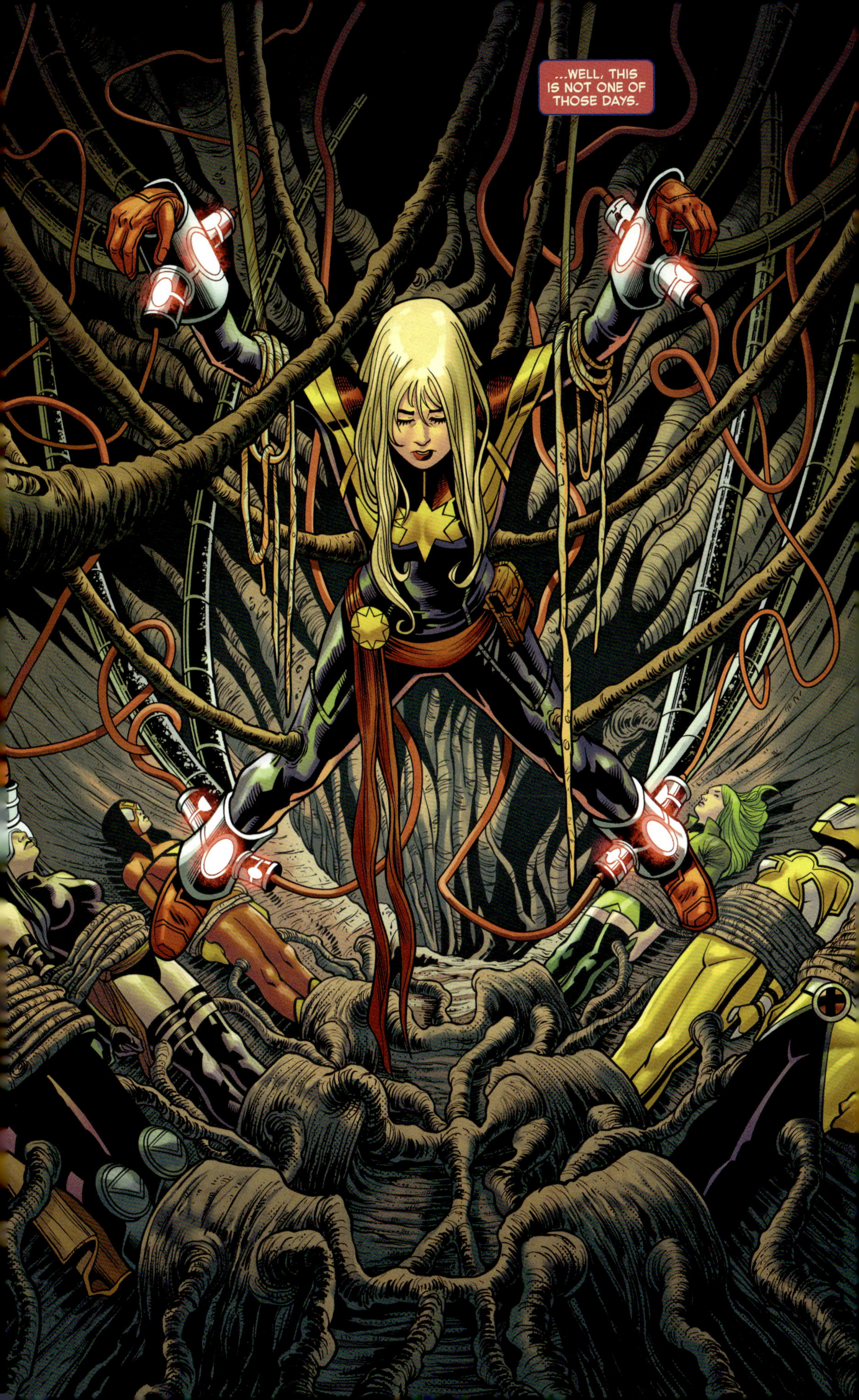
...WELL, THIS IS NOT ONE OF THOSE DAYS.

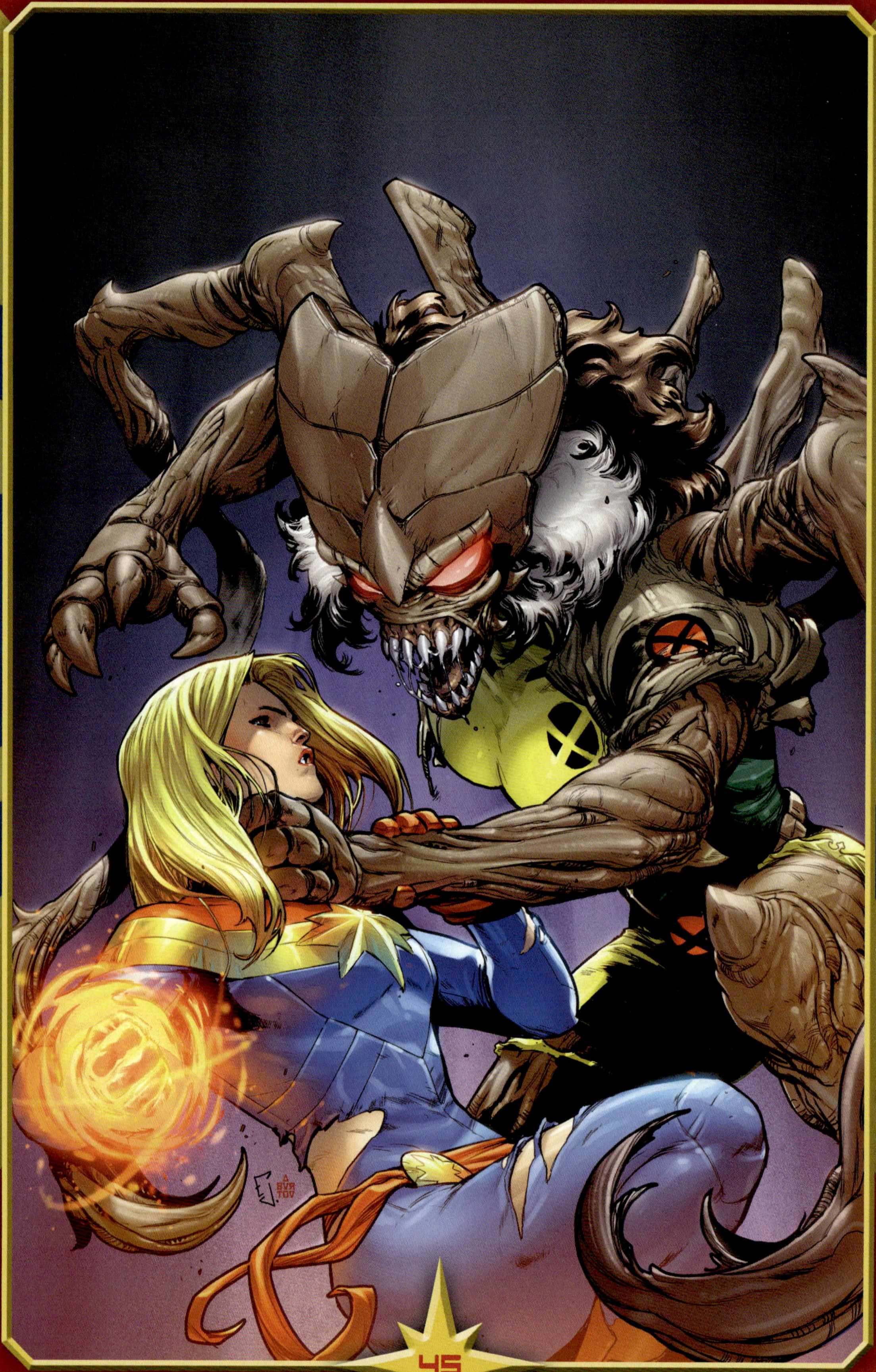

45

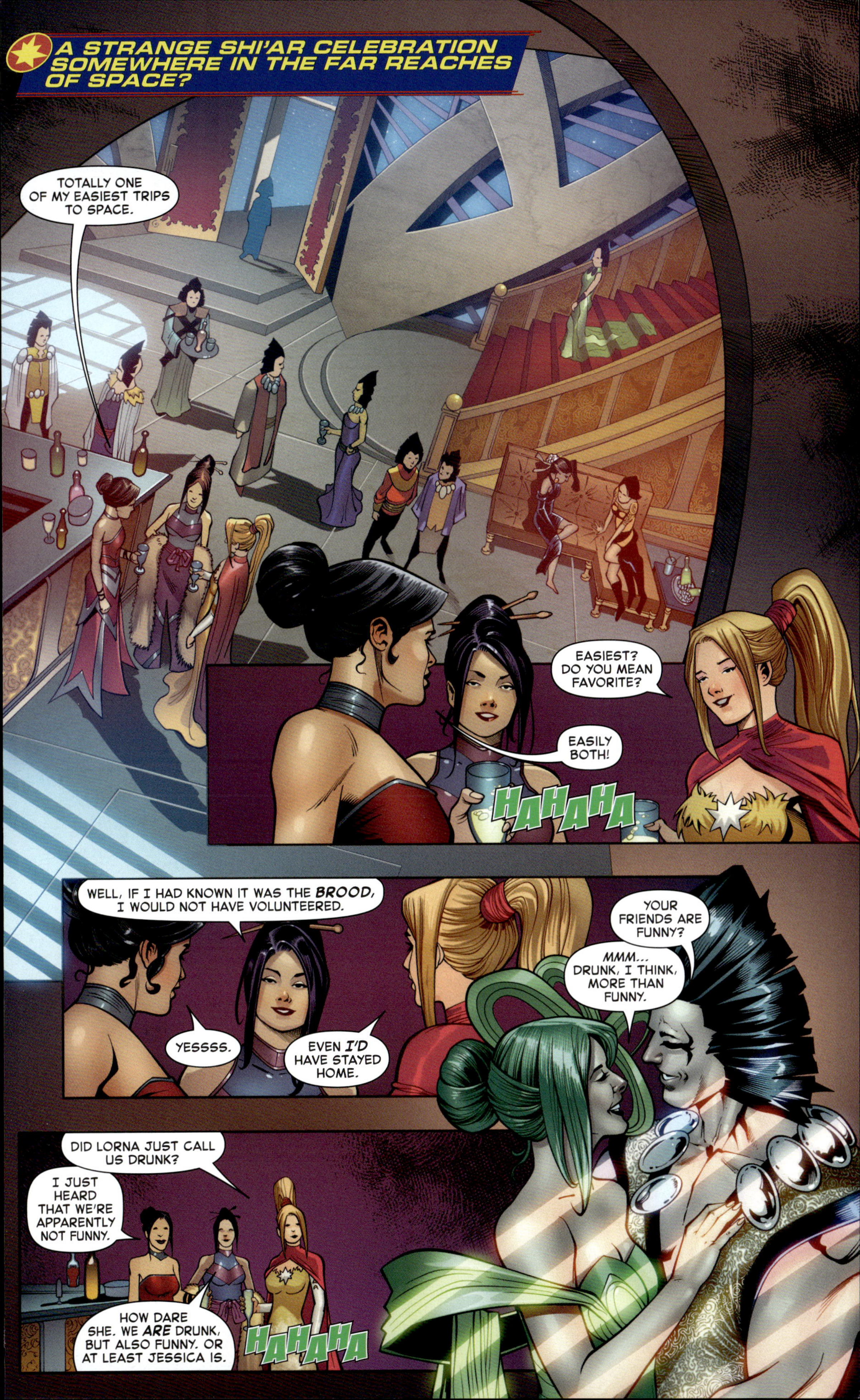
A STRANGE SHI'AR CELEBRATION SOMEWHERE IN THE FAR REACHES OF SPACE?
TOTALLY ONE OF MY EASIEST TRIPS TO SPACE.
EASIEST? DO YOU MEAN FAVORITE?
EASILY BOTH!
HAHAHA
WELL, IF I HAD KNOWN IT WAS THE BROOD, I WOULD NOT HAVE VOLUNTEERED.
YESSSS.
EVEN I'D HAVE STAYED HOME.
YOUR FRIENDS ARE FUNNY?
MMM... DRUNK, I THINK, MORE THAN FUNNY.
DID LORNA JUST CALL US DRUNK?
I JUST HEARD THAT WE'RE APPARENTLY NOT FUNNY.
HOW DARE SHE. WE ARE DRUNK, BUT ALSO FUNNY. OR AT LEAST JESSICA IS.
HAHAHA

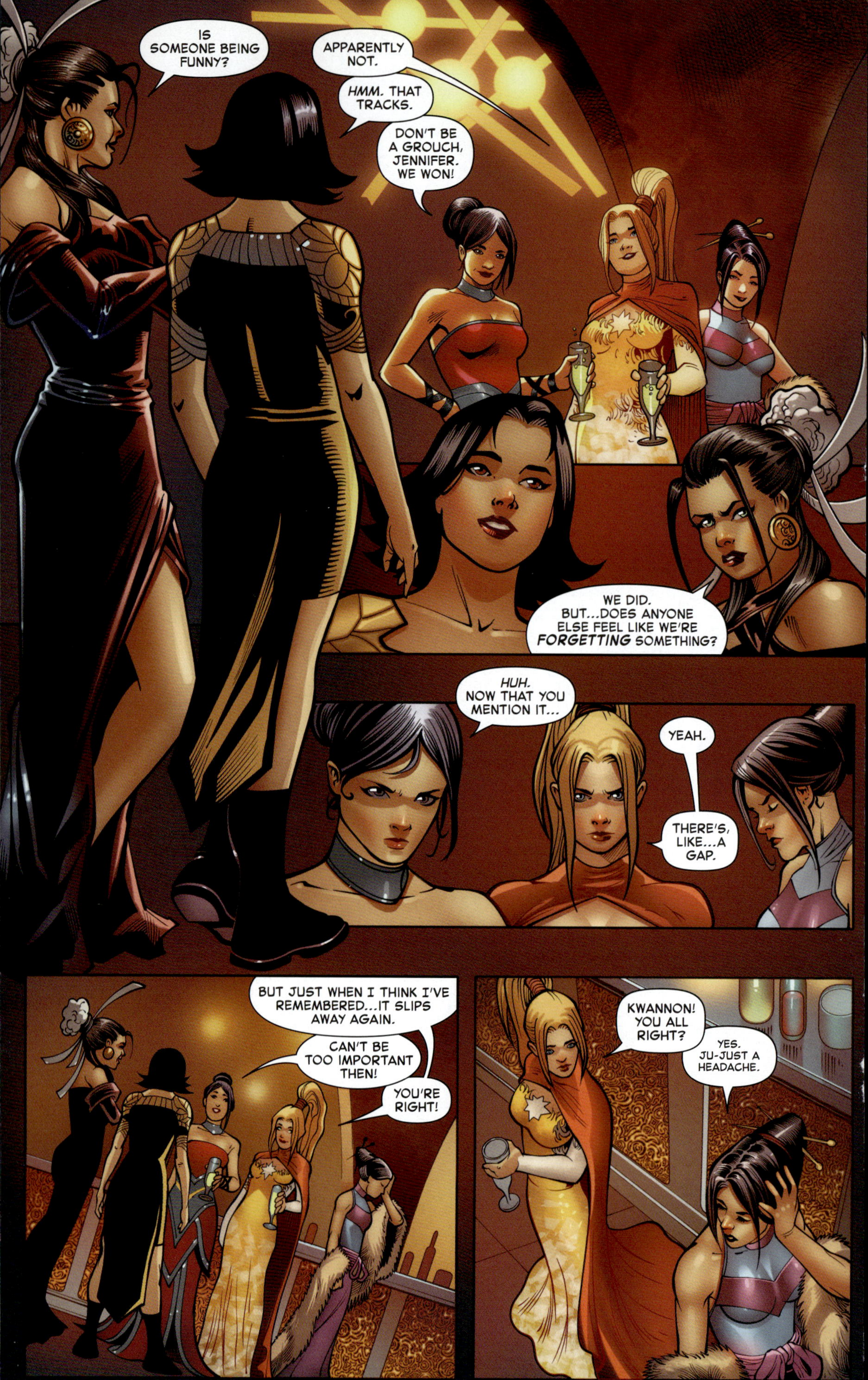
IS SOMEONE BEING FUNNY?
APPARENTLY NOT.
HMM. THAT TRACKS.
DON'T BE A GROUCH, JENNIFER. WE WON!
WE DID. BUT...DOES ANYONE ELSE FEEL LIKE WE'RE FORGETTING SOMETHING?
HUH. NOW THAT YOU MENTION IT...
YEAH.
THERE'S, LIKE...A GAP.
BUT JUST WHEN I THINK I'VE REMEMBERED...IT SLIPS AWAY AGAIN.
CAN'T BE TOO IMPORTANT THEN!
YOU'RE RIGHT!
KWANNON! YOU ALL RIGHT?
YES. JU-JUST A HEADACHE.

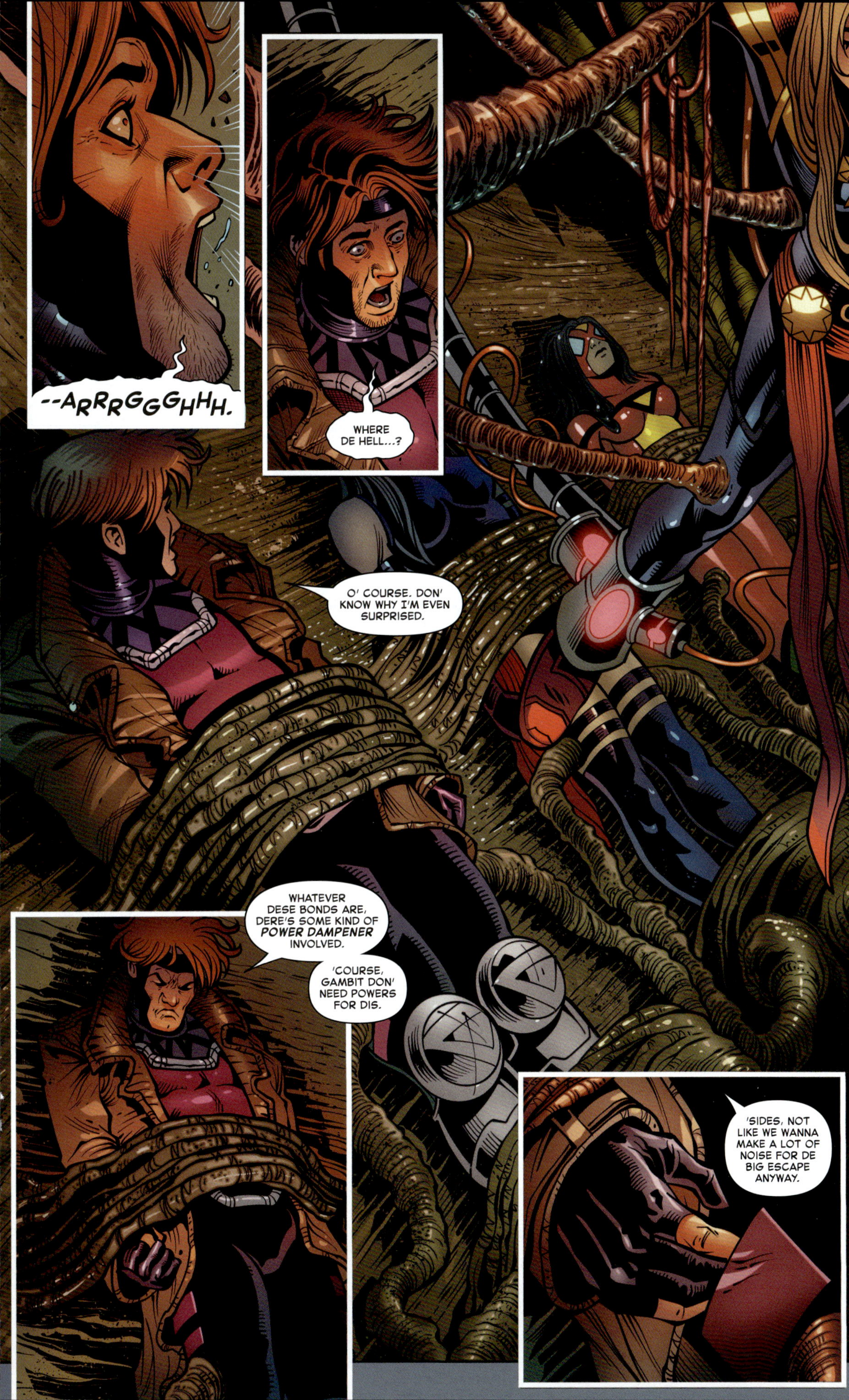
--ARRRGGGHHH.
WHERE DE HELL...?
O' COURSE. DON' KNOW WHY I'M EVEN SURPRISED.
WHATEVER DESE BONDS ARE, DERE'S SOME KIND OF **POWER DAMPENER** INVOLVED.
'COURSE, GAMBIT DON' NEED POWERS FOR DIS.
'SIDES, NOT LIKE WE WANNA MAKE A LOT OF NOISE FOR DE BIG ESCAPE ANYWAY.

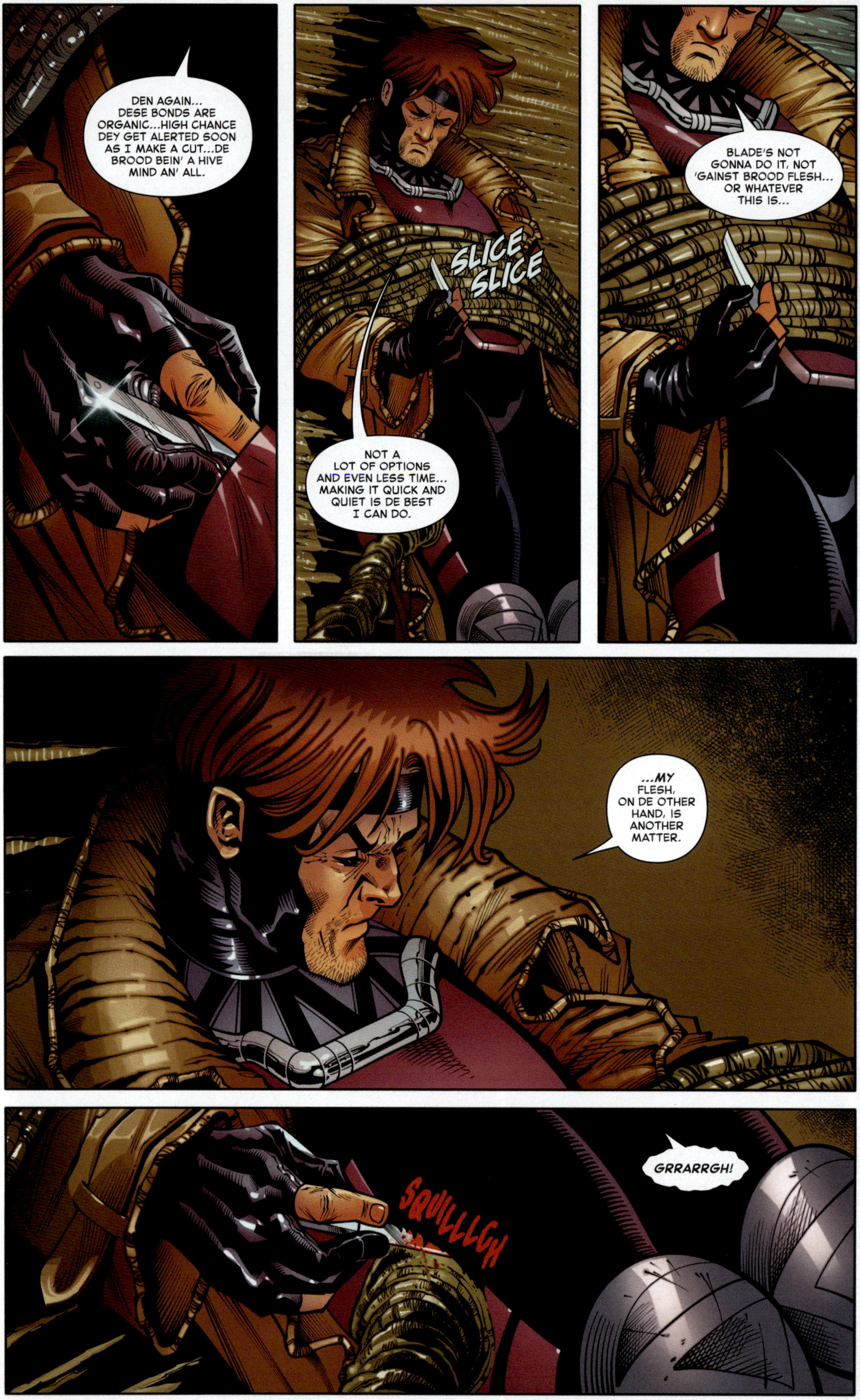
DEN AGAIN... DESE BONDS ARE ORGANIC...HIGH CHANCE DEY GET ALERTED SOON AS I MAKE A CUT...DE BROOD BEIN' A HIVE MIND AN' ALL.
SLICE SLICE
NOT A LOT OF OPTIONS AND EVEN LESS TIME... MAKING IT QUICK AND QUIET IS DE BEST I CAN DO.
BLADE'S NOT GONNA DO IT, NOT 'GAINST BROOD FLESH... OR WHATEVER THIS IS...
...MY FLESH, ON DE OTHER HAND, IS ANOTHER MATTER.
SQUILLLCH
GRRARRGH!

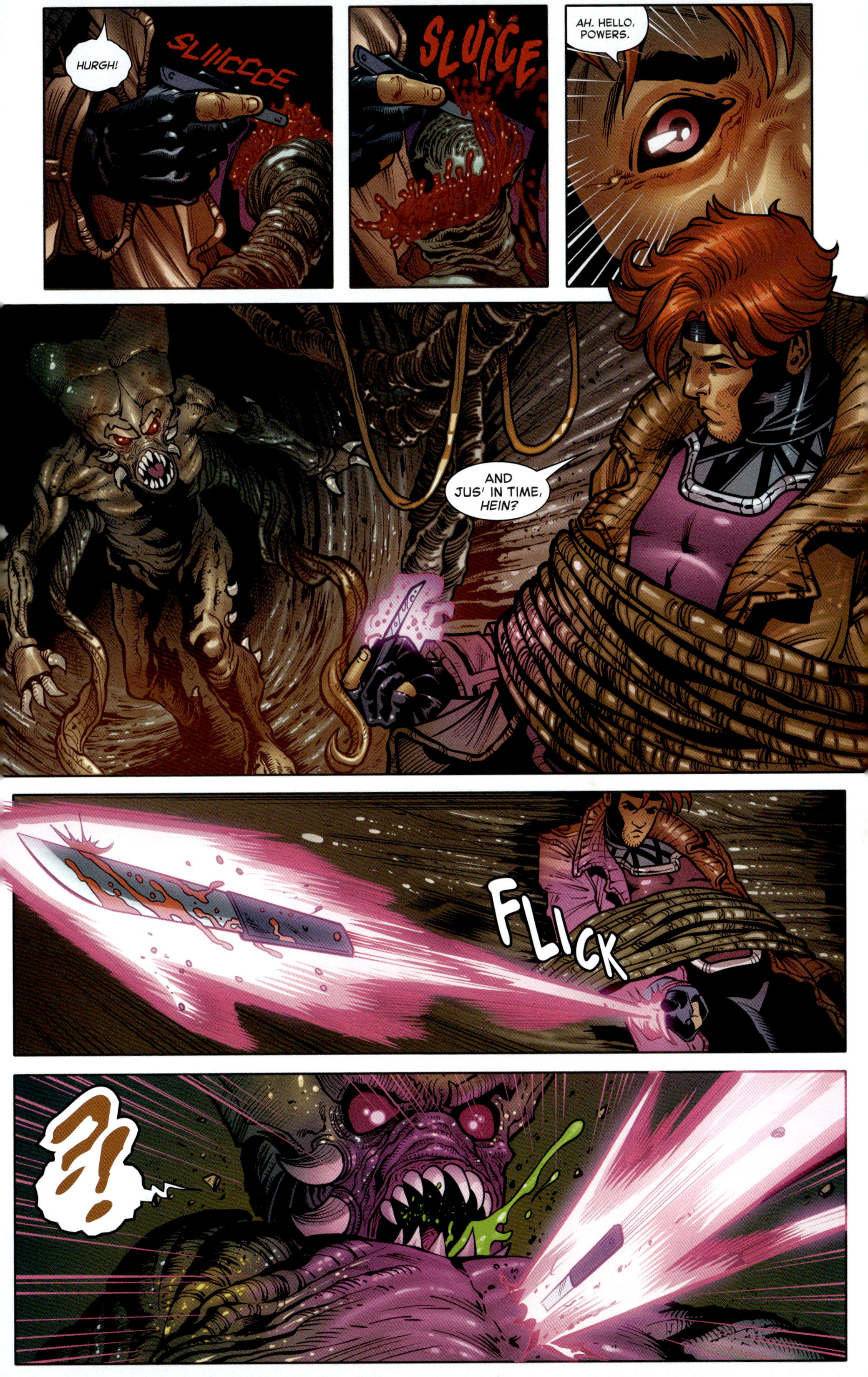
HURGH!
SLIIICCCCE
SLUICE
AH. HELLO, POWERS.
AND JUS' IN TIME, HEIN?
FLICK
?!

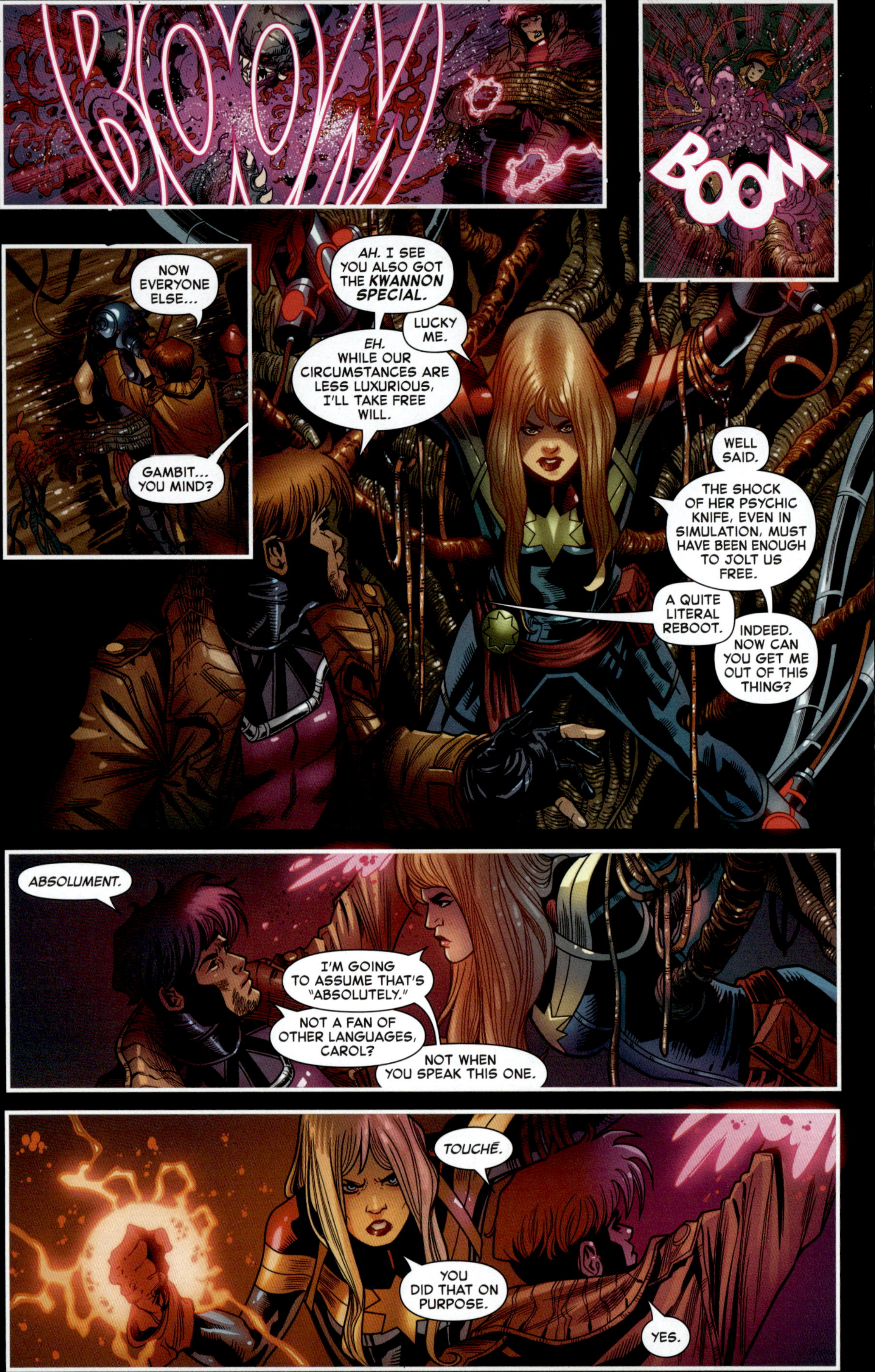

BOOM
BOOM
NOW EVERYONE ELSE...
GAMBIT... YOU MIND?
AH. I SEE YOU ALSO GOT THE *KWANNON SPECIAL.*
LUCKY ME.
EH. WHILE OUR CIRCUMSTANCES ARE LESS LUXURIOUS, I'LL TAKE FREE WILL.
WELL SAID.
THE SHOCK OF HER PSYCHIC KNIFE, EVEN IN SIMULATION, MUST HAVE BEEN ENOUGH TO JOLT US FREE.
A QUITE LITERAL REBOOT.
INDEED. NOW CAN YOU GET ME OUT OF THIS THING?
ABSOLUMENT.
I'M GOING TO ASSUME THAT'S "ABSOLUTELY."
NOT A FAN OF OTHER LANGUAGES, CAROL?
NOT WHEN YOU SPEAK THIS ONE.
TOUCHÉ.
YOU DID THAT ON PURPOSE.
YES.

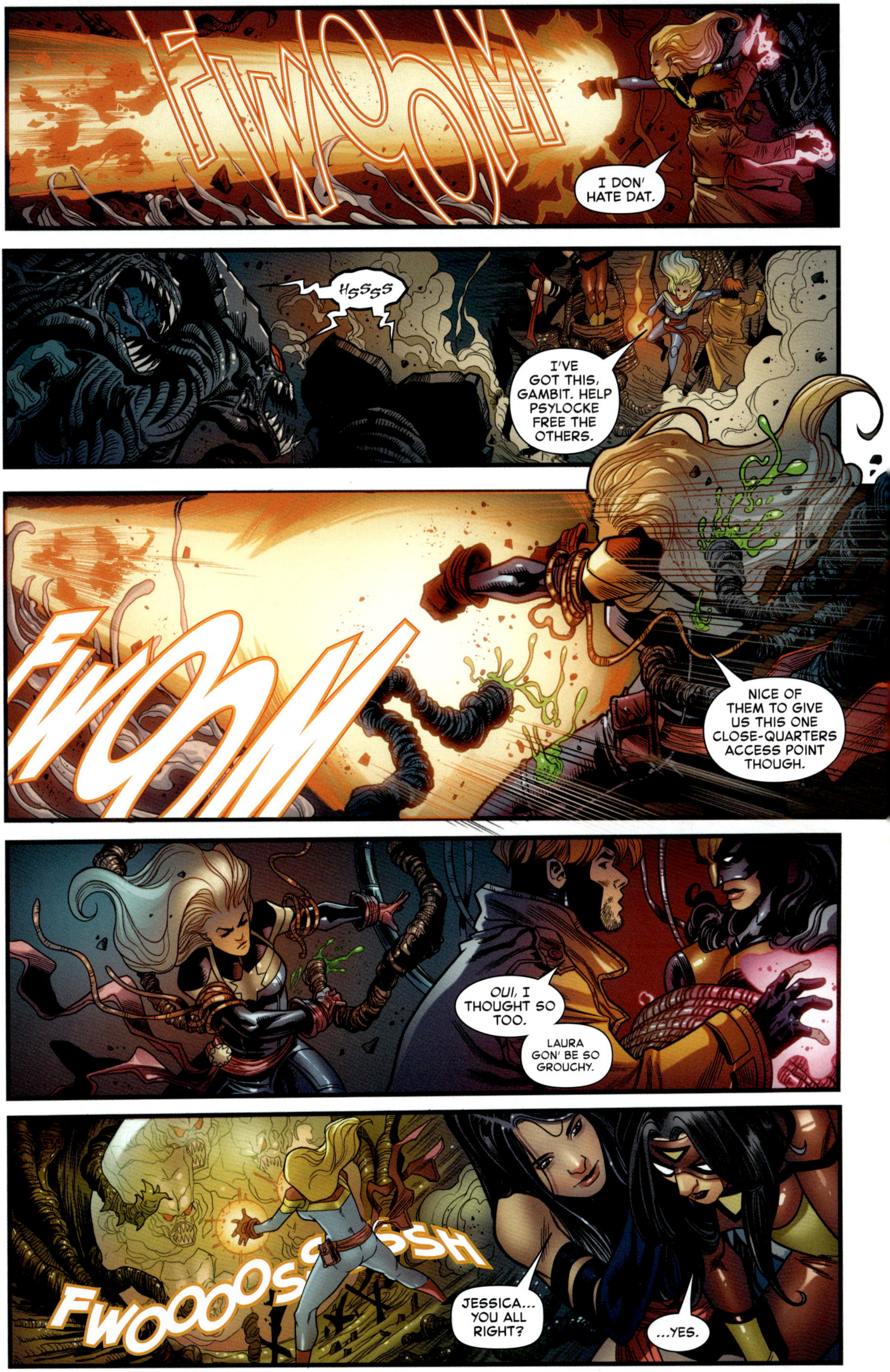
FWOOM
I DON' HATE DAT.
HSSSS
I'VE GOT THIS, GAMBIT. HELP PSYLOCKE FREE THE OTHERS.
FWOOM
NICE OF THEM TO GIVE US THIS ONE CLOSE-QUARTERS ACCESS POINT THOUGH.
OUI, I THOUGHT SO TOO.
LAURA GON' BE SO GROUCHY.
FWOOOOSSSSH
JESSICA... YOU ALL RIGHT?
...YES.

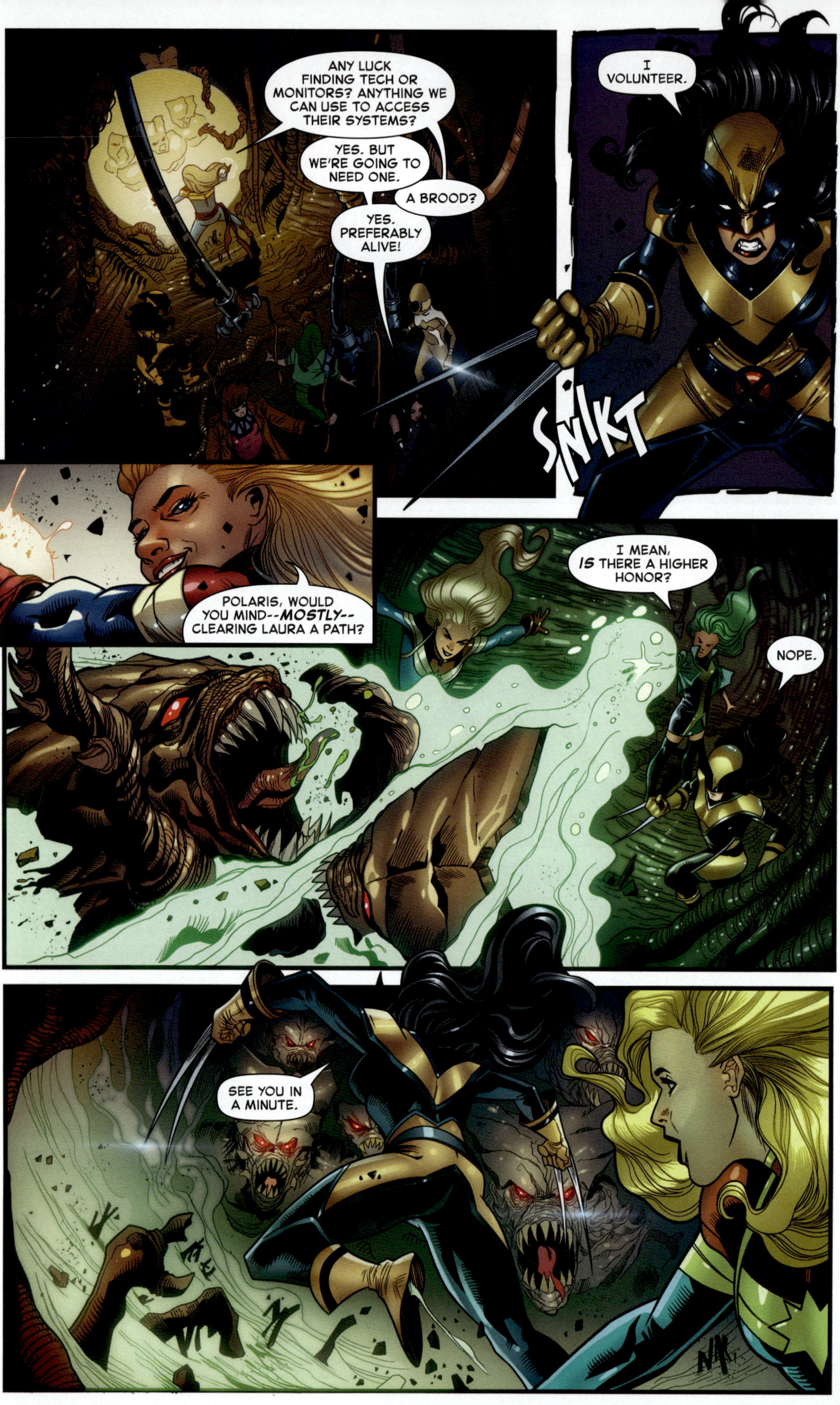
ANY LUCK FINDING TECH OR MONITORS? ANYTHING WE CAN USE TO ACCESS THEIR SYSTEMS?
YES. BUT WE'RE GOING TO NEED ONE.
A BROOD?
YES. PREFERABLY ALIVE!
I VOLUNTEER.
SNIKT
POLARIS, WOULD YOU MIND--*MOSTLY*--CLEARING LAURA A PATH?
I MEAN, *IS* THERE A HIGHER HONOR?
NOPE.
SEE YOU IN A MINUTE.

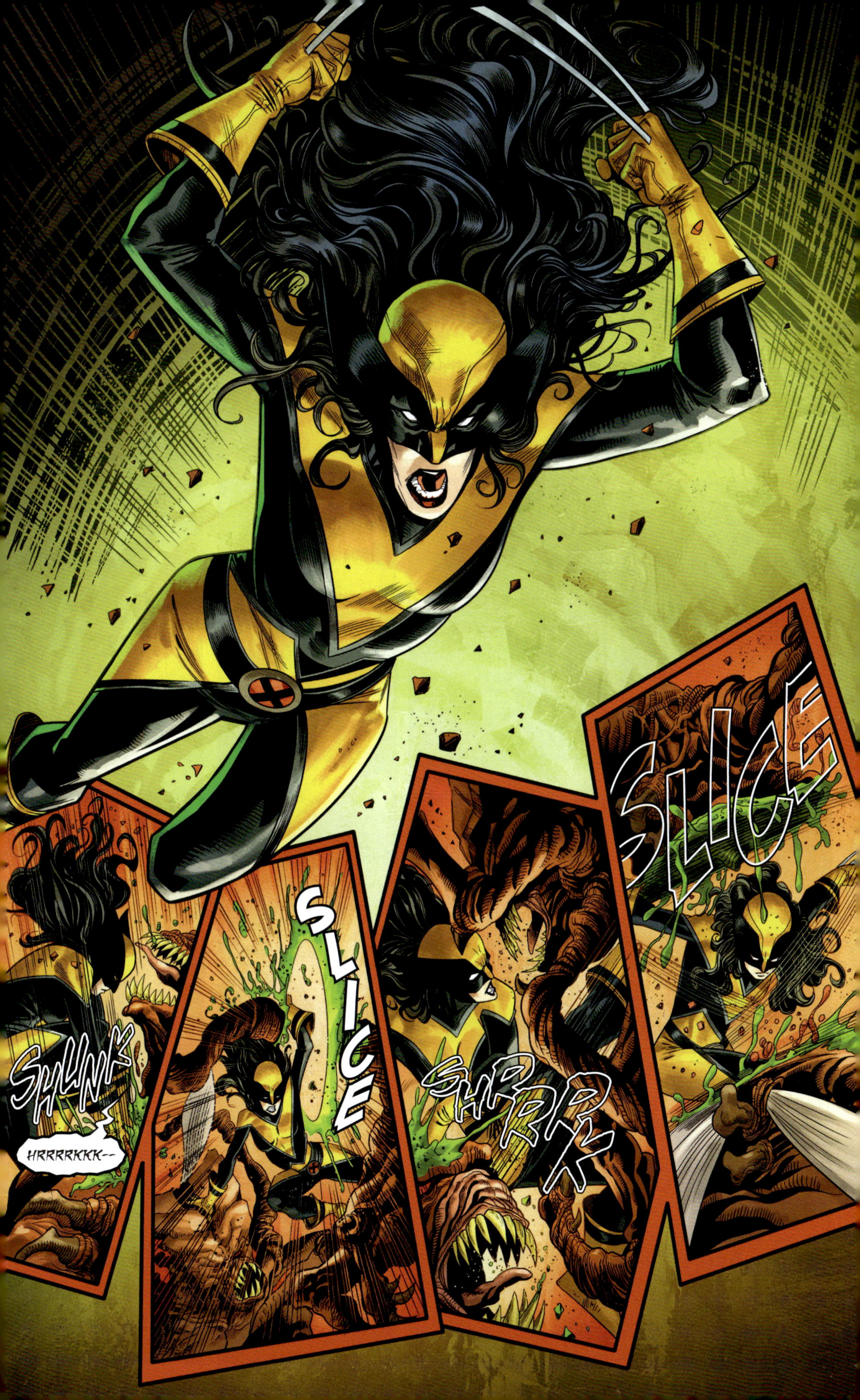
SHUNK
HRRRRKKK--
SLICE
SHRRRK
SLICE

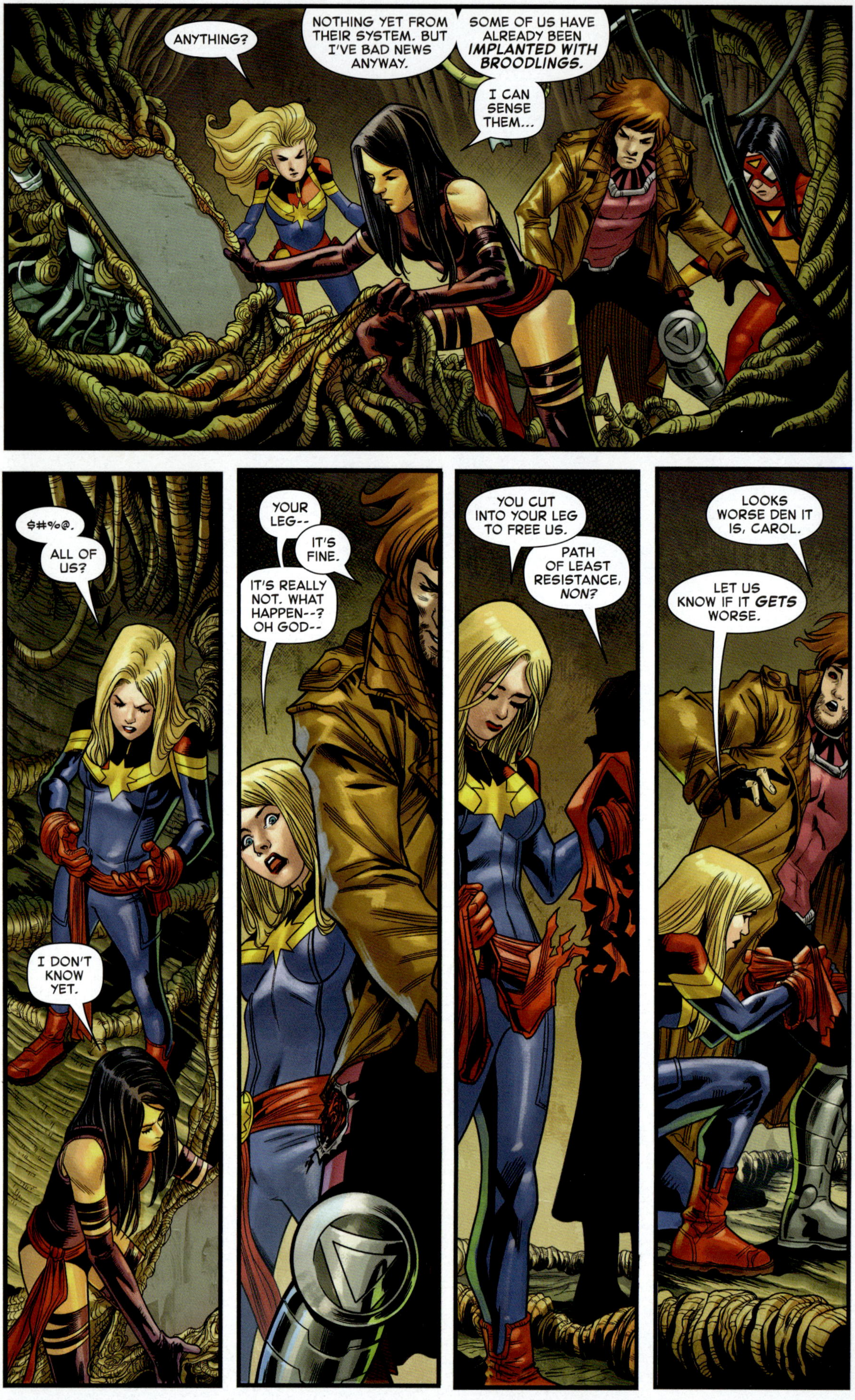
ANYTHING?
NOTHING YET FROM THEIR SYSTEM. BUT I'VE BAD NEWS ANYWAY.
SOME OF US HAVE ALREADY BEEN *IMPLANTED WITH BROODLINGS.*
I CAN SENSE THEM...
$#%@. ALL OF US?
I DON'T KNOW YET.
YOUR LEG--
IT'S FINE.
IT'S REALLY NOT. WHAT HAPPEN--? OH GOD--
YOU CUT INTO YOUR LEG TO FREE US.
PATH OF LEAST RESISTANCE, *NON?*
LOOKS WORSE DEN IT IS, CAROL.
LET US KNOW IF IT *GETS* WORSE.

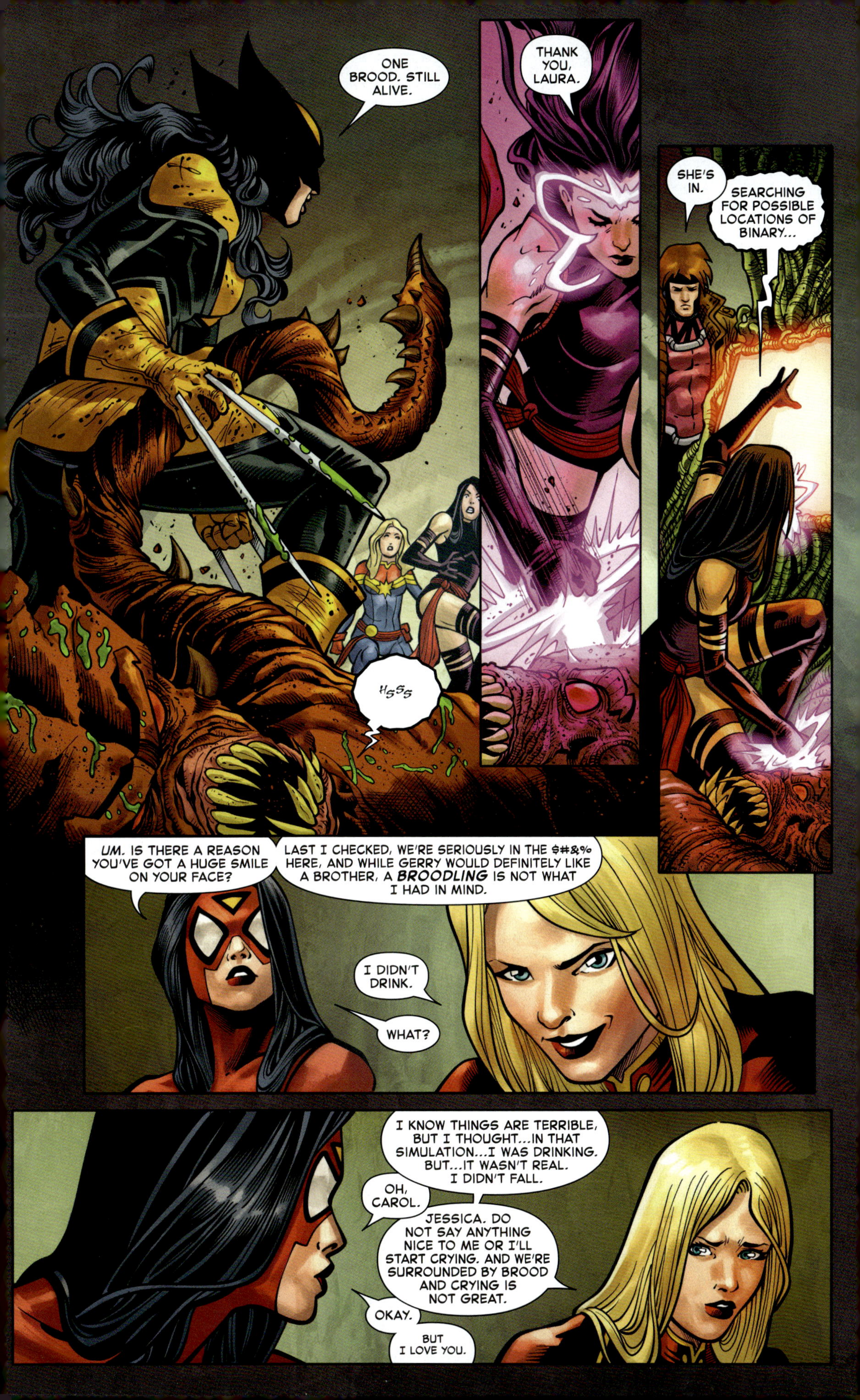
ONE BROOD. STILL ALIVE.
THANK YOU, LAURA.
SHE'S IN.
SEARCHING FOR POSSIBLE LOCATIONS OF BINARY...
HSSS
UM. IS THERE A REASON YOU'VE GOT A HUGE SMILE ON YOUR FACE?
LAST I CHECKED, WE'RE SERIOUSLY IN THE $#&% HERE, AND WHILE GERRY WOULD DEFINITELY LIKE A BROTHER, A BROODLING IS NOT WHAT I HAD IN MIND.
I DIDN'T DRINK.
WHAT?
I KNOW THINGS ARE TERRIBLE, BUT I THOUGHT...IN THAT SIMULATION...I WAS DRINKING. BUT...IT WASN'T REAL. I DIDN'T FALL.
OH, CAROL.
JESSICA. DO NOT SAY ANYTHING NICE TO ME OR I'LL START CRYING. AND WE'RE SURROUNDED BY BROOD AND CRYING IS NOT GREAT.
OKAY.
BUT I LOVE YOU.

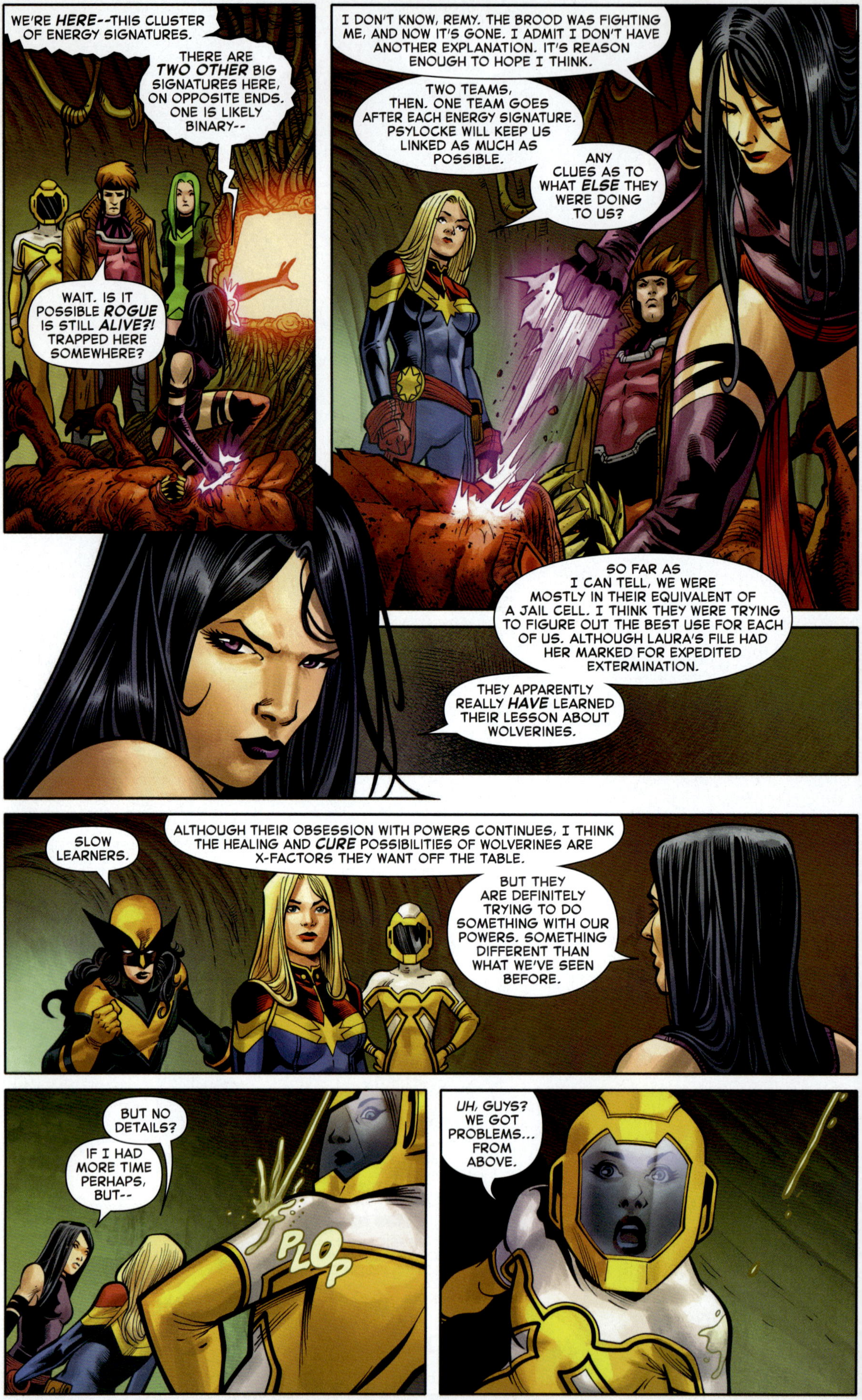
WE'RE HERE--THIS CLUSTER OF ENERGY SIGNATURES.
THERE ARE TWO OTHER BIG SIGNATURES HERE, ON OPPOSITE ENDS. ONE IS LIKELY BINARY--
WAIT. IS IT POSSIBLE ROGUE IS STILL ALIVE?! TRAPPED HERE SOMEWHERE?
I DON'T KNOW, REMY. THE BROOD WAS FIGHTING ME, AND NOW IT'S GONE. I ADMIT I DON'T HAVE ANOTHER EXPLANATION. IT'S REASON ENOUGH TO HOPE I THINK.
TWO TEAMS, THEN. ONE TEAM GOES AFTER EACH ENERGY SIGNATURE. PSYLOCKE WILL KEEP US LINKED AS MUCH AS POSSIBLE.
ANY CLUES AS TO WHAT ELSE THEY WERE DOING TO US?
SO FAR AS I CAN TELL, WE WERE MOSTLY IN THEIR EQUIVALENT OF A JAIL CELL. I THINK THEY WERE TRYING TO FIGURE OUT THE BEST USE FOR EACH OF US. ALTHOUGH LAURA'S FILE HAD HER MARKED FOR EXPEDITED EXTERMINATION.
THEY APPARENTLY REALLY HAVE LEARNED THEIR LESSON ABOUT WOLVERINES.
SLOW LEARNERS.
ALTHOUGH THEIR OBSESSION WITH POWERS CONTINUES, I THINK THE HEALING AND CURE POSSIBILITIES OF WOLVERINES ARE X-FACTORS THEY WANT OFF THE TABLE.
BUT THEY ARE DEFINITELY TRYING TO DO SOMETHING WITH OUR POWERS. SOMETHING DIFFERENT THAN WHAT WE'VE SEEN BEFORE.
BUT NO DETAILS?
IF I HAD MORE TIME PERHAPS, BUT--
PLOP
UH, GUYS? WE GOT PROBLEMS... FROM ABOVE.

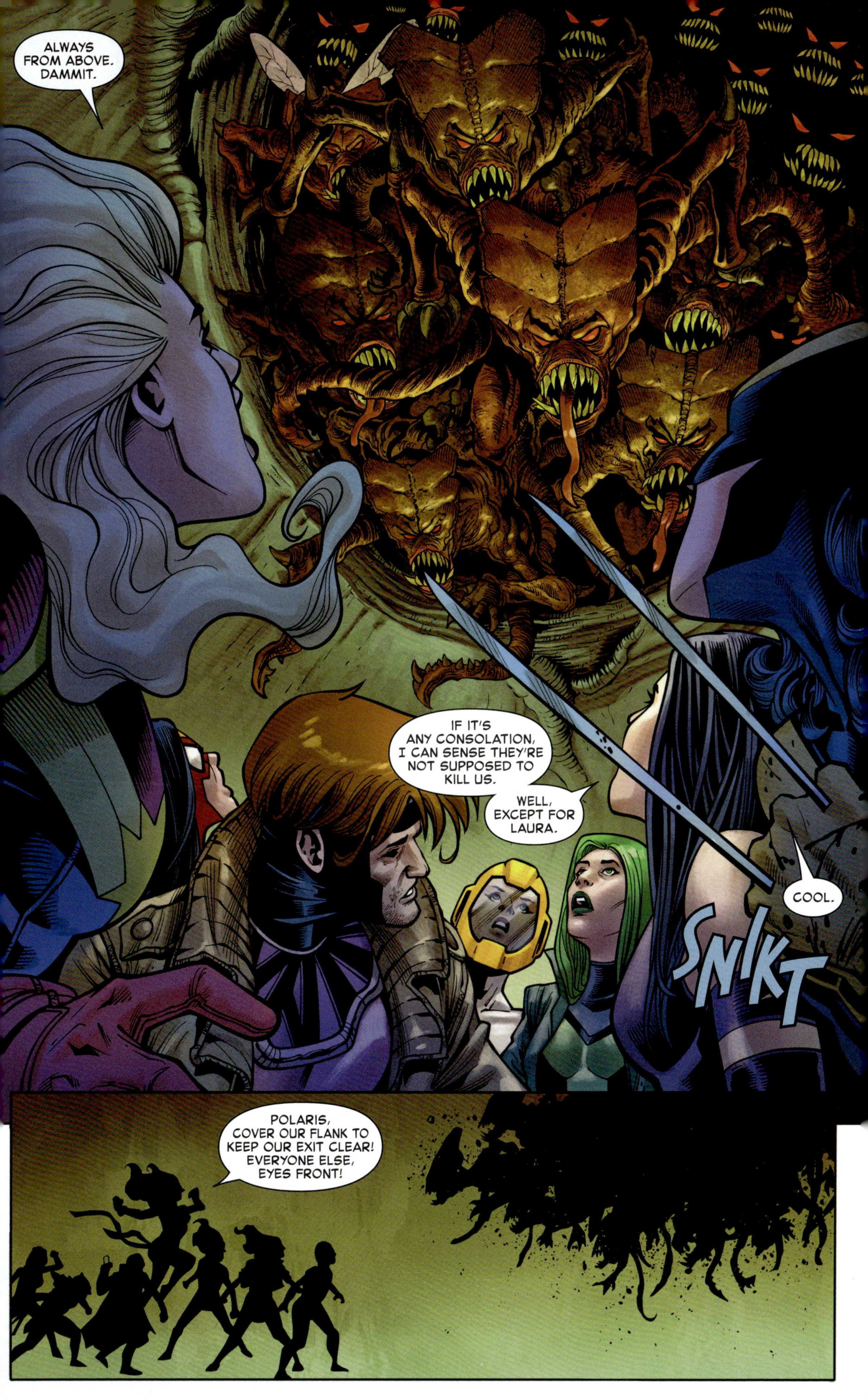
ALWAYS FROM ABOVE. DAMMIT.
IF IT'S ANY CONSOLATION, I CAN SENSE THEY'RE NOT SUPPOSED TO KILL US.
WELL, EXCEPT FOR LAURA.
COOL.
SNIKT
POLARIS, COVER OUR FLANK TO KEEP OUR EXIT CLEAR! EVERYONE ELSE, EYES FRONT!

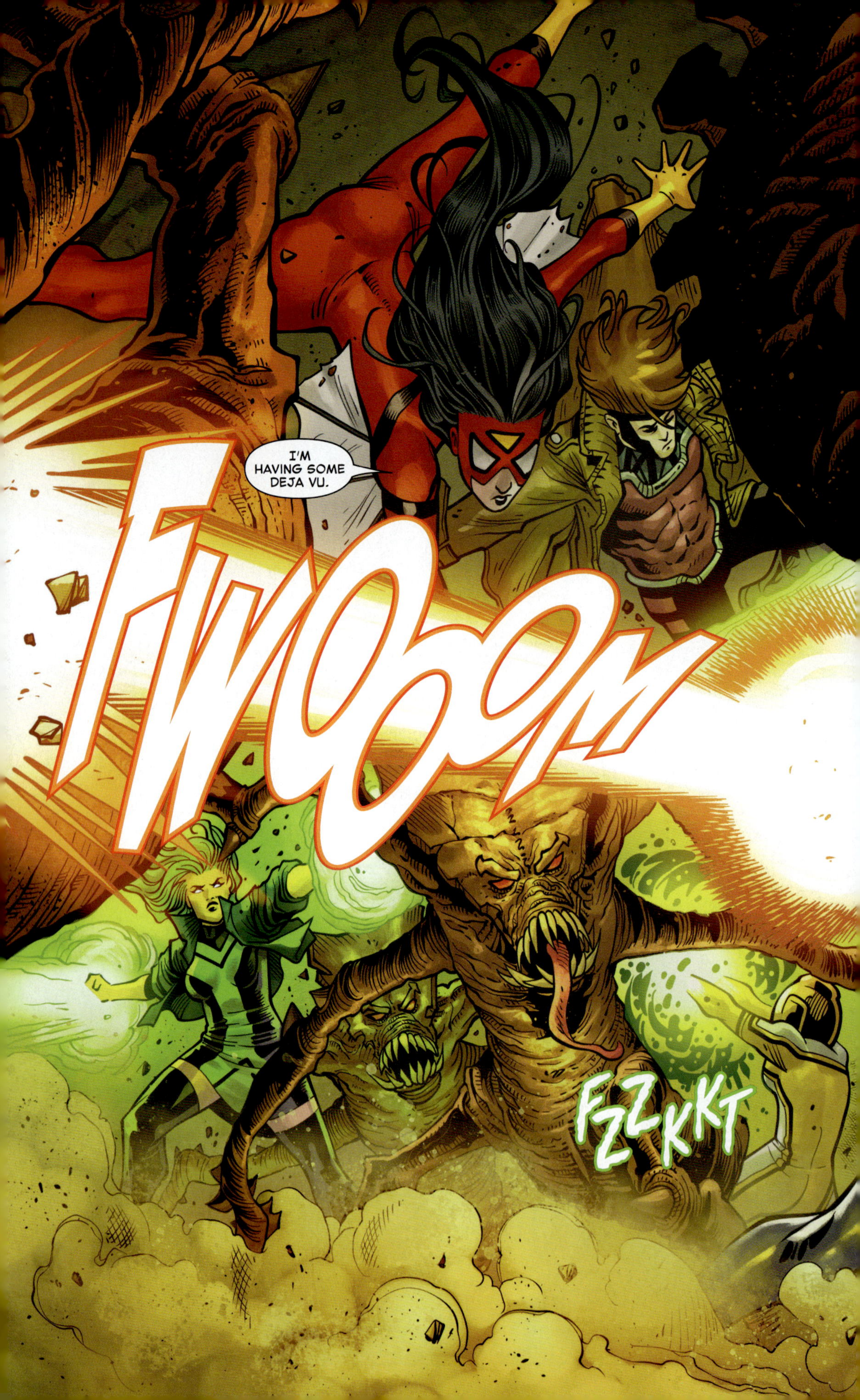
I'M HAVING SOME DEJA VU.
FWOOOM
FZZKKT

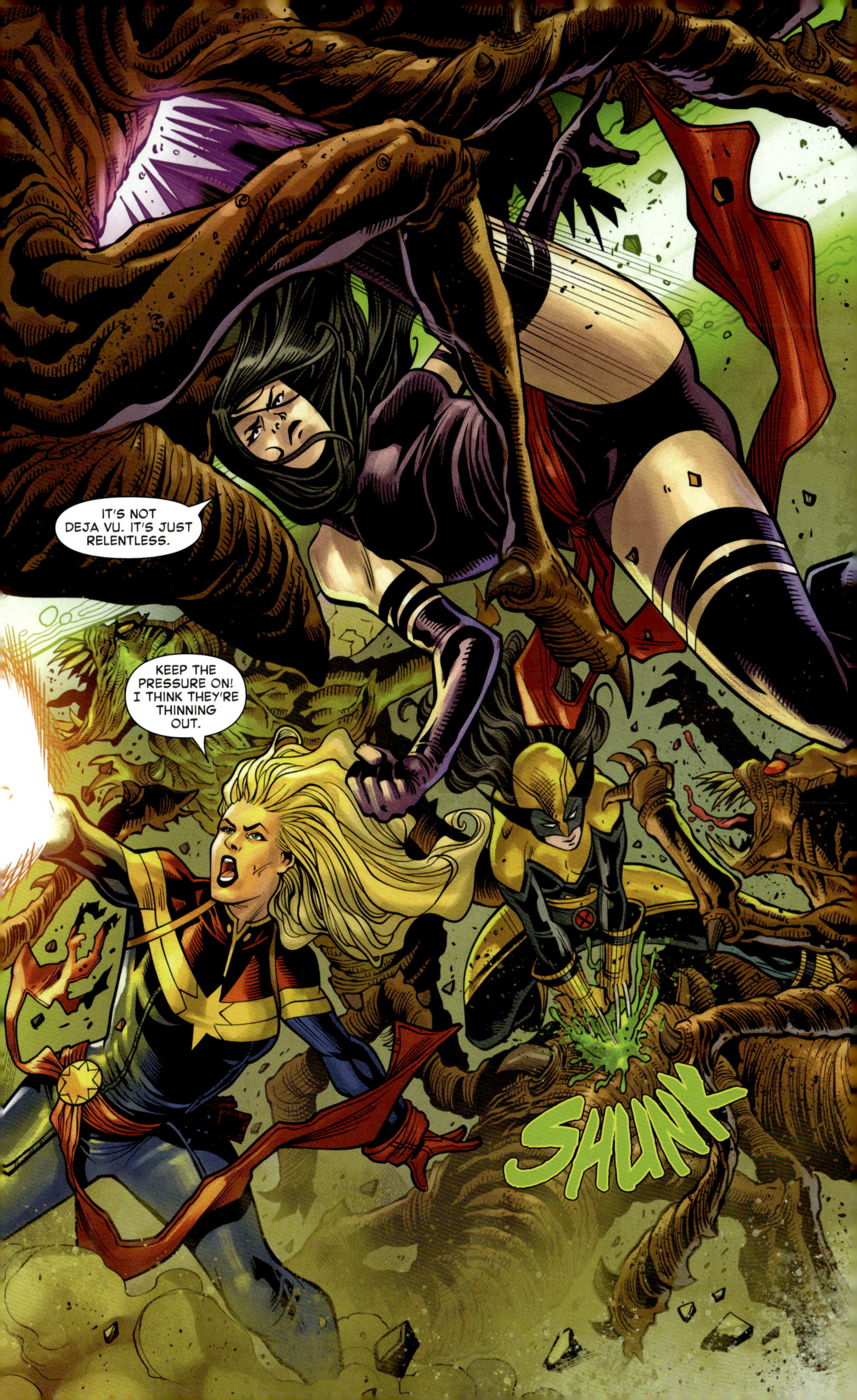
IT'S NOT DEJA VU. IT'S JUST RELENTLESS.
KEEP THE PRESSURE ON! I THINK THEY'RE THINNING OUT.
SHUNK

EVERYONE HIT THE GROUND!
EVERYONE ALL RIGHT?
OUI.
YES.
YEAH.
YOU KNOW, SOMETIMES YOU ALMOST FORGET WHY SHE'S IN CHARGE. THEN SHE REMINDS YOU.
YEAH, IT DOESN'T SUCK.
I'M SUPER INTO IT.

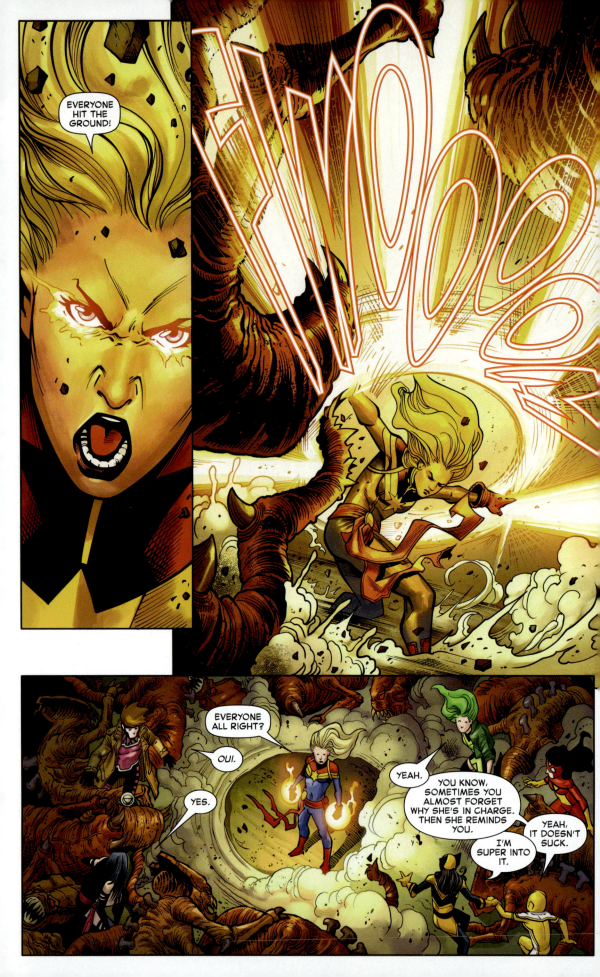

ALL RIGHT. IT'S GOING TO BE ME, PSYLOCKE, AND SPIDER-WOMAN ON TEAM ONE. POLARIS, GAMBIT, WOLVERINE, AND HAZMAT ARE TEAM TWO.

PSYLOCKE'S GOING TO MIND-LINK US, BUT THAT WILL PROBABLY FAIL AT SOME POINT, GIVEN THE RESISTANCE WE EXPECT TO ENCOUNTER.

RENDEZVOUS AT OUR SHIP'S COORDINATES IN TWO HOURS. ANYTHING MORE THAN THAT, AND WE RISK THAT THOSE OF US INFECTED WITH BROODLINGS WILL BEGIN TURNING. UNDERSTOOD?

UNDERSTOOD.

SHE'S SO BOSSY. I THINK I LIKE IT.

YOU WOULD.

I HESITATED SEPARATING FROM HAZMAT.

I DON'T LIKE HER NOT BEING UNDER MY EYE, BUT THE X-MEN WILL PROTECT HER LIKE SHE'S THEIRS.

I WOULDN'T DOUBT THEM EVEN IF THEY COULDN'T LITERALLY CHEAT DEATH, BUT IT DOESN'T HURT.

AND I NEEDED PSYLOCKE WITH ME, IN CASE WE DO FIND BINARY.

THEIR PROGRESS IS SWIFT, EMPRESS. SHOULD WE NOT BE MORE CONCERNED?
CONCERNED THAT THEY ARE MARCHING DIRECTLY INTO THE TRAPS WE HAVE CAREFULLY LAID FOR THEM?
TELL ME WHAT ELSE WE SHOULD HAVE HOPED FOR, YOU FOOL.
OUR BRAVE NEW WORLD ORDER DEMANDS POWERS... AND THEIR POWERS WE SHALL HAVE!
THAT, AND SO MUCH MORE.
HSSSSSS!

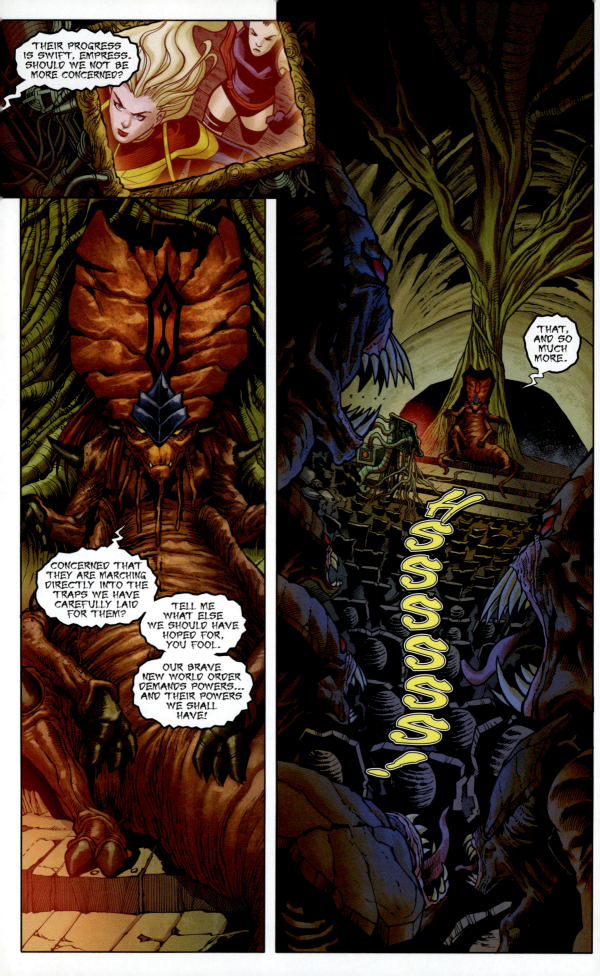

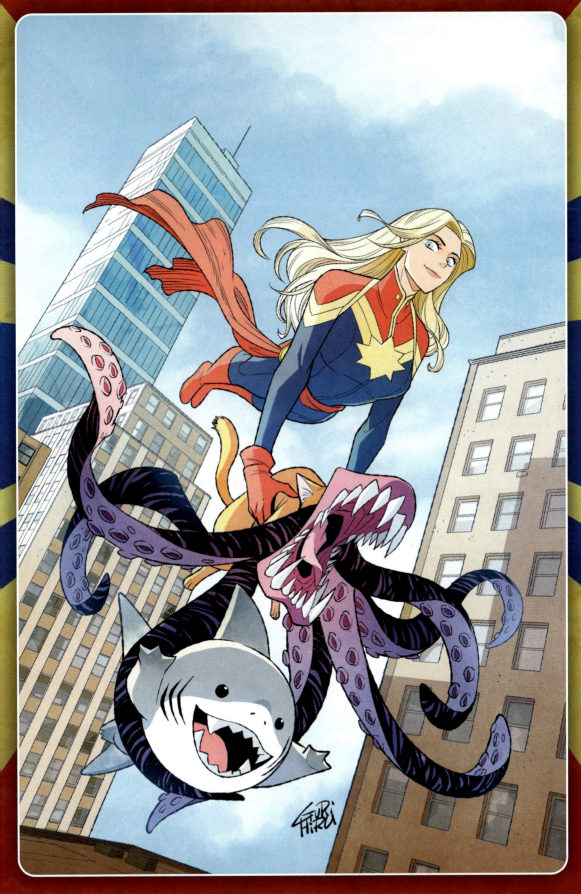

GURIHIRU
#42 JEFF THE LAND SHARK VARIANT

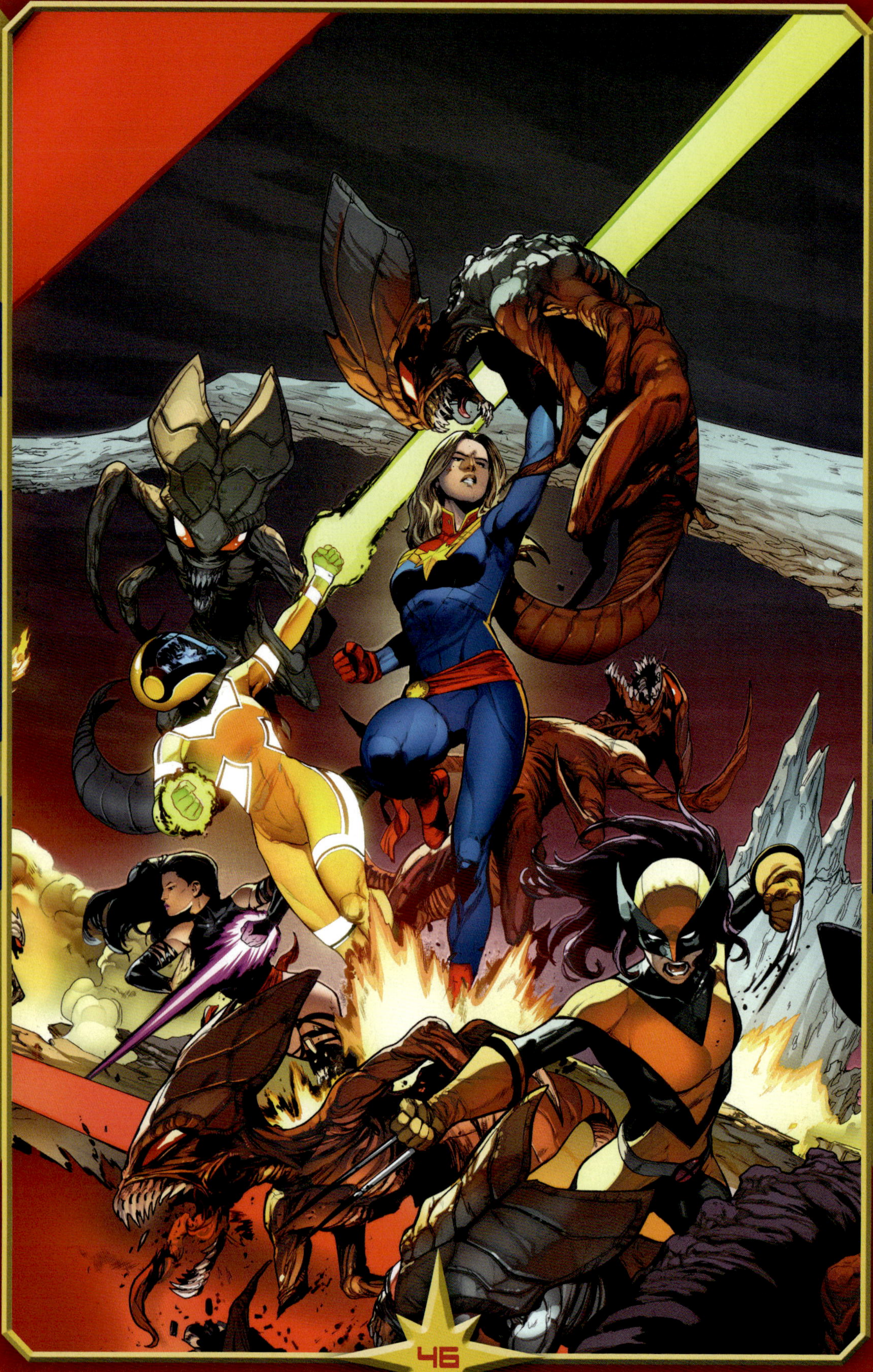

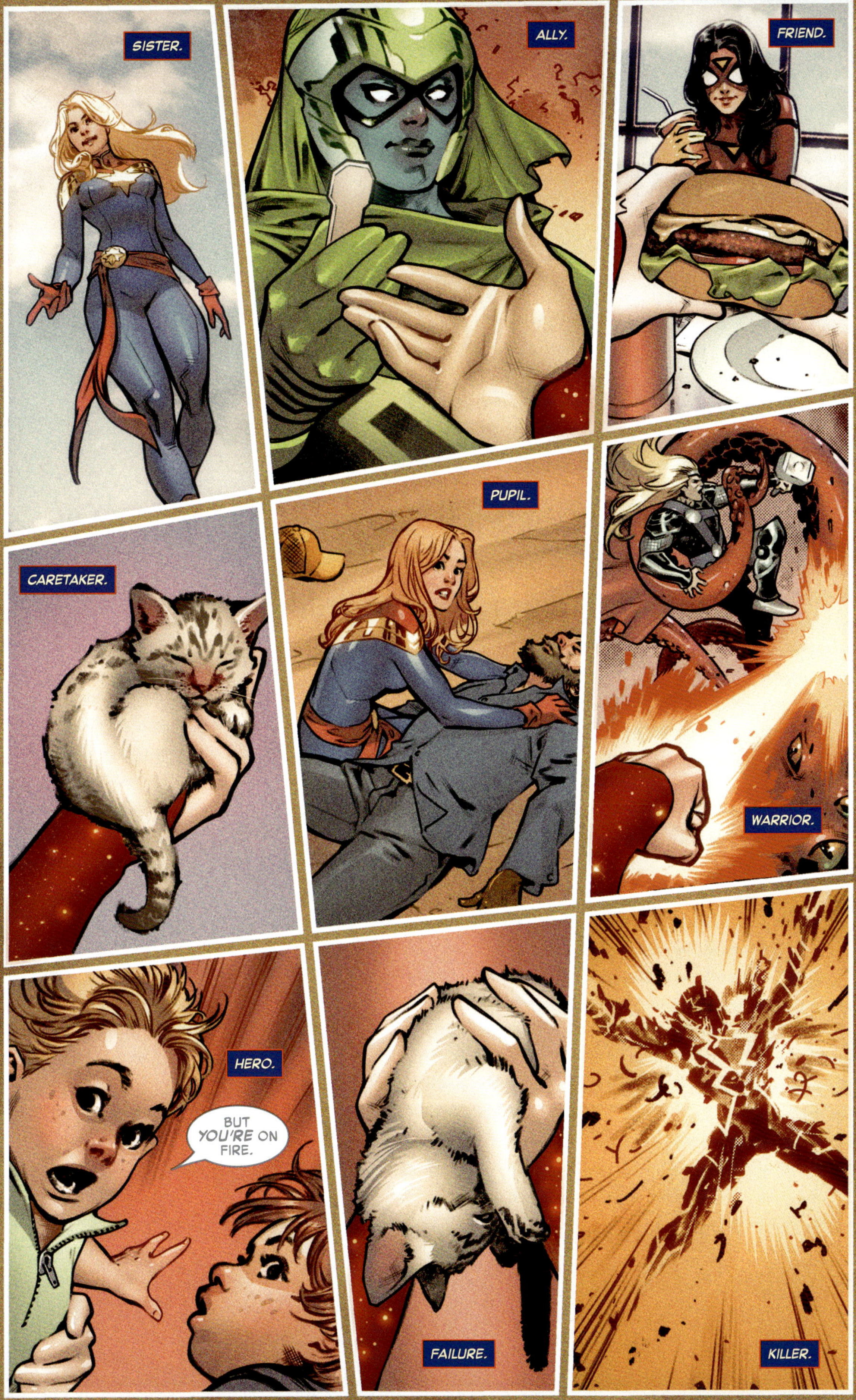
SISTER.
ALLY.
FRIEND.
CARETAKER.
PUPIL.
WARRIOR.
HERO.
BUT YOU'RE ON FIRE.
FAILURE.
KILLER.

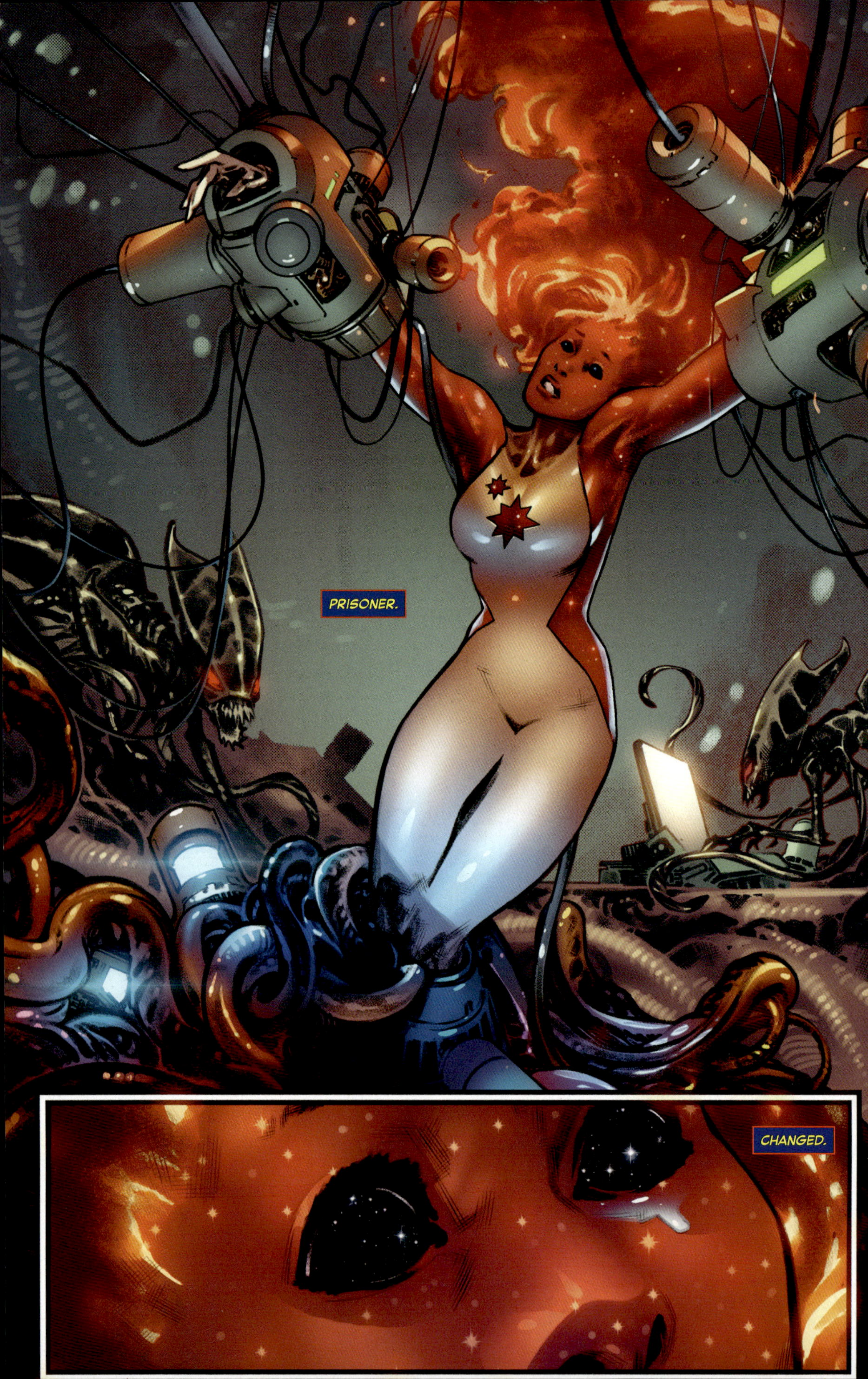
PRISONER.
CHANGED.

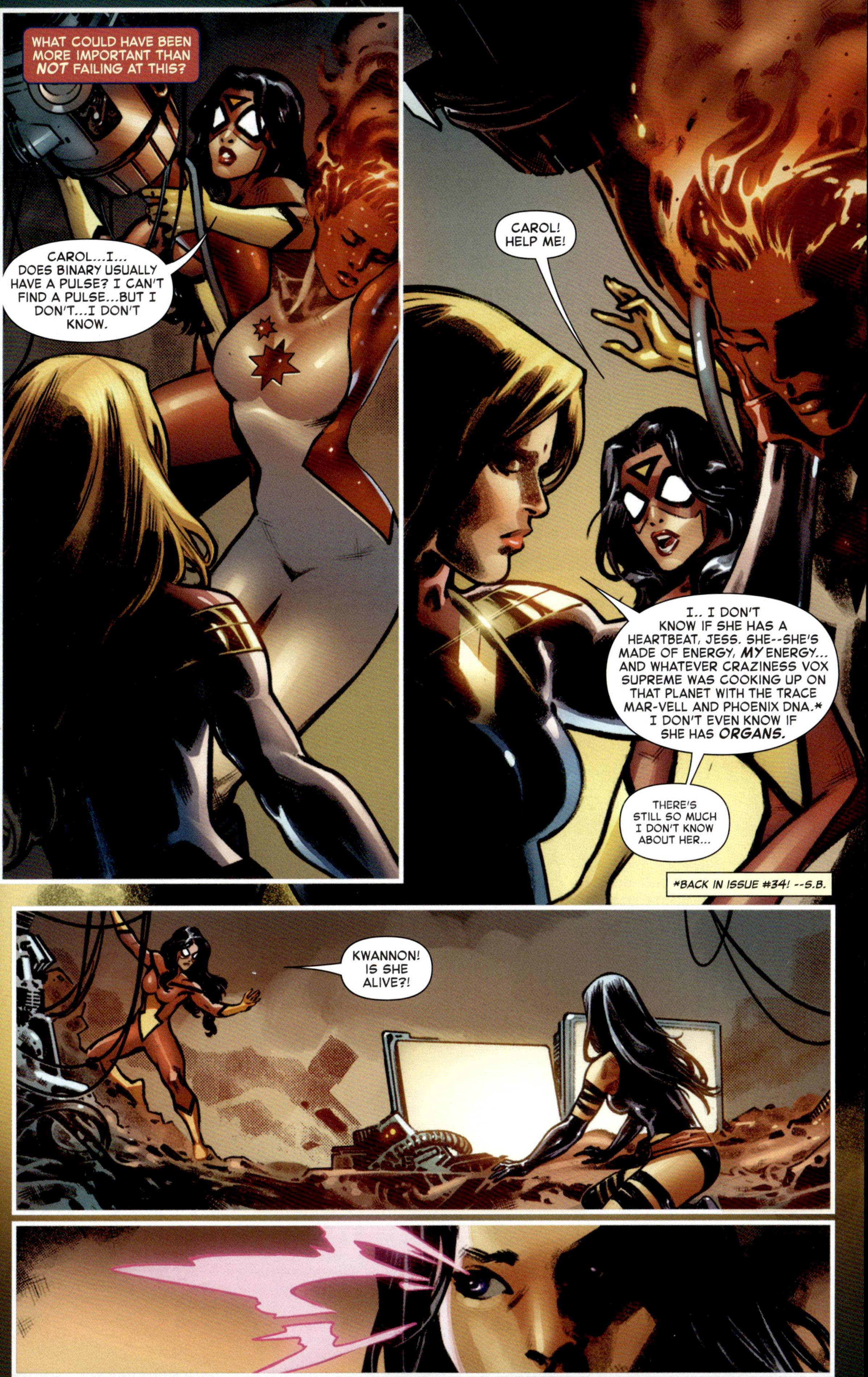
WHAT COULD HAVE BEEN MORE IMPORTANT THAN NOT FAILING AT THIS?
CAROL...I... DOES BINARY USUALLY HAVE A PULSE? I CAN'T FIND A PULSE...BUT I DON'T...I DON'T KNOW.
CAROL! HELP ME!
I.. I DON'T KNOW IF SHE HAS A HEARTBEAT, JESS. SHE--SHE'S MADE OF ENERGY, MY ENERGY... AND WHATEVER CRAZINESS VOX SUPREME WAS COOKING UP ON THAT PLANET WITH THE TRACE MAR-VELL AND PHOENIX DNA.* I DON'T EVEN KNOW IF SHE HAS ORGANS.
THERE'S STILL SO MUCH I DON'T KNOW ABOUT HER...
*BACK IN ISSUE #34! --S.B.
KWANNON! IS SHE ALIVE?!

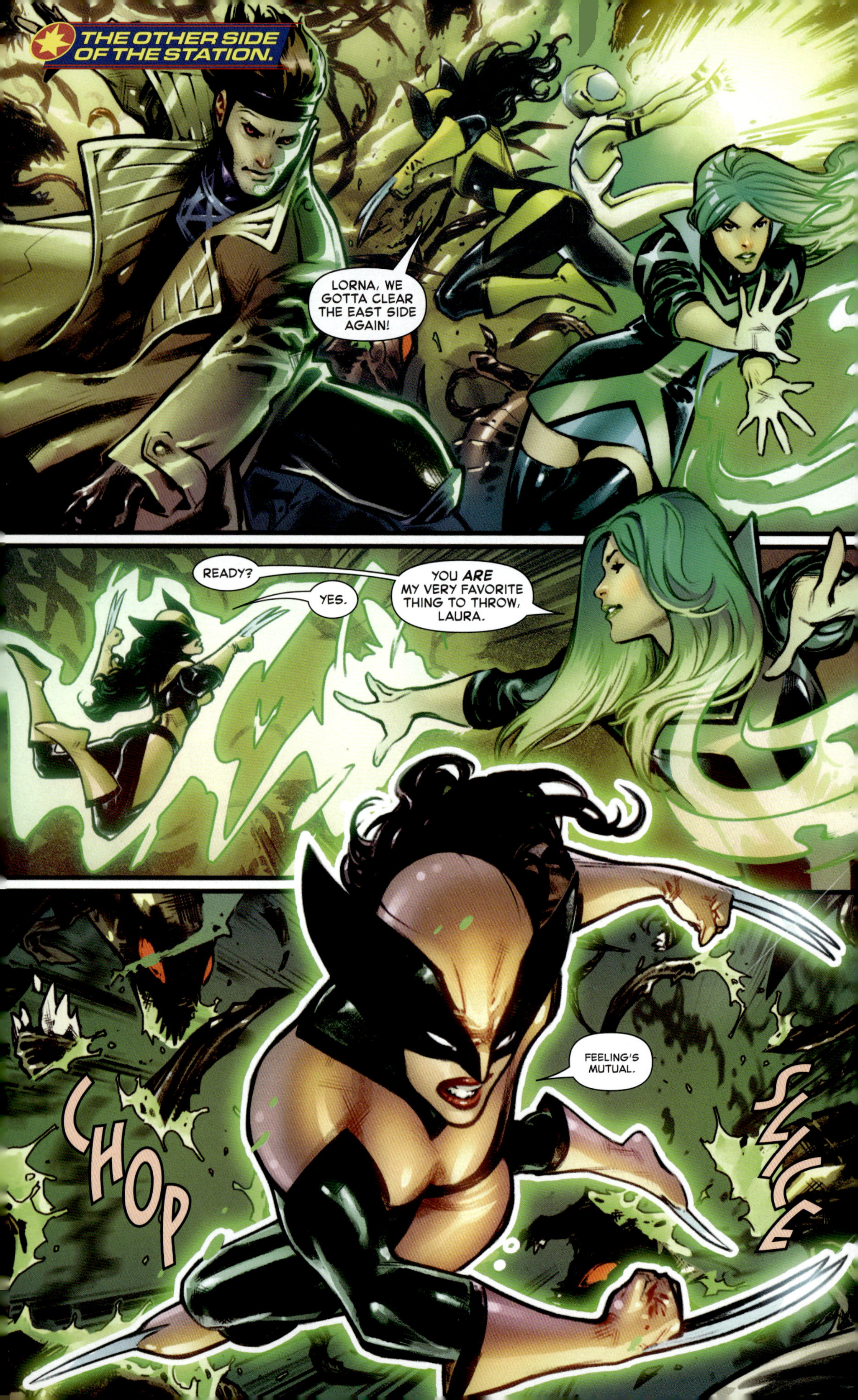
THE OTHER SIDE OF THE STATION.
LORNA, WE GOTTA CLEAR THE EAST SIDE AGAIN!
READY?
YES.
YOU ARE MY VERY FAVORITE THING TO THROW, LAURA.
FEELING'S MUTUAL.
CHOP
SLICE

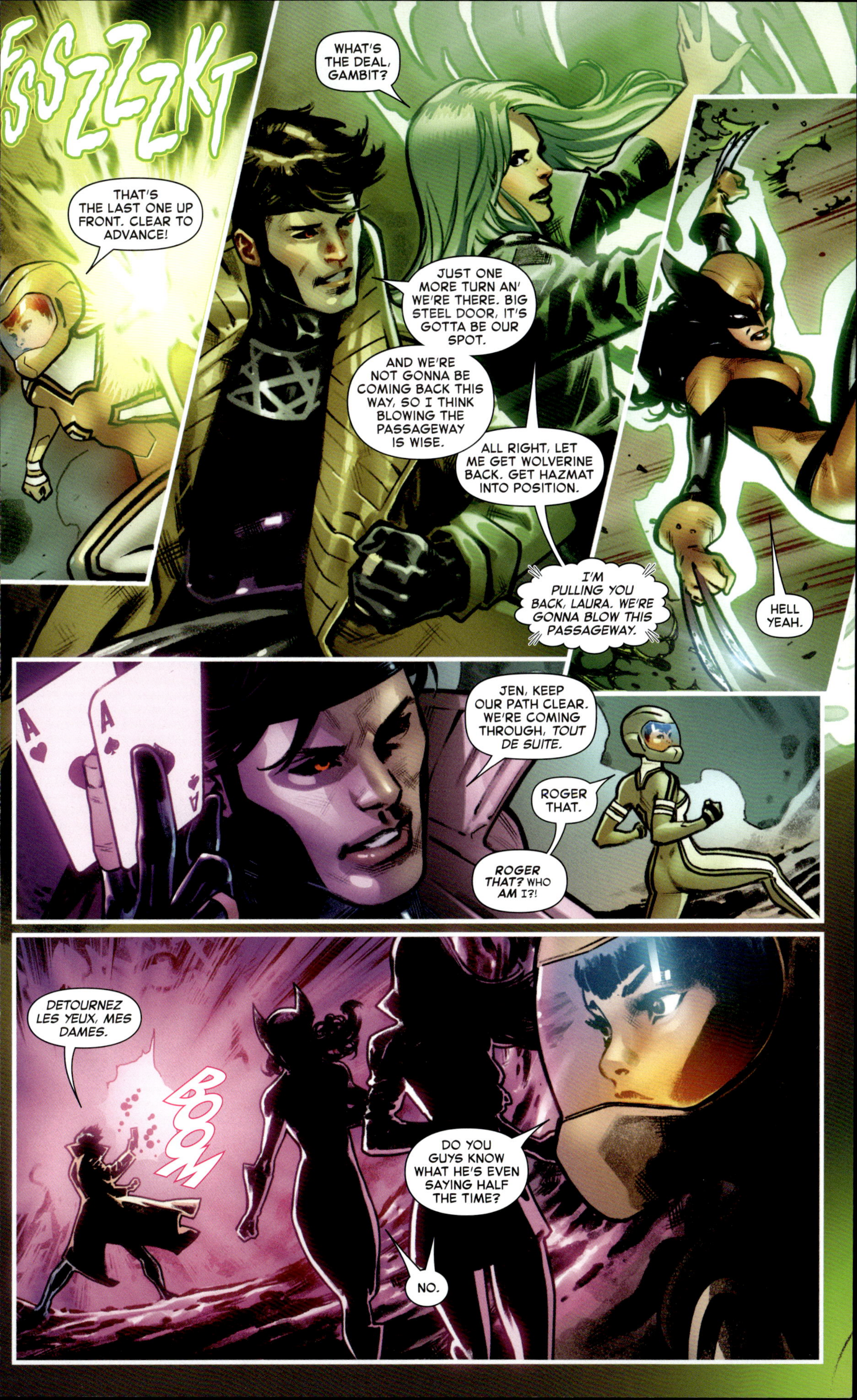
FSSZZZKT
WHAT'S THE DEAL, GAMBIT?
THAT'S THE LAST ONE UP FRONT. CLEAR TO ADVANCE!
JUST ONE MORE TURN AN' WE'RE THERE. BIG STEEL DOOR, IT'S GOTTA BE OUR SPOT.
AND WE'RE NOT GONNA BE COMING BACK THIS WAY, SO I THINK BLOWING THE PASSAGEWAY IS WISE.
ALL RIGHT, LET ME GET WOLVERINE BACK. GET HAZMAT INTO POSITION.
I'M PULLING YOU BACK, LAURA. WE'RE GONNA BLOW THIS PASSAGEWAY.
HELL YEAH.
JEN, KEEP OUR PATH CLEAR. WE'RE COMING THROUGH, TOUT DE SUITE.
ROGER THAT.
ROGER THAT? WHO AM I?!
DETOURNEZ LES YEUX, MES DAMES.
BOOM
DO YOU GUYS KNOW WHAT HE'S EVEN SAYING HALF THE TIME?
NO.

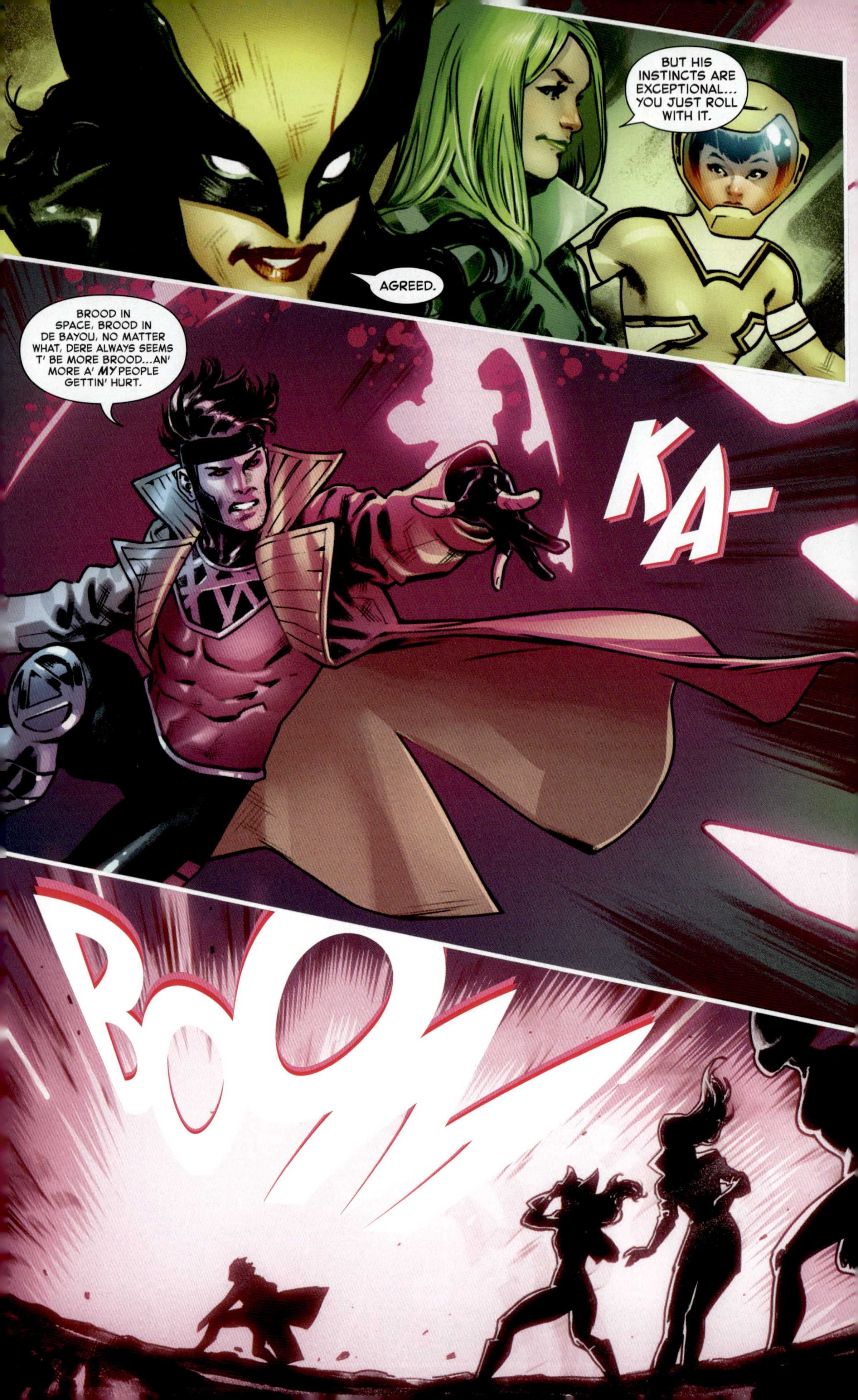
BUT HIS INSTINCTS ARE EXCEPTIONAL... YOU JUST ROLL WITH IT.
AGREED.
BROOD IN SPACE, BROOD IN DE BAYOU, NO MATTER WHAT, DERE ALWAYS SEEMS T' BE MORE BROOD...AN' MORE A' MY PEOPLE GETTIN' HURT.
KA-
BOOM

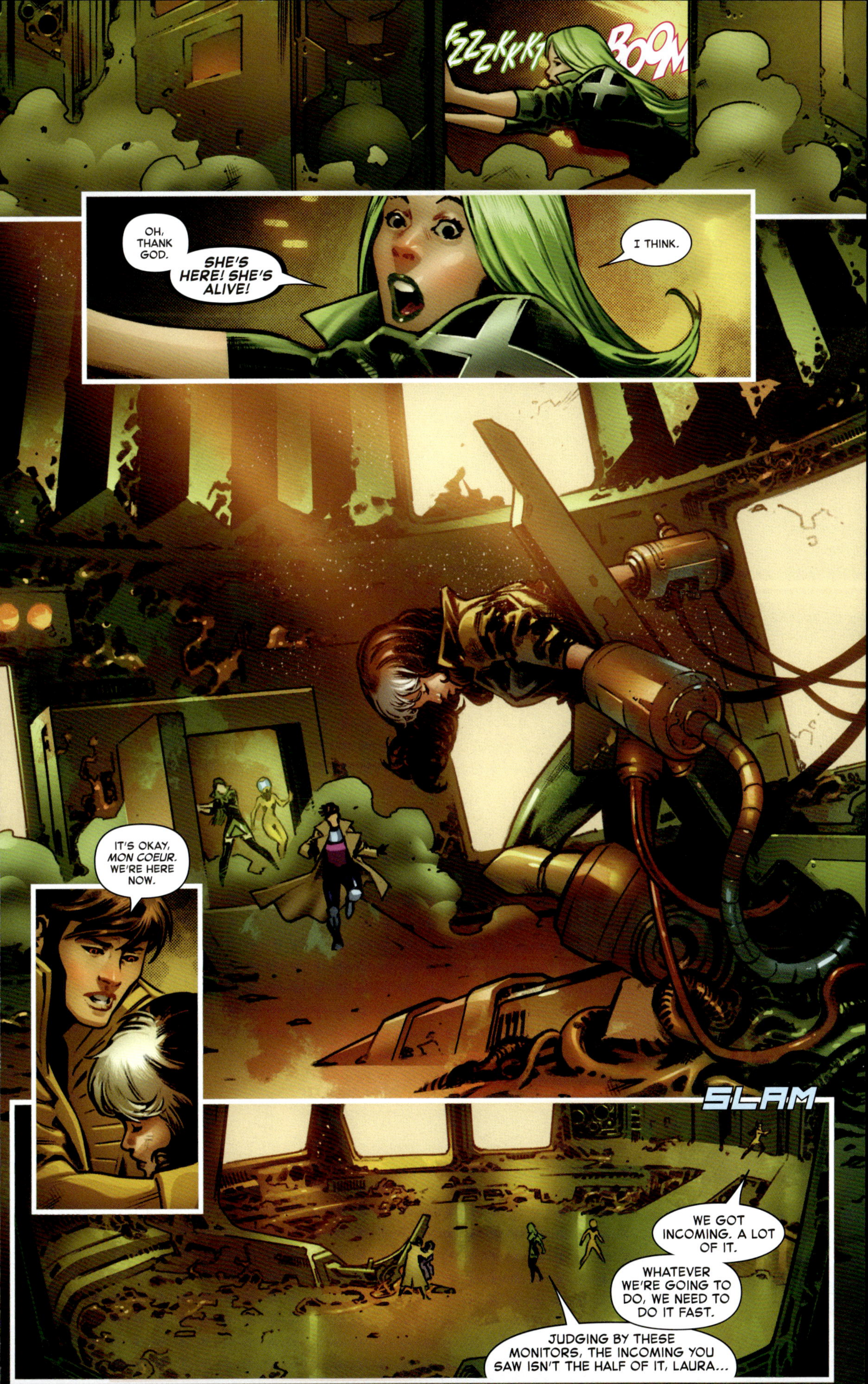
FZZZKKKT
BOOM
OH, THANK GOD.
SHE'S HERE! SHE'S ALIVE!
I THINK.
IT'S OKAY, MON COEUR. WE'RE HERE NOW.
SLAM
WE GOT INCOMING. A LOT OF IT.
WHATEVER WE'RE GOING TO DO, WE NEED TO DO IT FAST.
JUDGING BY THESE MONITORS, THE INCOMING YOU SAW ISN'T THE HALF OF IT, LAURA...

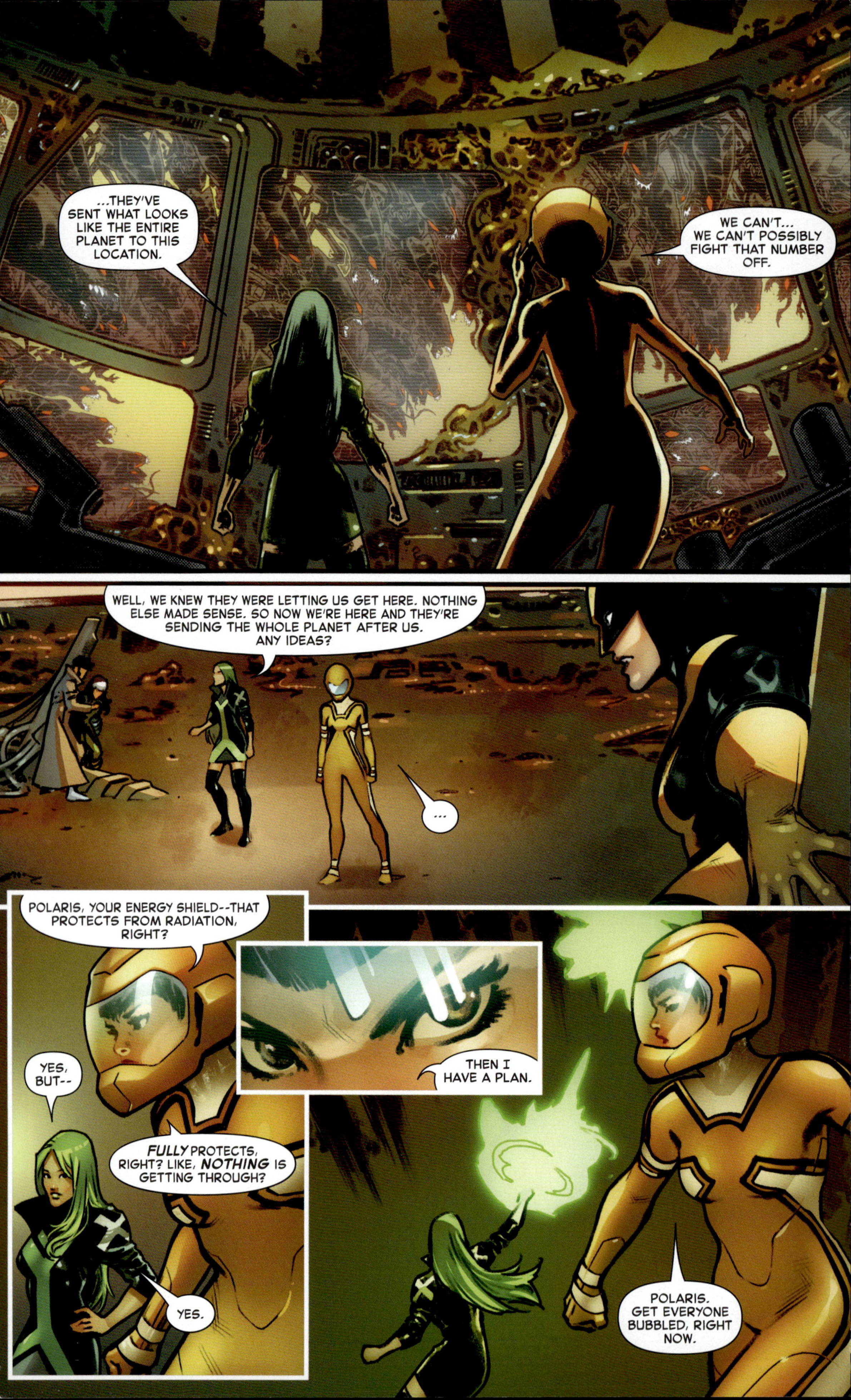
...THEY'VE SENT WHAT LOOKS LIKE THE ENTIRE PLANET TO THIS LOCATION.
WE CAN'T... WE CAN'T POSSIBLY FIGHT THAT NUMBER OFF.
WELL, WE KNEW THEY WERE LETTING US GET HERE. NOTHING ELSE MADE SENSE. SO NOW WE'RE HERE AND THEY'RE SENDING THE WHOLE PLANET AFTER US. ANY IDEAS?
...
POLARIS, YOUR ENERGY SHIELD--THAT PROTECTS FROM RADIATION, RIGHT?
YES, BUT--
FULLY PROTECTS, RIGHT? LIKE, NOTHING IS GETTING THROUGH?
YES.
THEN I HAVE A PLAN.
POLARIS. GET EVERYONE BUBBLED, RIGHT NOW.

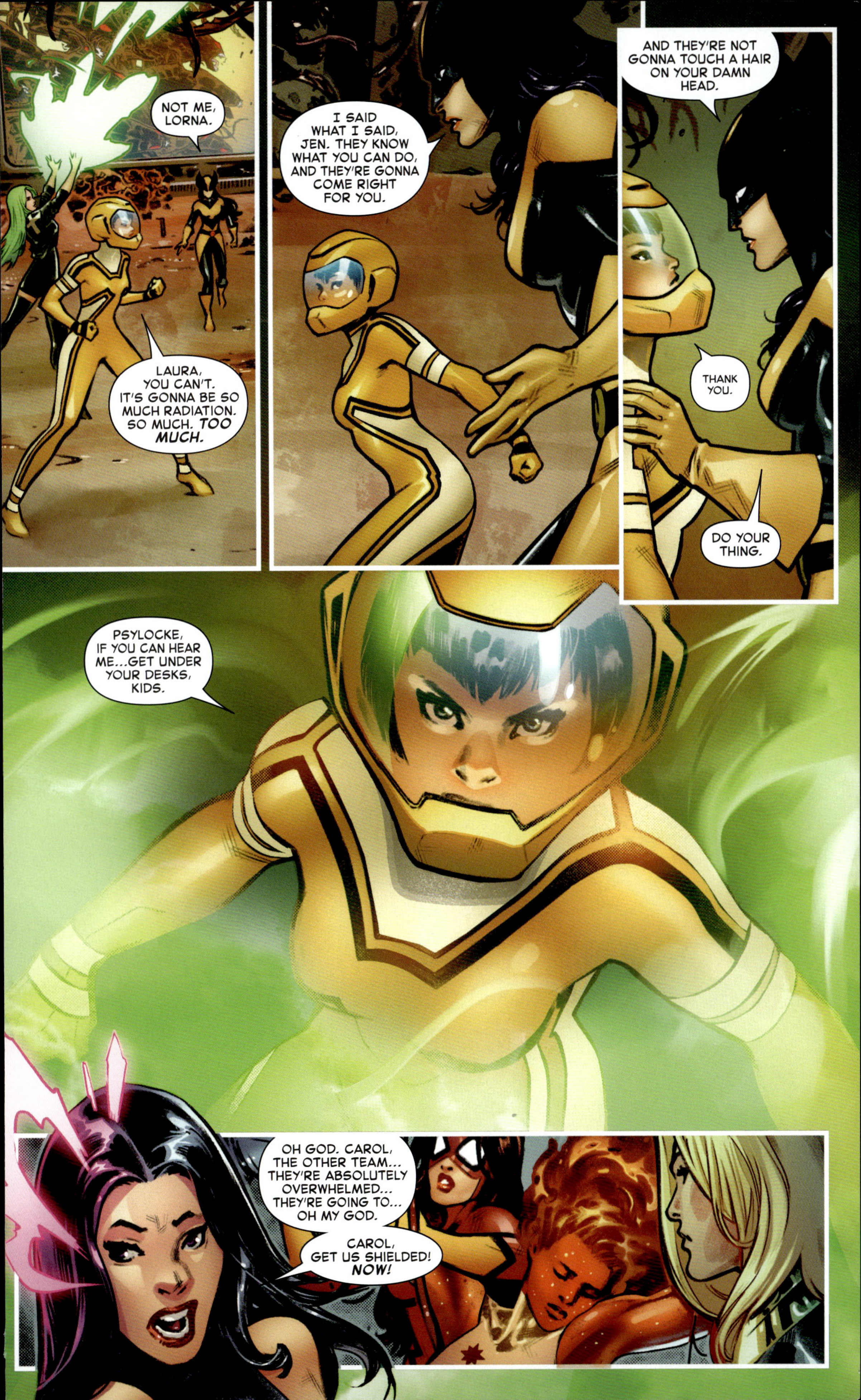
NOT ME, LORNA.
LAURA, YOU CAN'T. IT'S GONNA BE SO MUCH RADIATION. SO MUCH. TOO MUCH.
I SAID WHAT I SAID, JEN. THEY KNOW WHAT YOU CAN DO, AND THEY'RE GONNA COME RIGHT FOR YOU.
AND THEY'RE NOT GONNA TOUCH A HAIR ON YOUR DAMN HEAD.
THANK YOU.
DO YOUR THING.
PSYLOCKE, IF YOU CAN HEAR ME...GET UNDER YOUR DESKS, KIDS.
OH GOD. CAROL, THE OTHER TEAM... THEY'RE ABSOLUTELY OVERWHELMED... THEY'RE GOING TO... OH MY GOD.
CAROL, GET US SHIELDED! NOW!

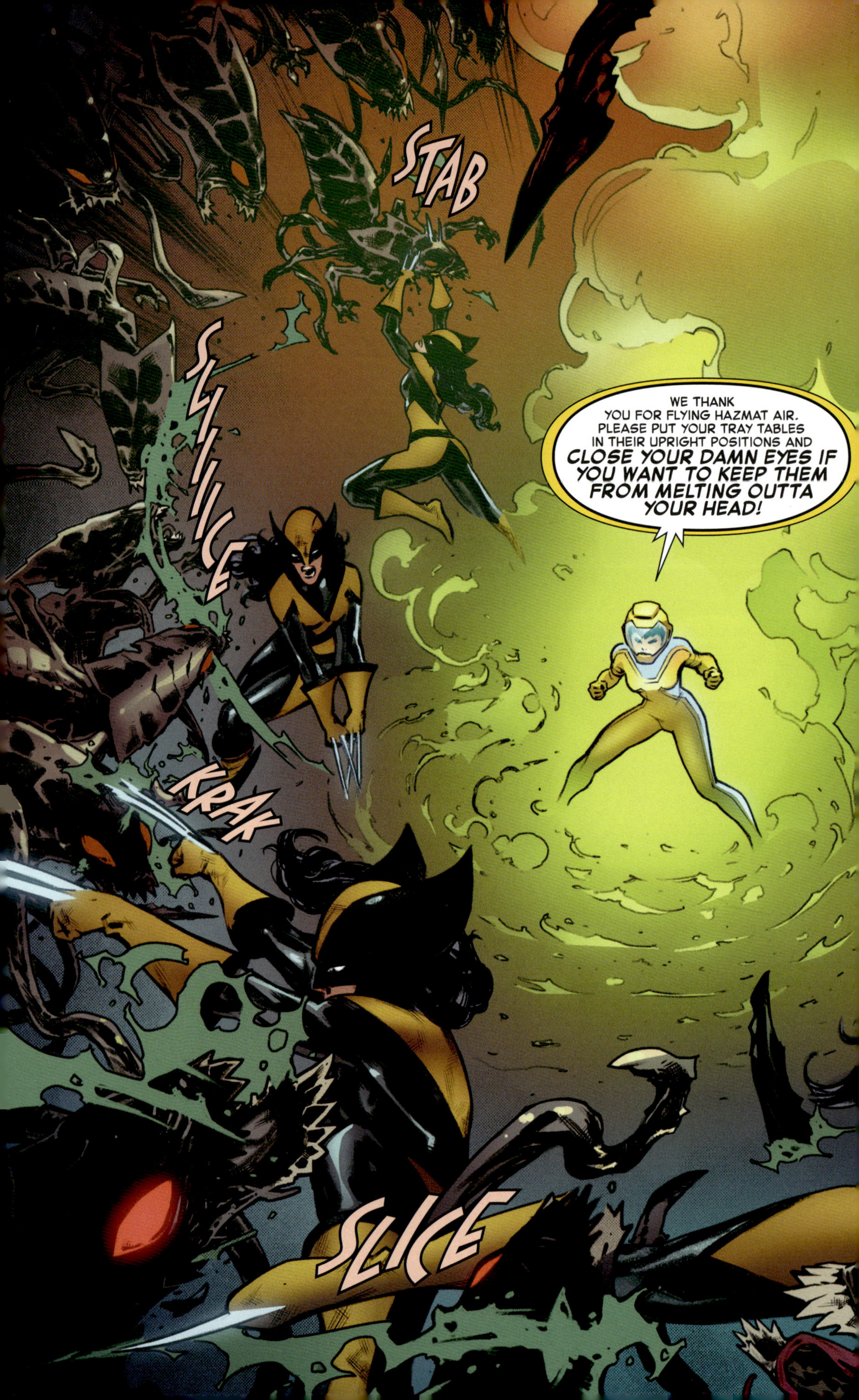
STAB
SLIIIICE
WE THANK YOU FOR FLYING HAZMAT AIR. PLEASE PUT YOUR TRAY TABLES IN THEIR UPRIGHT POSITIONS AND **CLOSE YOUR DAMN EYES IF YOU WANT TO KEEP THEM FROM MELTING OUTTA YOUR HEAD!**
KRAK
SLICE

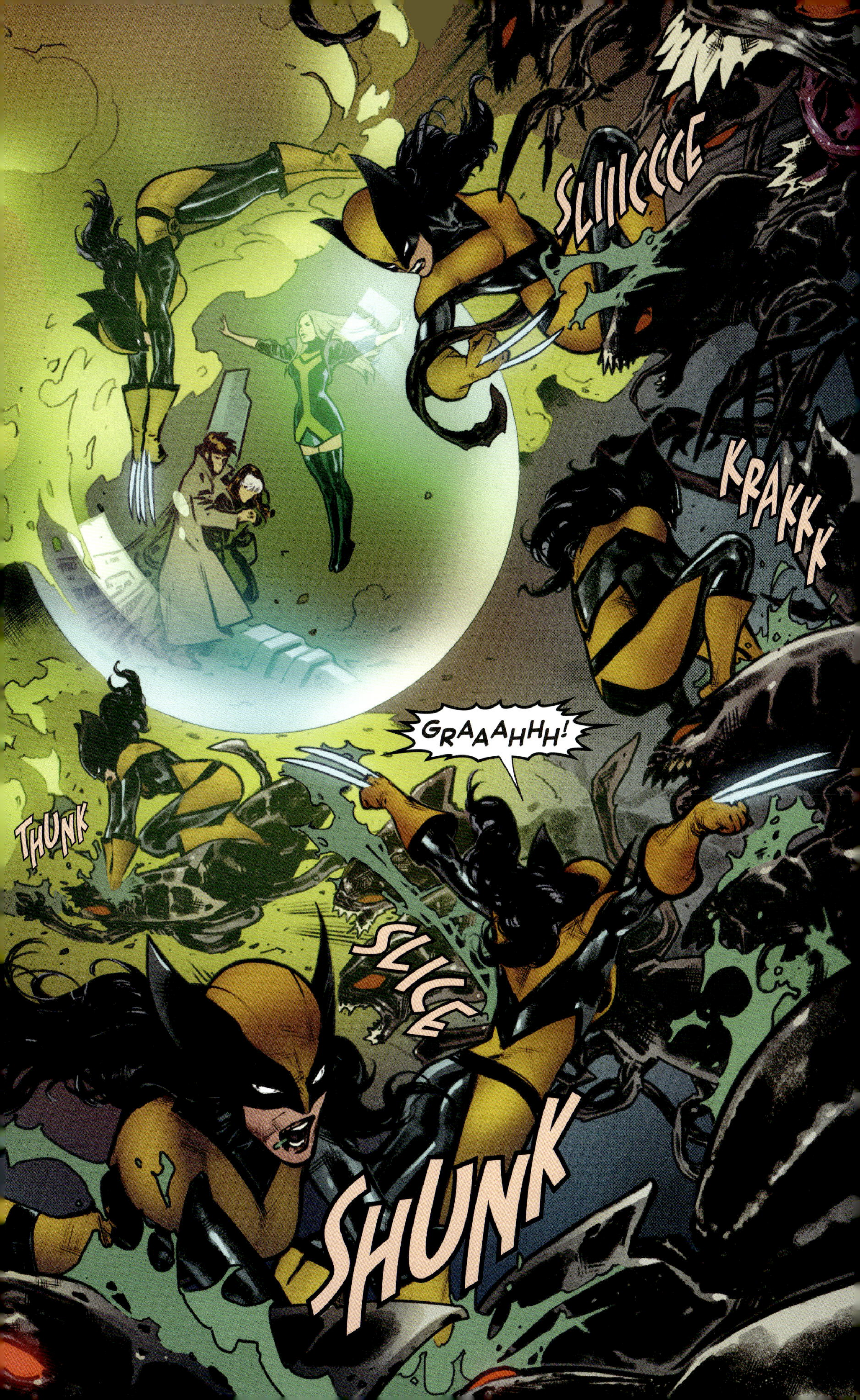
SLIIICCCE
KRAKKK
GRAAAHHH!
THUNK
SLICE
SHUNK

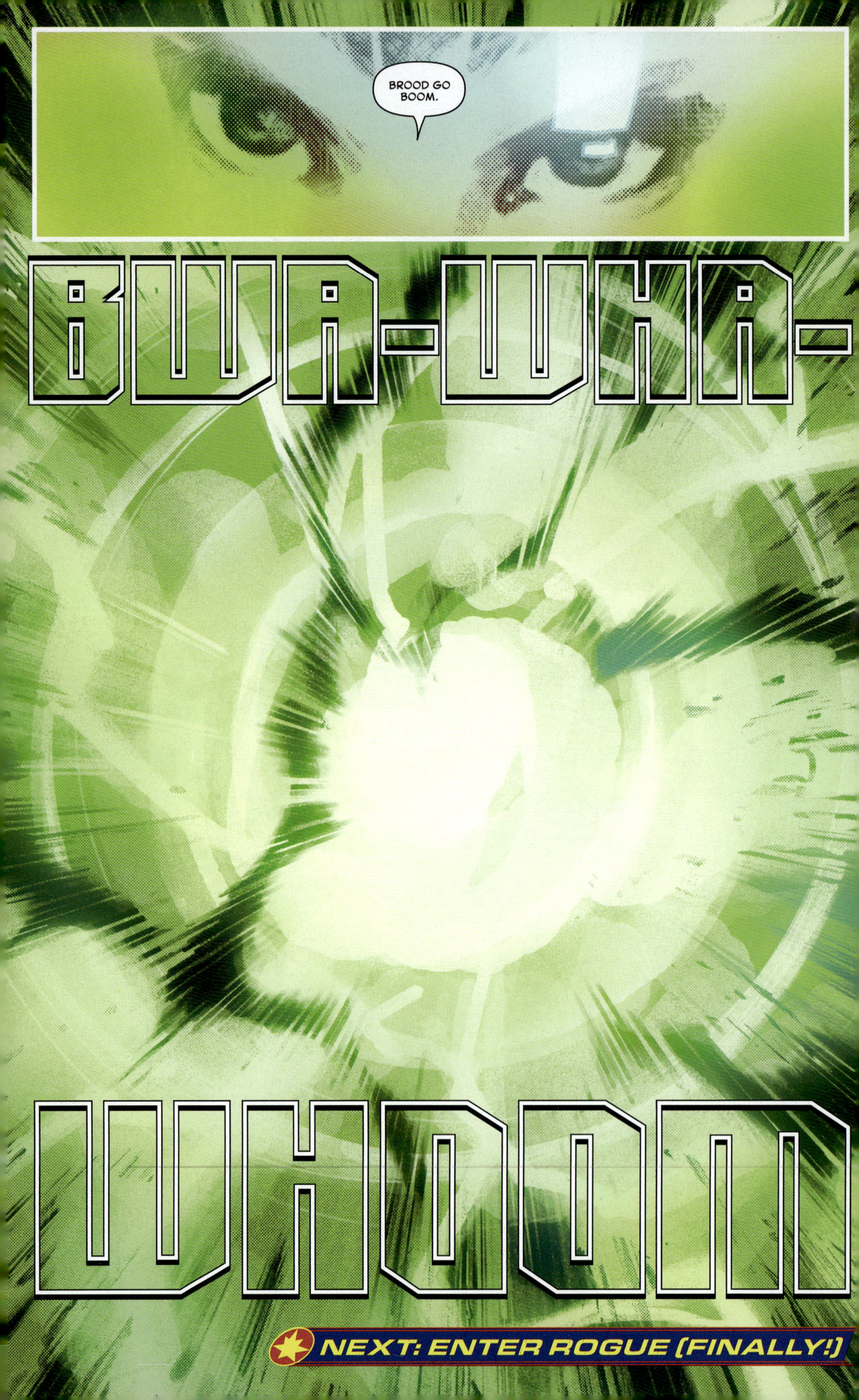
BROOD GO BOOM.
BWA-WHA-
WHOOM
NEXT: ENTER ROGUE (FINALLY!)